Coming Home

Judith Keim

BOOKS BY JUDITH KEIM

THE HARTWELL WOMEN SERIES:
> The Talking Tree – 1
> Sweet Talk – 2
> Straight Talk – 3
> Baby Talk – 4
> The Hartwell Women – Boxed Set

THE BEACH HOUSE HOTEL SERIES:
> Breakfast at The Beach House Hotel – 1
> Lunch at The Beach House Hotel – 2
> Dinner at The Beach House Hotel – 3
> Christmas at The Beach House Hotel – 4
> Margaritas at The Beach House Hotel – 5 (2021)
> Dessert at The Beach House Hotel – 6 (2022)

THE FAT FRIDAYS GROUP:
> Fat Fridays – 1
> Sassy Saturdays – 2
> Secret Sundays – 3

SALTY KEY INN BOOKS:
> Finding Me – 1
> Finding My Way – 2
> Finding Love – 3
> Finding Family – 4

CHANDLER HILL INN BOOKS:
> Going Home – 1
> Coming Home – 2
> Home at Last – 3

SEASHELL COTTAGE BOOKS:
A Christmas Star
Change of Heart
A Summer of Surprises
A Road Trip to Remember
The Beach Babes – (2022)

DESERT SAGE INN BOOKS:
The Desert Flowers – Rose – 1
The Desert Flowers – Lily – 2 (Fall 2021)
The Desert Flowers – Willow – 3 (2022)
The Desert Flowers – Mistletoe & Holly – 4 (2022)

Winning BIG – a little love story for all ages

For more information: **http://amzn.to/2jamIaF**

PRAISE FOR JUDITH KEIM'S NOVELS

THE BEACH HOUSE HOTEL SERIES

"Love the characters in this series. This series was my first introduction to Judith Keim. She is now one of my favorites. Looking forward to reading more of her books."

BREAKFAST AT THE BEACH HOUSE HOTEL is an easy, delightful read that offers romance, family relationships, and strong women learning to be stronger. Real life situations filter through the pages. Enjoy!"

LUNCH AT THE BEACH HOUSE HOTEL – "This series is such a joy to read. You feel you are actually living with them. Can't wait to read the latest one."

DINNER AT THE BEACH HOUSE HOTEL – "A Terrific Read! As usual, Judith Keim did it again. Enjoyed immensely. Continue writing such pleasantly reading books for all of us readers."

CHRISTMAS AT THE BEACH HOUSE HOTEL – "Not Just Another Christmas Novel. This is book number four in the series and my introduction to Judith Keim's writing. I wasn't disappointed. The characters are dimensional and engaging. The plot is well crafted and advances at a pleasing pace. The Florida location is interesting and warming. It was a delight to read a romance novel with mature female protagonists. Ann and Rhoda have life experiences that enrich the story. It's a clever book about friends and extended family. Buy copies for your book group pals and enjoy this seasonal read."

THE HARTWELL WOMEN SERIES – Books 1 – 4

"This was an EXCELLENT series. When I discovered Judith Keim, I read all of her books back to back. I thoroughly enjoyed the women Keim has written about. They are believable and you want to just jump into their lives and be their friends! I can't wait for any upcoming books!"

"I fell into Judith Keim's Hartwell Women series and have read & enjoyed all of her books in every series. Each centers around a strong & interesting woman character and their family interaction. Good reads that leave you wanting more."

THE FAT FRIDAYS GROUP – Books 1 – 3

"Excellent story line for each character, and an insightful representation of situations which deal with some of the contemporary issues women are faced with today."

"I love this author's books. Her characters and their lives are realistic. The power of women's friendships is a common and beautiful theme that is threaded throughout this story."

THE SALTY KEY INN SERIES

<u>FINDING ME</u> – *"I thoroughly enjoyed the first book in this series and cannot wait for the others! The characters are endearing with the same struggles we all encounter. The setting makes me feel like I am a guest at The Salty Key Inn...relaxed, happy & light-hearted! The men are yummy and the women strong. You can't get better than that! Happy Reading!"*

<u>FINDING MY WAY</u>- *"Loved the family dynamics as well as uncertain emotions of dating and falling in love.*

Appreciated the morals and strength of parenting throughout. Just couldn't put this book down."

FINDING LOVE – "I waited for this book because the first two was such good reads. This one didn't disappoint.... Judith Keim always puts substance into her books. This book was no different, I learned about PTSD, accepting oneself, there is always going to be problems but stick it out and make it work. Just the way life is. In some ways a lot like my life. Judith is right, it needs another book and I will definitely be reading it. Hope you choose to read this series, you will get so much out of it."

FINDING FAMILY – "Completing this series is like eating the last chip. Love Judith's writing, and her female characters are always smart, strong, vulnerable to life and love experiences."

"This was a refreshing book. Bringing the heart and soul of the family to us."

CHANDLER HILL INN SERIES

GOING HOME – "I absolutely could not put this book down. Started at night and read late into the middle of the night. As a child of the '60s, the Vietnam war was front and center so this resonated with me. All the characters in the book were so well developed that the reader felt like they were friends of the family."

"I was completely immersed in this book, with the beautiful descriptive writing, and the authors' way of bringing her characters to life. I felt like I was right inside her story."

COMING HOME – "Coming Home is a winner. The characters are well-developed, nuanced and likable. Enjoyed the vineyard setting, learning about wine growing and seeing the challenges Cami faces in running and growing a business. I look forward to the next book in this series!"

"Coming Home was such a wonderful story. The author has a gift for getting the reader right to the heart of things."

HOME AT LAST – "In this wonderful conclusion, to a heartfelt and emotional trilogy set in Oregon's stunning wine country, Judith Keim has tied up the Chandler Hill series with the perfect bow."

"Overall, this is truly a wonderful addition to the Chandler Hill Inn series. Judith Keim definitely knows how to perfectly weave together a beautiful and heartfelt story."

"The storyline has some beautiful scenes along with family drama. Judith Keim has created characters with interactions that are believable and some of the subjects the story deals with are poignant."

SEASHELL COTTAGE BOOKS

A CHRISTMAS STAR – "Love, laughter, sadness, great food, and hope for the future, all in one book. It doesn't get any better than this stunning read."

"A Christmas Star is a heartwarming Christmas story featuring endearing characters. So many Christmas books are set in snowbound places...it was a nice change to read a Christmas story that takes place on a warm sandy beach!" Susan Peterson

CHANGE OF HEART – *"CHANGE OF HEART is the summer read we've all been waiting for. Judith Keim is a master at creating fascinating characters that are simply irresistible. Her stories leave you with a big smile on your face and a heart bursting with love."*
~Kellie Coates Gilbert, author of the popular Sun Valley Series

A SUMMER OF SURPRISES – *"The story is filled with a roller coaster of emotions and self-discovery. Finding love again and rebuilding family relationships."*

"Ms. Keim uses this book as an amazing platform to show that with hard emotional work, belief in yourself and love, the scars of abuse can be conquered. It in no way preaches, it's a lovely story with a happy ending."

"The character development was excellent. I felt I knew these people my whole life. The story development was very well thought out I was drawn [in] from the beginning."

DESERT SAGE INN BOOKS
THE DESERT FLOWERS – ROSE – *"The Desert Flowers - Rose, is the first book in the new series by Judith Keim. I always look forward to new books by Judith Keim, and this one is definitely a wonderful way to begin The Desert Sage Inn Series!"*

"In this first of a series, we see each woman come into her own and view new beginnings even as they must take this tearful journey as they slowly lose a dear friend. This is a very well written book with well-developed and likable main characters. It was interesting and enlightening as the first

portion of this saga unfolded. I very much enjoyed this book and I do recommend it"

"Judith Keim is one of those authors that you can always depend on to give you a great story with fantastic characters. I'm excited to know that she is writing a new series and after reading book 1 in the series, I can't wait to read the rest of the books."!

Coming Home

A Chandler Hill Inn Book - 2

Judith Keim

Wild Quail Publishing

Coming Home is a work of fiction. Names, characters, places, public or private institutions, corporations, towns, and incidents are the product of the author's imagination or are used fictitiously. Any resemblance to actual events, locales, or persons, living or dead, is coincidental.

No part of this book may be reproduced or transmitted in any form or by any electronic or mechanical means, including information storage and retrieval systems, without permission in writing from the author, except by a reviewer who may quote brief passages in a review. This book may not be resold or uploaded for distribution to others. For permissions contact the author directly via electronic mail:

wildquail.pub@gmail.com

www.judithkeim.com,

Published in the United States of America by:

Wild Quail Publishing
PO Box 171332
Boise, ID 83717-1332

ISBN# 978-0-9992448-8-3

Dedication

For Ron and JoAnn Holec
How could I write so much about wine and not
think of you and our fun times together?

CHAPTER ONE

Camilla Chandler walked through the vineyards toward the grove of trees that meant so much to her at Chandler Hill in the Willamette Valley of Oregon. The ashes of her grandmother, Violet "Lettie" Chandler, now resided there along with the ashes of her mother, Autumn, Lettie's husband, Kenton, and Rex Chandler, Lettie's father-in-law and the original owner of the inn and winery Cami had just inherited.

The gray skies of this cool fall morning held a promise of rain, which suited her mood. The raindrops slated to fall would match the tears she'd somehow managed to hold onto after weeping for days at the loss of her grandmother, whom she called "Nonnee," a woman beloved not only by Cami, but by all who knew her. For eighteen months of Cami's first two years, Nonnee had raised her, forming an early, loving bond between them. And then, when Cami was only six, Lettie had stepped in to take the place of Cami's mother after Autumn had been struck and killed by a car while jogging one day near her home in South Africa.

Cami lifted her face to the sky and watched as a red-tailed hawk circled in the air above her and then glided down to perch on the limbs of a tall white oak, part of the collection of trees that was her destination. As her grandmother had done, Cami sought refuge and answers among the pine and hardwood trees that rose from the earth in a sturdy cluster— sentinels keeping watch over the grape vines that lined the hillsides with promises of good things to come.

Cami entered the inner circle of the trees and sat on the

stone bench that had been placed there long before her birth.

"What a mess," Cami blurted before she could stop herself. Wrapping her arms around herself, she wished she had worn her sweater. The crisp fall cold seeped into her bones as she began to cry. If Nonnee were here, she would hug her and tell her everything would be all right. But at the moment, nothing seemed all right. Especially after receiving the email from Bernard.

Cami rocked in her seat, wishing there was an easy way to get rid of the pain. "Bernard Arnaud is a ... a ... b ... jerk!" Her angry cry filled the air and bounced off the branches and boughs of the trees, making it seem as if their echoes confirmed her opinion of him.

She could hear her grandmother's words in her head. "Take a deep breath, darling, and begin at the beginning."

Following those silent instructions, Cami drew in air, straightened, and spoke aloud. "Nonnee, I thought he loved me. I thought he understood I had to come home to Chandler Hill, that I owed it to my family to be here. After our many months of being together, he called those days ... and nights ... a fun romance. And now, he doesn't want to see me anymore! After I helped to bury you, he told me this in an email ... an email for God's sake!"

Cami fisted her hands as fresh tears rolled down her cheeks. "I feel so ... so ... stupid!"

A sparrow landed on the ground not far from her and peered up at her with dark eyes, like a messenger sent by her grandmother. How she missed Nonnee!

Cami bowed her head. As strange as others might think of it, sitting in the grove, giving up her secrets brought answers. Though all of her Chandler relatives were deceased, they still spoke to her in memories and in stories others shared about them. They were fine people—her mother, grandmother, and the two Chandler men who'd given Nonnee the challenge of making the Chandler Hill Inn and Winery what they were today. Now, it was up to Cami to keep the enterprise healthy and strong. She knew it was an inheritance some people would love to have, but with the breakup with Bernard, it had already cost her dearly. And at twenty-three, Cami wondered how she could ever meet the challenge Nonnee had passed on to her.

The cool breeze blowing through the pines filled the air with whispers. Cami cocked her head to listen. No answers seemed clear but one. Somehow, she'd have to find the courage and strength within her to keep things going. If Nonnee, all five-feet-three inches of her, could do that, then so would she.

Cami stood to leave. Hearing a noise behind her, she turned to see Rafe Lopez walking toward her. Her lips curved, and she lifted a hand in greeting. Her grandfather was a striking man in his early seventies who was also struggling with Lettie's recent death. Cami and her grandfather, Rafe, had always had a close bond, and now that it was just the two of them living in Nonnee's house, they'd grown even closer.

She'd always called him Rafe, even as a child. When it was suggested she call him Grandpa, she'd stamped her toddler foot and said, "No! My Rafe!" He'd loved it then, and he loved it now.

"Thought I'd find you here," said Rafe. "Get a few things settled in your mind?"

She smiled sadly. "There are no simple answers, are there?"

He shook his head. "Life is anything but simple. May I sit with you?"

"Sure." She sat and indicated a place for him next to her. "What's up?"

"I just talked to Paloma. She's decided to leave Chandler

Hill to live in Arizona with her daughter and her family."

Cami's eyes widened. "But Paloma has been almost as big a part of Chandler Hill as Nonnee."

"Yes, but now that her best friend is gone, and with her new inheritance, Paloma is free to leave." The sadness in his eyes reflected her own. "A lot of things will never be the same."

"I heard Abby wants to retire by the end of the year." Cami let out a worried sigh. "Sometimes I feel so alone."

Rafe put an arm around her. "You've always got me. But I think it's time for me to move. I'd like to take over the cabin after Paloma is gone. What do you say?"

"You don't want to stay in the house with me?" Cami asked, genuinely surprised.

"Too many memories there. And the cabin is a special place for me. It's where I first spent time with Lettie. Of course, after all the renovations we've done, it's not a simple cabin anymore, but a very nice place for an old man like me."

Cami hugged him. "A very *special* old man. I'll miss you, but I agree. It's right for you to be on your own without worrying about me." She studied him with tenderness. "But I'll always be there for you, Rafe. A woman couldn't have a better grandfather than you."

He cupped her face in his broad, strong hands. "You'll never know what a gift you are to me, my granddaughter. I never suspected your mother was my child. When I found out, I cried with joy. And now I have you."

Cami had heard this story many times. It was a sweet one. She couldn't help wondering who her own father was. It was something her mother had refused to divulge. But someday, maybe when things were in better shape at the inn, Cami intended to find out. She needed to know.

Some families were complicated, she thought as she got to her feet once more. She held out a hand to her grandfather.

He took it and rose. "Ready to come home?"

"I guess so." *Home was as complex as her family.*

Cami sat in the office within the inn and stared out the window. The room and its history weighed heavily on her shoulders. She'd already met with Nonnee's lawyers regarding her inheritance of the inn and vineyards , but when she'd asked to see information from her grandmother's financial advisor, he'd sent her a summary accounting of Nonnee's investments and requested that the meeting she wanted with him be postponed for two weeks while he dealt with some other issues. Overwhelmed by all the new information thrown at her, Cami had readily agreed.

Now, it was time to decide which of her available funds she'd use for the upgrades to the guest rooms the inn manager, Jonathan Knight, was insisting be done. Jonathan, the young manager Nonnee had hired just before she was diagnosed with cancer, was not one of Cami's friends. He'd all but sniffed his disapproval when Cami told him he would now report to her.

"But you have no experience in the hotel business," he'd protested. "I understand you studied Fine Arts in college. That certainly doesn't qualify you to run an operation like this."

"Nevertheless, I own the entire business," said Cami sweetly, though inwardly she was seething at the insulting tone of his voice.

"Cami? Mr. Evans is here to see you," announced Becca Withers, her assistant, startling her out of her memory of that encounter.

Cami smiled. "Thanks, Becca. Please ask him to come on back." Cami had had a couple of telephone conversations with him. Dirk Evans had sounded smart, polished, and very cocky.

Becca showed Dirk into the office and, standing behind him, waved a discreet hand in front of her face to indicate she thought he was a hottie.

Tall, with sun-streaked brown hair and fine features, he swept into the room and beamed at Cami. Through lenses in black eyeglass frames, his blues eyes surveyed her.

From behind the desk, she rose to shake his hand. "Hello, Dirk. We meet at last."

"My pleasure. Photographs Lettie had of you on her desk don't do you justice."

"Yes, well, have a seat and let's get down to business, shall we?" Cami said briskly. "I want to talk to you about my grandmother's portfolio. We're about to start a renovation project at the inn, and I'm going to need to sell some more stocks."

All confidence seemed to evaporate from him. He sank into a chair and faced her with a look of despair. "We've had some disappointments. One in particular."

A niggling feeling crept through Cami like a python squeezing her insides. "You're not talking about the Montague Fund, are you? I directed you to sell that two weeks ago."

"Yes, I know. I tried to do that for you and all my clients, but there's a problem. It turns out that the Montague Fund was basically a Ponzi scheme. Most of the money is gone. I'm working on getting back what I can. I've already begun filling out claim papers with the SEC, but it's going to take time for the Feds to sort through it." He pushed his glasses further up on his nose. "I was given what I was assured was reliable information on the fund, so I'm not sure what went wrong."

Cami's mouth went dry. She gripped the arms of her desk chair so tightly her fingers turned white. "What went wrong? My grandmother was a very conservative woman. I don't believe she would have wanted you to invest her money in something like that. Was she aware of what you'd done? Did she approve?"

"She told me to go ahead and do whatever I could to ensure you'd have enough money to carry on with the inn. The fund promised exceptional returns ...." His voice trailed off.

She narrowed her eyes and studied him. "So Nonnee didn't know?"

He looked at her and then away. "Not exactly."

"I could have you reported and perhaps have your license taken away," said Cami, "but then I guess I'm not the only client of yours who feels that way."

"I did nothing wrong," Dirk countered. "I got the information for the fund from a very reliable source. Believe me, you're not the only person who has been hurt by this."

Cami's lips thinned. "So that makes it all right?"

He shifted in his chair and looked away from her.

"Did everyone in your office suggest their clients invest in this fund?"

He shook his head. "Mr. Berman didn't like it, warned his clients against it."

Cami leaned forward and gave him a steady stare. "I want this entire portfolio transferred to him immediately. Understand?"

"But ..."

"Stay right here. I'm calling him now."

Dirk let out a snort of disgust. "You don't have to do that."

"But I do," she said, with a calmness she had to force.

Cami scrolled through her contact list and tapped in the number on her cellphone. She was immediately put through to Russell Berman. He listened to her and then said, "I'd be honored to work with Lettie Chandler's funds, and now yours. I suggest going over everything, making sure that the remainder of the money is placed in safe, conservative funds."

"But Mr. Berman, what am I going to do? I need money to pay for the renovation of rooms." Cami felt like crying, but she refused to break down in front of Dirk.

"The market is volatile right now. Hold off on spending any money until I get things sorted out. Then, you and I can talk about funding the renovation of rooms."

"Okay, but the hotel manager isn't going to be happy about it," sighed Cami. As she hung up, she wondered why she felt as betrayed by Dirk as she had been by Bernard.

"Okay, Dirk," said Cami, getting to her feet. "I think we're done here."

He rose and turned to go, then turned back to her. "Maybe we could have dinner sometime."

Hysterical laughter bubbled inside her. *He'd ruined her future and was asking for a date?*

"Really? I don't think so. Goodbye, Dirk."

Later, repeating that conversation to Becca, she said, "Can you believe it?"

"Yes. Have you taken a look at yourself? Thin, but with curves any guy would go for, you're a stunning woman with that strawberry-blond hair and dark eyes. I'd kill for your looks."

Cami wrapped an arm around Becca. "You're adorable. Being short isn't bad, you know."

"And being a little round?" Becca said with an arched eyebrow.

"Cuddly and warm. I've seen the looks Jonathan Knight gives you."

Becca made a face. "Jonathan is in love with himself. Haven't you noticed?"

The two of them looked at each other and laughed. Tall and broad-shouldered, Jonathan carried himself with confidence. His dark hair, green eyes, and strong features were undeniably attractive. His attitude, not so much.

"For the time being, I've given up on men," said Cami with feeling.

"Not me." Becca grinned. "And you have to admit that Dirk Evans is one hot guy."

"Yeah, but looks aren't everything, Becca." Cami recalled how handsome she'd thought Bernard was. Now, the memory of his face as he leaned down to kiss her made her stomach fill with acid.

Cami's meeting with Jonathan went no better than her talk with Dirk.

"You can't tell me the renovation program I've planned is kaput," he groused, sitting in the office he'd assigned her. "The timing of it is perfect. Cold winter months are slow at the inn. And if we're going to raise rates, we need to refresh the rooms."

"I don't have any answers yet," Cami said. "But give me time to come up with a revised plan. Our renovations fund has been depleted and we may need to use our cash flow to get anything done."

Jonathan's lip curled with derision that matched his tone. "How can we do all the work I want that way? It'll take a miracle."

Cami held up a hand to stop him. "I'll get back to you as soon as I can, Jonathan. That's all I can promise right now."

His silence screamed his anger as he stormed out of the office.

Cami watched him leave, determined to show him just who she was. A Chandler and a Lopez.

CHAPTER TWO

Cami sat with Paloma at the pine kitchen table in the cabin and reminded herself to be strong. As her grandfather and she had agreed, life wasn't simple. This was another instance of it.

"I wish you weren't leaving," said Cami, setting down her mug of coffee. "Nonnee relied on you for so many things. I don't know how I can ever replace you."

Paloma smiled, reached over, and squeezed Cami's hand with affection. "Lettie and I helped each other and remained best of friends through everything. But, Cami, you'll find someone like that for yourself. I like Becca. She's smart and loyal. Give her a chance to grow with you."

Cami frowned at her. "I like her too, but it might not work. Jonathan doesn't think I can run Chandler Hill Inn because I don't have a degree in hotel management. Neither does Becca."

Paloma gave her a stern look. "And that opinion is going to stop you from learning what you need to know? Besides, you can call in a consultant whenever you need one. That's how Lettie met Abby. Long before she became manager of The Barn, Abby was a consultant to Lettie when she first took over the inn."

"For the past several years, Abby's done an outstanding job of handling all the merchandising for the inn and winery. And now she tells me she's ready to retire. I feel like the only one left on a sinking boat." Cami knew there was a whine in her voice, but she couldn't help it. The Chandler Hill world she'd envisioned not long ago was crumbling before her eyes.

"Think of how your grandmother felt at age nineteen when she was left the inn and vineyards with no experience to guide her. You, at least, spent your childhood here, know a great deal about growing grapes, and have an excellent business sense to help carry you through. Cami, you're every bit as capable as your grandmother. You can do what you have to do to keep the Chandler Hill Inn and Winery going. It's a pity Lettie trusted her new financial advisor to keep her money safe, but you can be creative about refreshing the guest rooms and making the inn look nice and inviting without spending all the money Jonathan requested."

Cami studied Paloma. Gray streaked her dark hair—a sign of experience and wisdom. Paloma returned Cami's gaze, her eyes shining with intelligence and unmistakable affection.

"Thanks. I needed to hear that." Cami rose and threw her arms around Paloma. "I know why Nonnee loved you so much. I do too."

Paloma returned Cami's hug. "Please understand. It's only right that I leave for Arizona to be with my family. And it's good for Rafe to be able to live here in the cabin. He could never leave Lettie. Now, he won't have to. He can simply walk across the fields to talk to her."

"They really loved one another." Cami's voice quivered. "I hope someday to find a man as perfect as my grandfather was for Nonnee."

"You will." Paloma smiled. "One often finds a few frogs before discovering the real prince."

Cami laughed. "Calling Bernard Arnaud that is about the best thing I can say about him."

"Sometimes, love finds a way to you when you're least expecting it," said Paloma. "Relax and enjoy finding new opportunities to make Chandler Hill even better. The rest will happen in time."

"You're right. Realistically, I want to be able to do things my own way. Nonnee trusted me to do that."

"Indeed. That's how she succeeded, and that's how you'll succeed." Paloma got to her feet. "Do you want to look around? I don't think you'll need to make any changes to the cabin beyond a fresh coat of paint. Heaven knows, it doesn't look at all like it did when Rafe met Lettie all those years ago."

"Sure, let's do a quick walk-through. I want to make sure he's going to be comfortable here."

Cami had heard stories of how her grandmother, Rafe, and Kenton had used the rustic cabin as a gathering place to taste and discuss wine and listen to music. It had been a humble abode then. Now, after Abby and her partner had expanded it, and with Paloma living there, what once was a simple cabin was a very lovely home in the woods. With two bedrooms, a den, a small office, a modern kitchen, and a large open area for living and dining, it was a comfortable haven for anyone who lived there.

Cami and Paloma quickly agreed that aside from painting the master bedroom, nothing else needed to be done to the house after Paloma left. Rafe could decide if he agreed.

"Though I'll miss it, I'm sure Rafe will love living here," said Paloma. "And it will be nice for you to have him around."

Cami kissed Paloma goodbye and headed back to the inn feeling a little stronger. She couldn't let people like Jonathan undermine her determination to move forward with some confidence. Sure, she'd make some mistakes, but she'd make some wise choices too.

Cami entered the inn and went directly to her office. When Nonnee was ill, Jonathan had taken over Nonnee's office in the inn instead of staying in the one designated for him in the hotel wing. But if Cami was going to oversee the entire operation along with the hotel, she wanted to be in the heart of things where she'd have a better handle on what was going on. Besides, her working in Nonnee's space was only right.

Jonathan was on the phone when she walked into the office he called his own, but which was now supposed to be hers. He looked up, frowned, and waved her to a chair.

She sat facing him as he discussed an advertising program he wanted to implement. As Cami listened, she grew alarmed at the costs Jonathan mentioned. Until things were straightened out, she needed to be very cautious about committing to any large expenditures.

"Okay, that's all set. I'll get the money to you later today," said Jonathan. He hung up the phone and turned to her. "That was the agreement to go forward with the travel campaign for the airlines."

Cami's stomach knotted. "We can no longer do that campaign. We agreed to do that before I learned about the losses in my grandmother's portfolio."

Jonathan slammed a hand down on the desk, startling her. "You can't keep undermining me this way. You make me look like a fool."

"We don't have the money," Cami said as calmly as she could while thinking he was a bigger fool than she'd thought. "Until we can review and agree on both a cash flow forecast and a budget, and while the accountant is going over the numbers, we can't spend any sizeable amount of money. I thought you understood that."

"*You* need to understand that you have to spend money to make money. It's time to take the Chandler Hill Inn up a step or two, even if you have to borrow the funds." He glared at her.

Cami hated confrontation, wished at times she'd never

promised Nonnee she'd come home to this mess. Drawing a deep breath, she gathered her thoughts.

"Things won't be easy for the next several months. I don't think now is the time to borrow money, when we're entering the slow season. We're going to have to improvise, be creative. It's not going to be a case of your making decisions on your own. If you don't like it ..." She stopped before she went too far.

His eyes widened. "Are you threatening to fire me?"

"No," she said calmly, "I'm merely telling you we need to be a team. I know things were thrown at you when Nonnee was ill. Now, I'll be back in her office, handling what I can while I assume her duties."

"You want me to change offices?" The disbelief in his voice was irritating.

"I was told that your being in this office was a temporary arrangement." Cami couldn't help wondering what other things Jonathan had assumed while her grandmother lay dying.

Jonathan jumped to his feet. "I've got to get out of here."

"Okay. I'll have Becca help me gather your things," Cami said as calmly as she could. Her mouth grew dry at the thought of losing him.

"Don't you touch a damn thing!" Jonathan shouted, shaking a warning finger at her.

Stunned, Cami sat back in her chair and watched him leave. As soon as he was gone, Cami rose to her feet and went to find Becca. "Please get me the number for Barnes and Associates."

"Everything all right?" Becca said. "I heard the yelling."

"I don't know, but I'm going to find out," said Cami. It was time to call in a lawyer.

After discussing the situation at Chandler Hill with her,

Cami was convinced Jamison Barnes Winkler was the right person to help her. According to her online bio, Lew Barnes' granddaughter was reputedly as clever and as honest as he had been. In her forties and the mother of teenage twin girls, she was a formidable foe to anyone who dared to challenge her.

Two days later, Cami stood inside Portland International Airport waiting for Jamison to arrive. At first, she had been hesitant to hire a woman to handle the situation. Even today in a man's world of business, it was too easy to dismiss a strong woman for those very qualities of leadership that were accepted in a man.

Cami scanned the California flight's disembarked passengers walking through the passenger terminal. When she finally realized the tiny blonde heading toward her with a friendly wave was Jamison, Cami chuckled. The booming voice she'd heard on the phone was that of a large, overpowering woman. This person looked like the kind of woman with whom you'd happily choose to chat over coffee.

"Cami?" said the woman, approaching her.

"Yes, and you're Jamison?"

Jamison smiled and nodded. "In person. I'm glad to meet you. My grandfather had such admiration for your grandmother."

"I've been left with big shoes to fill," admitted Cami. "That's why I'm glad you're here. I need to make sure things are in order. After Nonnee became ill, Jonathan assumed a lot of her responsibilities to handle at the inn. After a few conversations with him, I'm concerned about that."

"So you mentioned. We'll soon get everything straightened out. And if your Mr. Knight is not wearing a shining coat of armor, we'll take care of him." Jamison's blue eyes shown with humor.

As they waited for Jamison's luggage to arrive in baggage claim, Cami and Jamison chatted easily. Jamison talked about her daughters, who at age sixteen were a handful. She spoke lovingly of them and Wynton, her husband of many years and an artist who enjoyed some fame for his modern paintings in mixed media.

When Cami heard Jamison mention her husband's name, she clutched Jamison's arm with excitement. "You're married to Wynton Winkler? Oh my God! I'm such an admirer of his work. I studied some of his paintings in school."

"He'd be flattered," said Jamison. "I love his work too. We're as different as can be, but we somehow make it work. How about you, Cami? Anyone special in your life?"

"Besides my grandfather, Rafe?" Cami shook her head. "No, I'm through with men at the moment."

Jamison smiled knowingly. "We all have moments like that. Even when we're married."

Cami laughed at the wink Jamison gave her. She liked this spunky woman.

On the ride to Chandler Hill, they talked about what Cami would ask of Jamison while she was at the inn and what she wanted her to do going forward. Jamison then asked Cami lots of questions about growing grapes, running the inn, and managing the expectations of guests.

As she talked, Cami realized she knew a lot more about the overall operation than she'd thought. She glanced at Jamison, and seeing her smile, realized that's what Jamison had hoped for all along.

"Sounds to me like you're not the naïve newcomer

Jonathan thinks you are," said Jamison. "That's good. I like surprises. Let's see if he does."

Remembering the way Jonathan had dismissed her views on occasion, Cami laughed with delight.

Jamison looked around with interest when Cami drove up the long driveway to the inn. And when Cami pulled into the parking lot in front of it, Jamison let out a soft whistle.

"Online pictures can't compare to this. The inn and the setting around it are stunning."

Cami filled with a sense of pride. "It's beautiful, I know. But like my grandmother and the Chandler men, it's the land I love most. Probably because she walked me through it over and over again from the time I was little."

"I know enough about growing grapes to understand you need to be a skilled farmer."

"Yes," Cami agreed. "That's what Ken Kurey always said. Ken is gone now, but his son is still the winemaker here. As soon as I can, I'm going to begin training under him, but first I need to become more familiar with the details and daily routines of managing the inn, so I can get it running smoothly.

"Who's handling the grapes?"

"Sam Farley is in charge of the vines both here and at my grandfather's property. He recently hired his nephew, Drew, to help him."

"Sounds like a big, happy family," said Jamison.

"We'll see. We're still trying to get over the loss of Nonnee. She was a wizard at knowing exactly what needed to be done and when."

"You'll be fine," said Jamison. She patted Cami's shoulder and opened the car door, putting an end to the discussion.

Cami hurried to get Jamison's suitcase out of the back of the latest Lexus SUV that used to be Nonnee's. In Europe, she'd grown used to small cars. This vehicle seemed enormous, but Cami wasn't about to turn it in for something smaller or less comfortable.

She led Jamison inside the main building, which was the original house and inn. Looking at it through fresh eyes, she saw that the old pine floors in the living area gleamed with care. The red Oriental rug was a perfect example of the high quality of furnishings in the house, including several comfortable leather couches and chairs. It looked, she thought, like the large home of a successful owner of an estate, which was more or less the truth.

"Very nice," commented Jamison, looking around. "This has a quiet, understated elegance that is missing in so many places. You say Jonathan wants to change this?"

"Yes," said Cami. "He wants to step it up a notch, make it more attractive to young couples with a more contemporary look and vibe. I told him Nonnee wouldn't like that idea."

"And?" Jamison studied her.

"And he said that this was an excellent time to make some changes, to re-position the inn to bring in a different clientele. I don't agree with him. Anyway, we can't do anything because of the lack of money."

"I understand," said Jamison, smiling when Jonathan walked toward them.

"Welcome to the Chandler Hill Inn," he said. "I'm Jonathan Knight. And who, may I ask, are you?"

"Jamison Barnes Winkler," she said smoothly. "Nice to meet you."

"Ah, you're the lawyer who's going to help us sort things out. Well, Cami can show you to your room. I understand we're meeting after lunch." He gave her a little bow and left them.

Jamison turned to Cami. "Your Mr. Knight knows how to put on the charm even as he nicely puts you in your place."

Cami narrowed her lips. "That's why it's so difficult for me. Other people see his charm and assume that I, a woman, would naturally be the one working for him."

"For now," Jamison said sweetly. "Come along, and show me to my room."

"Oh, yes, sorry," said Cami. "I've chosen one of the original rooms for you rather than one in the north wing. The original rooms are not only my favorite ones, they're convenient to the kitchen and dining room. It's nice enough today that I thought we'd eat our lunch outside on the porch."

"Sounds perfect," said Jamison.

Cami showed Jamison to a large bedroom with a wide view overlooking the rolling hills to the west. With its crown molding, small, gas fireplace, and four-poster, canopied bed, the room oozed charm. The modern bathroom and private deck made it that much nicer.

Jamison clasped her hands and nodded her approval. "Lovely." She walked to the window and looked out at the scenery. "The rows and rows of grapevines are lined up perfectly."

"Yes, and they're all running north and south. That's so the grapes will get equal sunlight east to west."

"Ah, so much to learn," said Jamison.

"It's almost time to harvest," said Cami. "Too bad you can't stay to see it."

"Another time, perhaps. A school dance, first of the year, is an important event for my girls. I promised them I wouldn't miss it." Jamison chuckled. "I think they thought it was a threat."

Cami laughed with her. Nonnee had been like Jamison, making sure she didn't miss any special event of Cami's, even when the inn or vineyards needed her.

"May I get you anything before I leave?" Cami asked. She'd

already placed Jamison's suitcase on a luggage stand and checked to make sure a fresh pitcher of iced water sat beside a plate holding one of the inn's signature hazelnut muffins. Cookies, cheese, and crackers would be served in the afternoon.

"I'm fine, thank you," said Jamison.

"Okay, then I'll meet you downstairs shortly after noon." Cami smiled and made her exit. The afternoon promised to be exciting.

At noon, Cami waited at the bottom of the stairs for Jamison, thinking how the kitchen and staff had grown through the years as the inn had been enlarged and become more sophisticated. Where once it had been difficult to hire staff, the valley's growth made it easier to hire people who either lived in the region or were willing to move there.

"Hello," said Jamison, breaking into Cami's thoughts. "It's such a beautiful day, I took a quick nap outside in the sun."

"Nice. I love Indian Summer days like this. Shall we go have lunch?"

They walked out to the porch behind the house. Over the years, Nonnee had expanded it to accommodate the guests who came to the inn for the excellent food, wine, and views for which it had become known.

Jonathan was already seated at the table Cami had reserved. Seeing them approach, he rose to his feet. "Great day for lunch on the porch." He helped Jamison get seated while Cami sat nearby.

It being a weekday, the tables on the porch were not full. Cami was glad. She wanted privacy for the conversation that was to follow.

A young girl with a single long, brown braid came to serve

them. Her glance kept going to Jonathan, who gave her a wink. Cheeks flushed, she turned to Cami. "Our specials today are butternut squash soup, served with an open-faced, toasted brie-and-apple sandwich or chicken pot pie. And of course, we have our regular items on the menu."

"Thank you, Chelsea," Jonathan said, eying the waitress with obvious appreciation.

Uncomfortable watching the interchange between them, Cami shifted in her seat. Jamison caught her attention, and Cami knew by her eyeroll she was as put off by Jonathan's flirtatious behavior as she.

They quickly placed their orders, and then Jonathan turned to Jamison. "I hope you understand the position I'm being put in with the return of Cami to the property. Lettie Chandler relied upon me to carry on without her, and I've done exactly that."

Jamison nodded agreeably. "Yes, I do understand how difficult it might be for someone like you to relinquish your authority to someone you don't respect."

Jonathan's eyes widened. "I ... I ... never said that."

"Of course not," Jamison said pleasantly. "But your actions did and do. That's something we're all going to have to work on. Cooperation is the key. I trust you're willing to give me that as I sort through some of the contracts and business agreements on behalf of my client."

"I've made no new contracts since we discovered that a large part of Lettie Chandler's investments are now gone." Jonathan's voice held challenge.

"So, I understand," said Jamison, smiling at him. "Ah, here's lunch. It looks delightful."

Cami and Jamison ate their soup while Jonathan dug into a salad. The quiet was broken when Chelsea came to the table. "Mr. Knight, you have an important call from a supplier."

"Thank you." Jonathan dabbed a napkin to his lips and rose. "Let me take this. I'll be right back."

"Do you want me to come with you?" Cami asked, wondering why a supplier would be calling them. The bills had all been paid, hadn't they?

Jonathan waved her back to her seat. "I've got this."

After he left, Jamison turned to her with a frown. "I can see why you're concerned. But don't worry, as we discussed earlier, we're going to be in touch with all the suppliers. From this point forward, only you will be able to write checks or transfer funds. It will be annoying to Jonathan, but until we're sure of his cooperation that's how it'll have to be."

"Good," said Cami, happy she wouldn't have to face Jonathan's fury alone.

Jonathan returned to the table a few minutes later. "Got that settled. Just a dispute on a bill."

"What supplier?" Cami asked.

"Fresh Farm Foods," Jonathan said. "Now, let's get back to business." He faced Jamison. "You can see how frustrating it is for me to have to explain everything. Lettie hardly looked at the reports I prepared for her."

"My grandmother was dying," Cami reminded him.

"Yes, but she knew I could handle things," Jonathan shot back.

"As we talked about, I'll review all purchasing specifications, contracts, and procedures," said Jamison in a calming voice. "It's common to do that whenever there's a change in ownership."

"Did you know Lettie promised me part of the business?" Jonathan said, glancing at Cami and then focusing on Jamison.

"No, I wasn't aware of that." Jamison turned to Cami. "Were you?"

Shocked, Cami shook her head. "No, I wasn't."Nonnee certainly would have told her about that, wouldn't she?

Jonathan shifted in his chair. An intriguing blush crept up his cheeks. "Lettie was hoping that Cami and I would ..."

Cami raised a hand. "Don't even say it."

She and Jonathan scowled at each other.

"A grandmother's hopeful wish, nothing more," said Jamison, cooling the heated tension at the table. "The point is that you two have to work together, at least until Jonathan decides whether he wants to continue working here."

Both Cami and Jonathan stared at Jamison with surprise.

"That's the real issue. Right?" Jamison said.

Silent, Cami and Jonathan each nodded.

Still surprised by the idea Nonnee had thought they might get along, Cami glanced at Jonathan. She didn't like him, nor did she trust him. Why had Nonnee given him the job at the inn? It hit her then. Jonathan resembled a picture she'd seen of a young Rex Chandler. Maybe, as some had hinted, Nonnee was truly failing at the end. The thought made her sad.

They finished lunch and headed into Cami's office.

Jamison turned to Jonathan. "I'll need your computer for a couple of hours. Cami can accompany you to your office to get it."

"What in hell is going on?" Jonathan said. "Are you accusing me of something?"

"Not at all," Jamison said calmly. "It's all part of the review we talked about earlier. If things are in order, it shouldn't take that long. I understand Cami already has access to a lot of the files."

Cami reluctantly followed Jonathan out of the office. He looked like he wanted to slap her.

After he entered his office, he slammed the door behind them. "Go ahead. Try to find something wrong. You won't."

"I'm simply trying to understand our present situation," Cami said. "If I'm to take over for my grandmother, I need to understand everything about the operation. You know that."

"Yeah? Just so you are aware, that phone call wasn't from a supplier. I made that up. It was about a new job offer I have. And if any more of this shit goes on, I'm going to take it."

Hiding her anger, Cami picked up the computer from his desk. "I'll tell Jamison."

"You think it's easy to run a hotel like this? You're going to fail, Cami. You might be Lettie Chandler's granddaughter, but you're nothing like her."

His words, like needles in her heart, made her stumble as she headed for the door. She straightened and turned back to him. "You'd be surprised. You're not going to quit because as of this moment, you're fired."

She went back to the desk and lifted the phone to call Jamison. As soon as Cami told Jamison what had happened, Jamison said, "Get one of the male staff members up here as soon as you can. We need to remove Jonathan from the property."

Cami called down to the barn. Drew Farley answered the phone.

"Can you come to the manager's office right away? I need your help," she said, stifling a tremor to her voice.

"I'm on my way," he replied.

CHAPTER THREE

Cami stood in the office looking out the window at the figure walking toward the inn at a brisk pace. She'd met Drew Farley at the funeral service for Nonnee, but in her emotional blur she couldn't remember what he looked like beyond a tall, healthy male.

Watching his long strides, she wondered what lay behind the story she'd been told about him. His uncle, Sam Farley, who'd taken over from her great-grandfather, Jose Lopez, as the tractor man for Chandler Hill, had raised Drew single handedly. No mother, no aunt to do the job. She'd always liked Sam, who was a quiet, kind man.

Cami hurried to the office door to let Drew inside.

Tawny-colored eyes met hers when she greeted him.

"Glad you're here," she said quietly to Drew, glancing at Jonathan out of the corner of her eye as Jamison joined him in the hall. "We need you to escort Jonathan Knight off the property," she said quietly. "He announced he's taking another job, and before he could quit, I fired him."

Surprised to see Drew and Jamison enter the office, Jonathan frowned. "What's going on?" he said, trying to play it cool.

"My client has terminated your employment here," said Jamison. "Mr. Farley is going to escort you off the property. You can make arrangements with Cami to come back at a suitable time to pick up your personal belongings from the office, or we'll be happy to pack them up and have them delivered to your apartment in town."

"You can't do this," cried Jonathan, giving her a look so full of venom that Cami shuddered.

"We can, we will, and we are," said Jamison in a firm voice. "Grab your coat and go with Mr. Farley now."

"It's all your doing," Jonathan snarled at Cami. "Without me, you're going to bring this place down."

Drew stepped in front of her, forming a protective barrier. "Enough," he said in a deep bass voice that meant business.

Jamison handed Jonathan his blazer.

Jonathan stormed out of the room. Drew caught up to him, and they disappeared down the hallway toward the kitchen together.

Trembling, Cami lowered herself into a chair and drew several deep breaths.

"It's upsetting, I know, but this will prevent Jonathan from taking any confidential or proprietary information with him and give us a better opportunity to find out what, if anything, he might have done in an underhanded way."

Drew returned a few moments later and stood in front of her chair. "He's gone for now."

"Now, we need to warn the staff that he's not to be allowed back on property without an escort, " said Jamison.

Drew gave Cami a worried look. "He was pretty upset and said all kinds of threatening things about you. I'll go ahead and write it all down for you. Just in case you need it someday."

Cami looked up at him, seeing him clearly. His tawny-colored eyes matched what she would call hair the color of butterscotch—a warm, golden brown. His features were pleasing—straight nose, strong chin, and very kissable lips. Suddenly realizing she'd been staring, Cami blurted, "I'm really glad you were here to help us. Jonathan has resented me ever since I came home."

"Yeah, well if he bothers you again, let me know." He tipped his head and strode out of the room.

Jamison and Cami exchanged looks of admiration.

"Now that one," said Jamison, "is definitely not like your French friend."

Cami felt her lips curve. Maybe, with friends like this, she could succeed as the owner of this enterprise. In the meantime, she was definitely intrigued by Mr. Wonderful.

Thoughts of any man were dismissed as Cami and Jamison worked together to review all contracts with suppliers and their purchase specification, invoice, and statement files.

"I'm not sure what some of these surcharges are," said Jamison thoughtfully. She lifted the phone to call their meat supplier.

Cami continued to make a list of people to notify of the change in management. She'd make personal phone calls, followed up by emails. That way, no one could misunderstand that Jonathan was no longer able to conduct any business for Chandler Hill.

When Jamison got off the phone, she turned to Cami, working beside her. "That was interesting. Those surcharges were part of a kickback scheme Jonathan was using to benefit himself and a worker at the supplier who's already been fired. It's petty stuff, but very dishonest. We'll use it against the two of them if we have to. But I have a feeling we're not going to hear much from Mr. Knight when he realizes we know what's been going on. Let's see what else we can find. In the meantime, I suggest you start making phone calls to all the suppliers. And double-check with the bank to make sure Jonathan's name is off everything."

"What about the surcharges?" Cami asked.

Jamison smiled. "I've arranged for you to have a nice credit on the account."

Cami returned her smile and then grew serious. "Thanks. I'm calling the others now."

Cami's first call was to the bank. The vice-president to whom she was directed listened intently and then quietly said, "I'm glad you called, Ms. Chandler. I was about to get in touch with you. We've recently noticed a few irregularities on the account. Three different checks for fourteen hundred ninety-eight dollars and eighty-eight cents have been made out to a purveyor by the name of Paxton Fresh Foods. Ordinarily, we wouldn't think anything of it. But three different exact payments caught our eye, and when we looked up the name, we couldn't find such a business in the area.

"Thank you," said Cami, feeling sick to her stomach. "I'll have my lawyer follow through on this. In the meantime, only I will be responsible for any dealings with the bank."

"Understood," said the banker. "I'll be sure to remove Jonathan's name from all of your accounts immediately. Welcome aboard. We always enjoyed working with your grandmother. It will be a pleasure helping you."

Three days later, Cami stood inside the airport terminal in Portland. She gave Jamison a hug and stood back. "I wish you didn't have to leave. You've been such a great help to me handling the issues with Jonathan and assisting in setting things up properly."

"I'll be back. I promise. And next time, I'll bring Wynton with me. I think he'd love the landscape as much as we do."

"That would be fabulous," Cami said. "It would be such an honor to meet him."

Jamison's smile was warm. "I think he'd enjoy meeting you too." She waved goodbye and walked away.

Standing by herself in the bustling noise of the terminal,

Cami wished she could take off, fly anywhere to escape. The work ahead of her was daunting.

On the way back to the inn, her cell phone rang. *Bernard.*

Cami hesitated, then answered. "*Bonjour*, Bernard. What is it?"

Bernard let out a long sigh. "I miss you, *chérie!*"

Though her heart was doing a rebellious leap, Cami forced herself to stay silent.

"I was thinking I might come see you in Oregon. My job at the vineyards here has ended."

Cami's mind raced. "But I thought you were going to buy into the vineyards, have a piece of the action with your brother."

"Pouf! It ended up being nothing. That's why I thought I should come stay with you."

"I don't think that's a good idea. There are too many things to settle here. Give me a few weeks to get on my feet and then we'll see about that."

"But I thought you'd want me with you," Bernard said.

Resisting every urge to tell him to come immediately, Cami stopped him. "I'll let you know." She hung up before she could change her mind. At the sound of his smooth, sexy voice, her body had reacted with a familiar ache.

She found herself speeding along the highway as if she could hurry the time until she could call him. Slowing down before any cop could stop her, Cami realized Jamison was right. As far as romance was concerned, Bernard was a frog, not a prince. Besides, she had to devote all her time and efforts to getting a handle on the business, not trying to resurrect a one-sided love affair. Besides, who did Bernard think he was? He had broken her heart. He'd never even called her on the day of Nonnee's funeral.

When she realized she was gripping the steering wheel so

tightly her knuckles had turned white, Cami took a deep breath and relaxed her grip. Bernard had already shown his true self. Why would she ever want to see him again?

Her thoughts turned to issues at the inn. The staff, it turned out, hadn't been as impressed with Jonathan as he was with himself. After meeting with several of them, Cami felt they'd at least give her a chance to prove herself capable. When Nonnee had run it, the Chandler Hill Inn had been one of the best places in the valley for staff to work. She wanted that to happen again.

As she pulled into the driveway of her home, her grandfather was leaving. He approached her car with a smile. "Hi! I just finished loading the last of my belongings. Want to come over and see how things are going at the cabin?"

"Sure," Cami said, wishing she didn't have to face another change. She got out of her car and climbed into his silver truck.

In silence, Rafe drove the short distance to the cabin. When he pulled to a stop in front of it, he turned to her. "After I'm settled here, you and I need to talk about a few things. I want Drew Farley to begin working at the winery for me."

"I thought he was set to work for Chandler Hill."

"Scott's son, Adam, is training to take over for him. Drew wants an opportunity on his own. He'll continue to help Sam with the vines here at Chandler Hill and at Taunton Estates. Seems only appropriate since you will someday own both."

Silent, Cami nodded.

Rafe placed a hand on her shoulder. "I know it must seem like all these changes are too much to handle, but you can do it."

"I hope so. I don't want to disappoint Nonnee or you."

He smiled. "Don't worry. You couldn't. We both love you so much."

Cami climbed out of the truck and waited for him to join her. Together they went inside.

At the sound of hammering and a mumbled curse loud enough for her to hear, Cami followed her grandfather to the master bedroom.

Drew Farley looked up at them from where he was kneeling on the carpet. "Almost got this bed put together, but it isn't easy."

Cami stared at the huge four-poster bed partially assembled. Rafe had insisted on continuing to use the bed following Nonnee's death and had brought it with him to the cabin. She was happy to choose something simpler, more contemporary for the master suite at Nonnee's house.

Rafe and Cami held the headboard and the footboard while Drew slid the side rails into place.

"There, that's going to do it," said Drew standing.

"Help me get the mattress and box spring onto it and then the housekeepers from the hotel can do the rest," said Rafe.

Watching the men lift the heavy mattress onto the bed frame, Cami couldn't help staring at the way the muscles in Drew's arms knotted.

Her grandfather checked his watch. "Your bed is due to be delivered now, Cami. Better go. And, Drew, why don't you go with her to make sure everything, including the mattresses, are set in place."

Drew glanced at Cami and then nodded. "Sure, no problem."

"Want to borrow my truck?" Rafe asked.

Cami shook her head. "No, we'll walk. It won't take us long."

She and Drew left the cabin and headed for her house.

Outside, Cami drew in a breath of the crisp, fresh air. She loved this time of year—the autumn weather and the knowledge that the ripening grapes would soon be picked.

She turned to Drew. "Look, you don't have to accompany me to my house. I'm pretty sure I can handle things there."

He shook his head. "I'll go with you. I'd do anything for Rafe."

They headed toward her house, walking easily across the land.

"Pretty time of year, huh?" said Drew.

"Yes. Mother Nature does her best with colors in the fall. I never tire of looking at them. They make me want to sit with my paints and try to capture them."

"You're an artist?" Drew asked as they ambled along side by side.

"Not really. I studied fine arts, but don't fancy myself as anyone but a person who admires nice work." Bernard had made fun of the few paintings she'd tried of fields of flowers in the south of France. It had stung at the time, but she realized he was right. She'd never be anything but a novice at painting.

"In college I took an art appreciation course," Drew said. "It was an easy way to get a high grade."

Cami laughed. "Well, did it help you to understand some of the better-known art we see today?"

"Actually, it did," said Drew grinning. "Art galleries aren't quite so baffling anymore." His expression grew more serious. "Speaking of baffling, why does Jonathan Knight have such a thing against you? You seem pretty reasonable."

"My grandmother might have given him a wrong impression. I believe he actually thought he was going to end up owning a piece of the business. But that was never going to happen, especially when I have a strict duty to my grandmother to carry on for her. That's my reason for coming home."

"Where were you before you came here?"

"In France. Another long story. One I'm glad is over."

He stopped and studied her with the light-brown eyes she found intriguing. He was handsome—a Ryan Gosling lookalike. "Yeah. I have a long story too," he said. "Live and learn, I say."

"My grandfather told me you're going to become a winemaker for him. You realize that makes us rivals, don't you?"

He grinned. "Both Chandler Hill and Taunton Estates wines are superb. But I'm hoping to do a little experimenting for a new wine. We'll see."

Until now, Cami hadn't been anxious to get started on winemaking. The thought of trying to beat Drew in wine competitions suddenly made it seem exciting.

"Who's going to run the inn with Jonathan Knight gone?" Drew asked, bringing her back to reality. She couldn't think of getting overly involved in winemaking until the inn was in order.

"Becca and I are going to run it together. We'll hire a consultant to work with us for a few months, and then we'll be on our own."

Drew's eyebrows shot up. "Becca? She's really smart. She and I dated a few times, but I told her I'm not getting serious with anyone. No long-term relationships for me. Now, she's dating a friend of mine."

Cami hid her surprise. Becca had never mentioned it.

As they walked up to the house, a delivery truck rumbled toward them.

"Good timing," said Drew.

Cami hurried inside the house to make sure the master bedroom was ready to receive her new bed. Later, she'd move in her personal items. She hadn't wanted to disturb Rafe while he was packing up.

Drew stayed with her while she made sure the bed was placed correctly. After everything was put together and in place, he said, "Guess I'd better go."

"It's lunch time. Want to stay? I make a mean sandwich."

He laughed. "Sure. Why not? I wasn't scheduled to work today anyway."

Sitting on the deck, Cami swallowed the last bite of her sliced chicken and chutney sandwich. "Sorry, I don't have anything to offer you for dessert," she said to Drew.

"No worries. This was great. Now, I'd better go." His warm gaze remained on her. "Thanks for lunch. With harvesting about to begin, I'm sure we'll see each other around." He got to his feet. "See you later."

Cami rose and walked him to the door. "May I drop you off anywhere?"

Drew shook his head. "No, thanks. I'll go check on Rafe and then go home from there."

She stood at the doorway for a few moments, watching him stride away. If she were considering dating, he'd definitely be on her list. But he'd made it plain he wasn't interested in her or any other woman. Having that out in the open had made their lunch relaxing.

Cami hurried into her office and buzzed Becca. She and Jamison had discussed having Becca work beside her, much like Lettie and Paloma had done through the years. Now, it was time to work out some of the finer details.

Becca came into the office all smiles. "I heard you and Drew Farley had lunch together."

"How'd you hear that?" Cami asked.

Becca laughed. "Nothing goes unnoticed in a hotel. Not with staff everywhere. So, how was it?"

"If you're talking about my fixing a sandwich for Drew as a means of thanking him for helping Rafe and me this morning, that was it. Nothing more. He's not interested in anything between us, and neither am I."

"Oh." Becca sounded disappointed. "I thought the two of you would be great together. Drew's a good guy."

"Yes, he is. You're dating a friend of his?"

Becca's cheeks turned a pretty pink. "Dan Thurston and I have been dating a couple of months now. There's a spark between us that I've never felt with anyone before. I don't know for sure, but I think he may be 'the one.'" She made quotation marks in the air with her fingers. "He's a really great guy who is part of his family's construction business, and I respect his hard work."

"Nice," said Cami, remembering how she'd once thought she'd found "the one" with Bernard. "Is Dan okay with your taking on more and more responsibility here at the inn?"

"Yes, he's very busy, and I will be as well." Becca's green eyes studied her. "The first time I met you, I knew we'd be friends. And after watching you work with the staff the short time you've been on board, I know I can work with you as your personal assistant. In fact, I think I may have already found my replacement as an administrative assistant."

"Really? Fantastic!"

"Her name is Imani. I told her if you were interested, we'd call and ask her to come in for an interview. I already have her resumé."

"Okay, let's go over that, and if we like what we see, we'll set up an appointment. Then we need to talk about what needs to be done here at the inn. Paloma, my grandmother's friend, ended up running a lot of the daily details. I'm hoping that's what will happen with us."

"It sounds great," said Becca. "I want you to know how much your trust in me means. Jonathan always made it seem as if he was running the show while, in reality, I was doing a lot of the work behind the scenes."

"Yes, Jamison and I both are aware of that."

After agreeing to meet with Imani and going over a number of duties and a calendar of sorts for the year, Cami rose. "Let's go say hello to some of our guests. It's time for happy hour. I'm sure many of them will be at the reception."

CHAPTER FOUR

Circulating among the guests, seeing how happy they were, was the most pleasant part of the job for Cami. Years of standing by her grandmother's side as she greeted others at these occasions had always been a joy to her. Hard work went into creating the environment for even the most-easy-going visitor's stay, and this was a moment to reap the benefits of that.

Cami smiled at the memory of her grandmother and moved on to greet someone new.

Some guests were easy and pleasant. Others, not so much. But Cami made it a practice to listen to each one, storing information to be used later to improve their experiences at the inn.

Cami lingered to keep an eye on Becca. With her bubbly personality, Becca was a natural with the guests. Jamison had been quite right to urge her to take advantage of having Becca get more involved at the inn.

Abby, who handled the merchandise for The Barn and the rest of the complex, came into the room. Cami rushed over to her and gave her a hug. If Nonnee was the grandmother every young girl wanted, Abigail Wilkins was the great aunt one wished for. She'd always been more like a fairy godmother, appearing with gifts and games and other surprises from the store. Now in her late sixties and anxious to retire, Abby was eager for Cami to take over for her.

"Glad you're here," said Abby. "I've set up a meeting for us later this week. I want you to meet with the staff at The Barn, and then we can talk about the future. I'm sure Rex Chandler had no idea how a simple tasting barn could evolve. Today, The Barn is a major source of revenue and profit for us."

"The end of the week sounds fine. Again, thank you for staying until I get things organized. There's so much to think about."

Abby gave her a hug. "You're not Lettie's granddaughter for nothing."

Cami's smile wobbled. Everyone else but she was convinced she could easily do the job.

Rafe walked into the room, causing a stir among the older women. He was still a handsome man and was considered quite a "catch" in the valley.

He approached, gave Abby a quick hug, and kissed Cami on the cheek. "Looks like I'm all set at the cabin. To thank you, I have a surprise waiting at the house."

Cami grinned at him. "Really? I love surprises!"

Rafe laughed and winked. "I know, and it's a good one."

Anxious to get home, Cami looked around the room. The library was used for smaller groups, but with the inn full of guests, the reception area in the wing of the inn was being used for this occasion. Observing how the colors of the sunset shining through the double set of sliding-glass doors were reflected in the crystal chandelier, Cami thought of her grandmother. Just as she'd had a natural palate for wine, Lettie Chandler had had an instinctive ability to create environments of understated elegance. The beauty of the chandelier and plush carpeting in this area was enhanced by views of the rolling hills blanketed by vineyards outside.

Cami continued to make her round of guests, welcoming them. But her mind was on Rafe's surprise. As soon as she could gracefully excuse herself, she signaled Rafe, and they left together.

"Want a ride?" she said to Rafe.

"Sure. I walked over to the reception. It's nice the lay of the land gives privacy to the cabin and your house, yet they aren't that far away from the inn and The Barn."

"And not far away from our special grove of trees," amended Cami, giving him a warm smile as she got behind the wheel of her car.

He sat in the passenger seat and sighed. "I never dreamed I'd outlive Lettie."

"It was an awful surprise to everyone. She was such an active, strong woman."

He studied her. "You're a lot more like her than you think. But, Cami, she wasn't perfect. Don't let others intimidate you on that point. Be your own person, go your own way."

Tears stung her eyes. They were words she'd needed to hear. "Thanks," she managed to say. There were times she was scared to death of what lay ahead.

When she pulled up to her house, Rafe turned to her with twinkling eyes. "Okay, let's see to that surprise."

Cami got out of the car, and she and Rafe hurried up to the front door together. As Cami opened the door, she heard "Yip!"

Laughing, she turned to Rafe. "A dog? That's the surprise?"

"Come see." He led her to the kitchen.

Behind a gate in a section of the kitchen, a small, smooth-haired, black-and-tan puppy stared up at her and barked, "Yip!"

"A wiener dog?" she asked, already reaching for the bright-eyed puppy that was wagging her tail so hard she almost toppled over.

In her arms, the puppy squirmed until she could reach up and give Cami a lick on the cheek. "Oh, she's so sweet!"

"She's a ten-week-old dachshund from a reliable breeder in

the area. I remember how you were with one of the staff's wiener dogs when you were small. And of course, there was Babe. But I thought you'd want something smaller than a Lab."

"Nonnee once gave me a stuffed wiener-dog toy," Cami said remembering how she used to love it. "I'm going to call this one Sophie too." She hugged the dog to her chest. "Thank you, Rafe. It means so much to me to have her, especially with your moving out of the house."

"I thought you'd like the company." He gave her a teasing grin. "But don't call me when she makes a mess or does something worse."

Cami laughed. "It'll be worth all the training. Maybe the puppy will even come to my office with me."

Rafe gave her a hug. "It's nice to see you smile, *cariño*. Now, I will leave you. Time for me to get more settled."

Carrying the puppy, Cami walked Rafe to the front door. She stood and watched him as he walked away, not toward the cabin, but to the grove of trees.

Cami set the dog down in the grass. "Get busy!" she ordered.

The puppy cocked her head, started to run, and then squatted in the grass.

"Oh, you're so smart, Sophie! Good girl." She picked up the puppy and brought her inside, knowing it was going to take a lot more training to get Sophie to understand her commands.

When she put Sophie back in the kitchen and left to go change her clothes, Sophie gave an indignant bark that grew into loud, high-pitched yaps of fury at being abandoned.

A few days later, preparing for Friday's meeting with the staff at The Barn, Cami placed a small blanket inside the huge, canvas bag she sometimes used for travel and put Sophie inside. The puppy had made it clear she intended to be a bigger part of her life than Cami had imagined. But she didn't mind. Sophie was bright and responsive and adorable.

Abby met her outside the barn. "I love seeing you with the puppy like this. It reminds me so much of Lettie carrying you in a backpack as she went about business at the inn. Heaven knows how many miles she walked with you through the vineyards, but it was a lot."

Cami smiled at the memory. "I hope I was easier to carry than this little girl." She opened the bag wider so Abby could get a good look. "Isn't she the cutest puppy?"

Sophie wagged her tail, making a thumping noise against the canvas that made them break out in laughter.

"She sure is a sweetie," said Abby. "C'mon. Let's go inside. The staff knows you, of course, but they're anxious to learn how you envision things going forward."

"I have several ideas, but we'll have to work together to see how best to do things."

"Nice idea to be part of the group from the beginning," said Abby. "Don't hesitate to let us know when you see something you don't like or you want to do differently. With your artistic background, you might want to change things up, bring in some new merchandise, that kind of thing."

Cami let out the breath she hadn't realized she'd been holding. She hadn't wanted to offend Abby, but she wanted to do exactly what Abby had suggested.

When she entered the meeting room upstairs, twenty-one people smiled at her. She knew, of course, that six were full-time store employees, and eight were part-time. Two more worked on filling mail orders, three handled the wine-tasting bar, and two office workers handled invoicing, ordering, shipping, payroll, and other office procedures. Of different ages, all seemed friendly.

Abby had every person in the room tell a little bit about their background and interests and their role at The Barn. Cami was pleased to see both men and women were part of the operation and the entire staff had been trained to know about the wines they served at wine tastings.

After everyone had spoken, Abby said, "I'm going to give Cami a complete tour of The Barn, and then over the next week or so, she will spend time in all areas working with each of you so she understands every aspect of the operation. That will be your job."

Amidst the murmuring that followed, Cami said, "Don't worry. I'll be a hard worker." Laughter followed.

A woman she guessed was in her forties and who worked in the book section of The Barn smiled. "It will be a pleasure to have you."

"For all of us," added a gentleman. "I want to hear everything you have to tell me about our wines. You wouldn't believe the questions I get from visitors."

"Why don't we bring in Scott Kurey to talk to us?" said Cami. "He's our winemaker. He can tell us more about Chandler Hill wines than anybody I know." She could never get enough information about winemaking. Each vineyard, each grape was so different. She'd found that in France, too.

"Great suggestion to ask Scott to speak to us," said Abby. "I'll arrange it."

Sophie woke up from her nap and stared at Cami from inside the canvas carryall.

"Excuse me," she said, and raced to take the puppy outside.

As she was watching the puppy do her thing, Cami thought about all the work Abby did overseeing The Barn. Gone were the days of only T-shirts, trinkets, and baseball hats. Those still remained, of course, but the inventory had become more widely diversified, and activities now included wine tastings, sampling of appetizers, cooking demonstrations, and merchandising of every conceivable item for cooks and lovers of wines. As someone who appreciated art, she was interested in adding more of that to The Barn. She knew that artists in the valley were always looking for ways to display their work. What better place than The Barn at Chandler Hill? And perhaps there'd be opportunities to use reproductions of the work of local artists in some of the guest rooms that needed freshening.

From a distance she watched guests enter The Barn with enthusiasm. Others left carrying packages and brochures. One man lugged a case of wine. No doubt he'd joined the wine club at Chandler Hill.

Later, Cami and Becca interviewed Imani Patel. Short and petite with lively smiles that frequently lit her tan face, her bright dark eyes seemed to miss nothing as she sat in Cami's office to discuss the role of assistant and the necessary qualifications to fill it.

As the three of them talked, Cami was impressed by how competent and confident Imani was with her office skills. More than that, she was a nice person with a great personality and a willingness to get along. From the smile on Becca's face, Cami knew Becca liked Imani as much as she. Together they asked Imani to join their team, pleased with the idea of the extra help. They needed it. The inn was continuing to be busy.

As the holiday season approached, Cami vowed to keep to Nonnee's traditions.

Thanksgiving Dinner at the Chandler Hill Inn had become one of the best events in the valley. Darren Bullard, his wife Liz, and the entire kitchen crew worked for days in advance to create a meal worthy of the inn's reputation.

Darren, a long-time alumnus of the Culinary Institute, was a wonderful chef and a true find for the inn. His wife, Liz, assisted in the kitchen and did most of the work on the morning shift while he took on the dinner duties. In their fifties, they'd moved to the Willamette Valley to have a simpler life from the competitive rat race they'd experienced in the restaurant business in metropolitan areas.

As her grandmother had done every year, Cami stood at the entrance to the dining room to welcome her guests. This year, three different seatings were scheduled: eleven thirty; three o'clock; and six p.m.

By the time the last of the guests had completed their dinners, she was exhausted from standing on her feet greeting guests, making small talk, and overseeing the wait staff. Good service was as important as the food to some people, and she didn't want to disappoint anyone.

Darren waved her into the kitchen with a grin.

Cami eagerly joined him and the other staff members to celebrate with a glass of wine. Tomorrow, she knew, would be another hectic day when she and the staff would turn the inn and The Barn into a winter wonderland.

Outside, small, white, holiday lights twinkled on trees and bushes. Inside, cinnamon-scented candles, fresh pine boughs, and wine-colored velvet ribbons brightened rooms everywhere.

Cami stood in the reception area, studying the huge Christmas tree they'd put up there. It glistened and glowed with assorted, colorful glass balls and sparkly ornaments from the Christmas gift shop at The Barn and complemented the burgundy color of the Oriental rug.

Her spirits soared. Christmas was the one day of the year the inn was closed so staff members could be with their families. Growing up, she'd always loved this holiday best because it meant she could be home with Nonnee and Rafe and have them to herself.

"Looks nice," said Becca, coming to stand beside her in front of the tree.

"It's such a wonderful time of the year. The Barn looks fabulous, and sales are going crazy."

"Are you sure you don't mind if I take a few days off after Christmas?" Becca said.

"I'm sure. As long as you're back for New Year's Eve, it shouldn't be a problem." She placed an arm around Becca's shoulder. "The good thing is we have full-time jobs. The bad thing is these jobs are 24/7."

Becca laughed. "Growing up in New England, I never dreamed I'd be so involved with an inn in Oregon. But I love it."

"I love it too," Cami said automatically, fighting the knowledge of forever being tied to a property, never able completely to escape again. She understood now why Nonnee had been so eager for her to travel and be away from home while she could.

Christmas Day dawned bright and sunny. Cami stood in her kitchen adding champagne to two glasses of orange juice. Her grandmother had started the tradition of serving mimosas and eggs benedict on Christmas morning, and even though she and Rafe would be alone, Cami wanted to continue the custom. It made her feel as if Nonnee were there with her in spirit. Sophie barked when the doorbell rang, and Cami hurried to the door. She opened it and stared in surprise at

Rafe and Drew standing together.

"Hope you don't mind, but I've invited Drew to join us," said Rafe. "Seems he didn't have anywhere else to go."

"That's fine. Come on in. The more the merrier, as Nonnee would say." A thread of excitement quickened her pulse. She'd forgotten how mesmerizing Drew's light-brown eyes could be.

"Thanks," Drew said, giving her a broad, white smile. "Rafe insisted I join you."

"I'm so glad he did," she said sincerely. She'd made plenty of hollandaise sauce, and poaching an extra egg or two was no problem. The baker at the inn had given her a coffee cake as a gift—one she'd put to good use.

While the men greeted Sophie, Cami took their coats and laid them on a chair in one of the rooms in the guest wing. When she walked back into the living room, Rafe and Drew were standing in front of one of the paintings on the wall.

She froze.

"Lettie and I are so proud of Cami's work. This was a study she did in college," Rafe was saying.

"Very nice," said Drew. "I like the colors."

Rafe turned to her. "I've discovered another admirer of yours."

Cami felt her cheeks grow hot. Embarrassed to be described as a real artist, she said, "It's just a piece of homework, really."

Drew shrugged. "I like it. As I said, I've learned to appreciate art, and this is talent."

Remembering Bernard's cruel laughter, tears unexpectedly stung her eyes. She blinked furiously and quickly changed the subject. "How about joining me in the kitchen?"

The men followed her and stood by the kitchen bar. She handed mimosas to them and fixed herself another. Raising her glass, she said, "Here's to us! Health and happiness!"

"Hear! Hear!" cried Rafe, clicking his glass against hers and turning to Drew. "Here's hoping our new partnership works out."

"Partnership?" Cami said.

Her grandfather and Drew clicked their glasses in a mutual salute and turned to her.

Rafe cleared his throat. "I was going to tell you later, but you might as well know now that Drew and I are going to change up a few things in our winemaking. I'm renaming a section of my land and will produce wines under the label of Lettie's Creek Wines. Drew will be in charge of these grapes and the end product. It's an exciting time for both of us."

Surprised but pleased, Cami grinned. "How nice." She hadn't seen Rafe so happy for weeks. This would be a great way for him to move on.

They took their drinks to the living room and sat in front of the fire. With Sophie curled up between Rafe and her on the couch, a peaceful quiet filled the room.

"Abby and her partner, Lisa Robbins, would ordinarily be here with us, but they flew to Arizona to make sure their house was ready for the move," she explained to Drew.

"Yes, I know," said Drew. "Once they leave, I'll rent their place here."

"Oh, that's a great house, nestled between our two properties, convenient to both."

"That's important because I'll continue to help Sam with the vineyards on both your property and Rafe's."

Cami couldn't hold back her curiosity. "I understand your Uncle Sam raised you."

"Yes. My mother took off when I was a toddler, and who knows who my dad is. So, Sam took me in. He's a great guy."

"And he's never married?" she continued to ask even though Rafe had begun to frown at her.

"He was married briefly and has no intention of ever doing it again. I think living with him and seeing how happy he is without a woman in the house is one reason why I'm not eager to settle down with anyone."

"Interesting. Neither one of us knows who our father is."

"I'm not sure we could ever have gotten the whole story from your mother," Rafe said to her. "Autumn could be pretty stubborn, and she wasn't about to share any information about your father." He turned to Drew. "Autumn was killed by a car as she was jogging when Cami was just six."

Drew's glance shot to her. "Sorry. That must have been hard. I was too young when my mother left to be able to remember her."

"I say we have another mimosa," said Rafe, rising to his feet. "I'll make them."

"Great," said Cami, watching him leave the room. She stared into the flames of the fire feeling a sense of loss. Her father, a man she didn't know, was somewhere.

"Here we are," said Rafe, carrying in a pitcher of mimosas. "We can take our time, though I do have a gift for you, Cami."

"Not another dachshund," she teased. "I'm not sure I could handle another Sophie."

When Sophie heard the sound of her name, she wagged her tail and barked.

Rafe laughed. "No, something a little easier to take care of. I'll give it to you later."

After they'd eaten their eggs benedict and each had enjoyed a last sip of hot coffee, Drew got to his feet. "Great breakfast. Before I go, can I help you with the dishes?"

Cami shook her head and rose from her chair. "Thanks, but I'll take care of them."

She walked him to the front door. "I'm glad you could join us, Drew. It made for a very nice morning."

"I really enjoyed it." He gave her a smile that reached his eyes, adding a sparkle to them, drawing her in. He leaned over and gave her a quick kiss on the cheek. "See you around."

Watching him head to his truck, Cami lifted a hand to the spot on her face that still tingled.

CHAPTER FIVE

After doing the dishes, Cami sat in the living room with Rafe, watching the glow of the fire. Above it, the mantelpiece was lined with a collection of Santa Clauses that Nonnee had started. In the corner of the room sat an Alberta spruce in a pot. Cami had decorated it with family ornaments. Now, it hid a few presents for Rafe. Later, she would plant it a distance from the deck.

Rafe smiled at her and squeezed her hand. "Before we begin our gift exchanges, I need to tell you that I wasn't entirely truthful when I mentioned I was simply devoting land for Lettie's Creek Wines. I intend to give that land to Drew when I die. He has no idea this is what I have in mind, and I have no intention of ever mentioning it to him. But I need to be sure you'll be okay with it. You'll inherit most of my land, vineyards, and the winery."

Cami understood that what he planned to leave her was a gift from the heart, but the thought of taking on more responsibility seemed overwhelming at the moment. "It's fine with me, Rafe. We've always talked about combining the two properties one day, and I will have more than enough to handle."

"If you don't mind, I'm asking you not to mention this conversation to Drew. I want him to get started in his own business for all the right reasons. Drew reminds me so much of myself at that age—anxious to succeed and eager to work with the land. You know, it was your grandmother's love of the land that bound her to Rex Chandler and then to Kenton. She always felt at home on these acres."

"Yes. That, and the fear of flying kept her here," said Cami.

Rafe stared out the window. "I would never have left the valley if Maria hadn't insisted on living in California. She couldn't understand my ties to the place." He turned back to her with a smile. "But Lettie always did."

Cami's lips curved. "It's nice you two had all those good years together."

She rose from the couch and from behind the Christmas tree extracted her gifts to him.

His eyes rounded when he saw the collection of packages. "All those for me?"

She laughed. He loved surprises as much as she. "Yes, for you from Sophie and me."

"I only have two gifts for you," he said, rising. "They're in my jacket. I'll get them and be right back."

Cami lowered herself onto the couch and waited impatiently for him to return. One of the gifts for Rafe was something Nonnee had asked Cami to do for her, and she couldn't wait to give it to him.

Rafe entered the room and sat down beside her. He handed her one small box and set another on the coffee table.

"Lettie and I talked about this before she died. She wanted you to have this."

With trembling fingers, Cami tore the silver wrapping paper off the box, opened it, and stared at the velvet covered case inside. Her heart began to pound as she recognized the case. Opening it, she let out a gasp and turned to Rafe with blurred vision. "It's the grapes necklace. Oh, thank you so much! I know how much it meant to her and to you, Rafe."

She lifted the necklace and stared at the pendant. Several diamonds clustered together on a gold grape leaf, like the grapes they portrayed. As bold as the design was, it was small enough to be worn for any occasion. Nonnee had worn it almost every day.

Tears shone in Rafe's eyes. "We both wanted you to have it. Here, I think you'll like these too. I picked them out."

Cami opened the gift he handed her and stared at the earrings that winked at her from a bed of black velvet. Simple, but elegant, the pear-shaped diamonds sparkled like fresh spilled tears. They were, she thought, so perfect for this moment. She and Rafe were missing Nonnee so much neither could speak.

She set down the box and gave him a hug she never wanted to end. She'd been so lucky to be raised by two such wonderful people.

When she pulled away, she reached for the gift that Nonnee had chosen for him. "This is for you, from Nonnee."

His eyebrows shot up. "When did she have time to do this?"

"She left me a list of things she wanted me to do. This was among them. Go ahead. Open it."

He tore the red-foil paper off the box and opened it. A toy boat stared up at them. His brow wrinkled. "What's this?"

"Read the note that comes with it," she urged.

He took out the piece of paper and read the words out loud.

"This card entitles Rafe Lopez to a river cruise of his choice, including airline tickets to and from its location. We almost made it, didn't we? Love, Lettie."

His voice quavered on the last words. Shoulders shaking, he lowered his head into his hands.

Cami rubbed his back. "I'm so sorry. Nonnee was working with a new psychologist to deal with her fear of flying and hoped to surprise you with tickets. Then she became ill. But she thought you might like to go yourself. It's something you've wanted to do for a while."

Rafe lifted his tear-streaked face. "Without her? Impossible."

"Give the idea some thought. It might work for you later," said Cami with sympathy. She handed him another gift.

He laughed when he saw the electronic device that responded to voice commands. "I can really use Alexa's help. I have a bad habit of going back to sleep after the alarm goes off."

The tension and sadness that had hovered in the room dissipated as Rafe opened his other gifts—practical, useful ones that Cami knew he needed.

"Thanks for everything, sweet girl," said Rafe after he'd opened the last one. "If you don't mind, I'm going to take a nap."

"Not at all," said Cami. "I'm going to take Sophie for a walk."

She realized they both needed some time alone after the emotional experience of opening gifts that triggered treasured memories.

Moments later, she left the house with Sophie and headed for the grove of trees.

Though the two days before and after Christmas were usually slow, the days that followed were busy as guests started to arrive for the New Year's festivities. Each year, the Chandler Hill Inn put on a party that had become the talk of the Northwest Coast. Fabulous food, champagne, fireworks, dancing, and a morning-after brunch people raved about created a very special celebration for all of their guests, who made reservations weeks, sometimes months in advance.

As she went about overseeing all aspects of the event with the staff, Cami hoped she'd be able to beat the challenges of the new year. First things first, she reminded herself as she headed to The Barn to talk to the staff there. The New Year's gala included special deals for guests at The Barn—an important step in getting rid of the old items so new merchandise could be brought in.

As she always did after stepping inside the building, Cami took a moment to look around. While Abby was in charge, she'd kept quiet about changes she wanted to make. Now, Cami savored the ideas of adding a little reading corner next to the book section, working with local artisans to expand their offerings, and moving displays around. It was an ideal time to do it.

She thought of the recent changes in personnel. Abby's assistant manager, Gwen Chapman, had agreed to take over as manager. A woman in her forties, Gwen had come to the valley for a vacation after a messy divorce and decided she loved the lifestyle enough to move there permanently. But after a few months of recovering, Gwen begged for a job at the inn. She'd been working at The Barn ever since, doing a great job of helping with the merchandising. Gwen had a good eye for quality items and a well-developed instinct about what would sell. Cami was thrilled she was on board.

Abby's partner, Lisa Robbins, had handled growing vegetables and herbs for the inn's kitchen and the cooking classes at The Barn and for producing a number of specialty products such as salad dressings, soaps, and other unique gifts. At the last minute, Cami and Abby were able to convince a friend of Gwen's, Laurel Newson, to take over Lisa's job, with the understanding that she could have a couple of winter months off to go to Palm Springs. Cami jumped at the chance to make a deal with her. Chandler Hill products were doing well online as well as locally, and she needed Laurel to oversee the gardening crew. More importantly, Laurel, who came from a privileged background, was the perfect person to help oversee weddings.

Several staff members waved and called greetings to her as she joined the group climbing the stairs to the staff room for their meeting. It was a superb crew, Cami thought, wondering how they'd react to her ideas.

She waited until everyone had grabbed a bottle of water or cup of coffee and taken their seats before going to the front of the room. "Happy New Year, everyone! We're off to what I hope will be another successful year at Chandler Hill Inn. Over the past couple of months, I've watched and worked with you, and I've come up with a number of things we all can do to add even more appeal to The Barn."

Cami smiled and held up her hand. "I can hear your silent groans, but it should be fun and educational. Let's consider a different layout to the store. Nothing major, merely rearranging space so we can have a reading nook in the book section, more room upstairs in the wine-tasting area, refreshing and relocating some of our displays, and things like that."

The tension in the room eased. "However, before any of these changes take place, I'm going to ask each of you to work in a different section, so we have fresh eyes looking at each area of The Barn. It'll be for a few days only, but each of us will then respect one another's job a little more. I don't know of a better group of people to make this work."

Cami stopped talking and waited for the barrage of questions she was sure would be coming her way.

One of the men who tended bar said, "I don't know much about the books."

Cami smiled. "Exactly. Let's see if you can come up with a

way to attract non-reading customers to that section."

The audience in the room broke out in conversation. There was laughter as some staff members tried to make bargains with one another over which jobs they wanted. Cami smiled. This was exactly what she'd hoped. She left the meeting pleased with the exchange of ideas.

Gwen was going to deal with the staff and the handymen, who would do the heavy work of moving display cabinets and tables and other items.

During this quiet time at the inn, Cami and Becca took inventory of all thirty rooms. There was no question that the carpeting in twenty-four of the rooms needed replacement and their walls painted. Surprisingly, the soft goods—bedspreads, duvets, draperies, and towels—were in excellent shape. Better yet, the case goods—overstuffed chairs, bureaus, headboards, desks, and chairs—were in similar condition.

Making a note of it, she bit her lip. Why had Jonathan insisted on a complete renovation? The rooms definitely needed refreshing, but not a full transformation as he'd insisted. Maybe he was about to make another deal with suppliers. Thankfully, Jamison had put an end to that unsavory business.

Cami returned to her office deep in thought. Russell Berman, her new financial advisor, had initially told her not to spend any significant amount of money, and then, after going over the numbers, he'd worked with Cami to develop a budget so small the project seem impossible. But as Jonathan had said, this was the perfect time to work on the guest rooms.

Carpet would be the biggest expense. Cami looked through the old-fashioned rolodex Nonnee had used. Under C for carpeting, she found the card for Donovan's Carpet and Flooring. On a whim, she called them. When she explained who she was and why she was calling, she was put through to

Gene Donovan.

After they exchanged pleasantries, Cami explained what she needed.

Gene listened to her and said, "Tell you what. I was heading down that way anyway. Why don't I stop at the inn, and we can talk face to face?"

"That would be great," she exclaimed. Bubbling with excitement, she hung up the phone. If they could get a great deal on carpeting and find some painters hungry for work, she just might be able to pull off refreshing the rooms. The public areas were fine for now.

Cami was working in her office when Imani buzzed her. "Mr. Donovan is here to see you."

"Thank you. Please send him in," she responded and got to her feet.

The door opened, and an older man entered the room carrying a briefcase.

Hurrying to greet him, Cami smiled. "Mr. Donovan, thank you for coming. I appreciate it. Won't you have a seat? And may I get you some coffee or something to drink?"

"Thanks, I'm fine for now." He lowered himself into one of the two leather chairs in front of her desk and set his thick briefcase down with a sigh.

She sat and faced him, worried about his response to her plea. "I have to be up front with you. We find ourselves in a difficult situation. There's been a lot of news about the Montague Fund recently."

"Yes, I've read all about it. Several investors lost a lot of money in the scheme. It's such a shame."

"Unfortunately, my grandmother's estate was among those hurt terribly by this. So, I need to find out if there's a way you can provide us with the best, most price-sensitive carpet to redo all twenty-four guest rooms in the wing and possibly the reception area and be open to a payment plan over the coming months."

"Let's take a look at those areas, and then we can talk about it," Gene said, his expression giving nothing away.

Cami led him out of the office and to the guest wing of the inn. "I figure it will be cheaper to have the same carpeting in all the rooms. We like that continuity anyway."

He nodded his agreement. "Makes sense."

After examining and taking measurements in several guest rooms and seeing they were the same size with the same layout, Gene said, "I think I've seen enough."

They went down to the wing's open reception area. Though the carpet was in good shape, the sun streaming in through the tall windows facing west had faded it in spots.

"What do you think?" she asked.

He studied the carpet, knelt down to run his hands over it and stood. Gazing at the windows, he shook his head. "We have rug material that resists sunlight fading better than this. I think, though, we need to be a little more creative here. I'd recommend a patterned, commercial carpet. It will show the dirt and wear less."

They went down to her office. Once more sitting and facing each other, Gene maintained a neutral expression she found unnerving.

Gene opened his briefcase and took out a calculator. He started to fill out a service contract. "Let's see what we've got here. Give me a minute or so to gather all the information. You say the reception area is 20 x 30 feet? I'll double check, but we'll work with that."

Cami caught the corner of her lip, certain the numbers he was working on were getting too large to handle.

"I think I've got the yardage figured out. Let me get some of my samples from the car and we can talk then."

"Okay," Cami said agreeably, but she wished he wouldn't keep her waiting for numbers.

Looking at the samples he thought best in terms of value and wear and tear, she breathed more easily. The attractive beige rug he suggested for the rooms was exactly right—bland, but rich enough in color to carry off the ideas she had for paint colors.

"A very nice option for you," Gene said, rubbing his fingers over the nap of the carpet.

"And the reception area?"

Gene smiled. "I've got a roll of carpet left over from another commercial project I just oversaw in Seattle. I think it'll be perfect for that area here." He lifted his cell phone, scrolled through some photos and handed the phone to her. "What do you think?"

She studied the rug with growing approval. It was unlike anything she might have chosen herself, but the more she studied it, she decided it would be perfect. The warm-green carpet with a muted pattern of cabbage roses was interesting, but not too obtrusive, and suited the old-fashioned flavor of the inn.

"I think the reception area would accommodate this carpet very well," said Gene.

"So do I," said Cami, clasping her hands together with growing excitement.

Gene smiled again and sat back in his chair. Studying her, he said, "You're a lot like your grandmother, you know. We at Donovan's credit her with saving our business."

"You do?" she said, startled to see Gene's face flush with emotion.

"In the '90s, when the economy turned bad, our business

was about to fail. I called every commercial enterprise, every business, every person in the area asking them for help by placing an order. Lettie Chandler invited me to come to the inn to see what I could do for her. The minute I walked in and saw the condition of the carpets in the main areas, I knew she didn't need new carpeting. But I accepted her offer to sit with her for a cup of coffee. We talked about many things, how tough business was and so on. When we were through, she said she wanted all the carpeting replaced in the inn, and she would donate the used carpet to a church-school project in the area. She gave me a steady look and asked me if I could do it. I, of course, said yes. But I've never forgotten what she did for me. And I'm not the only one, believe me."

Cami felt the sting of tears. It sounded so much like Nonnee.

"Why am I telling you this?" said Gene. "Because I have a deal for you. I will give you the carpeting for the rooms fifty percent off, no labor costs, no padding costs. And as for the reception area? I'll donate the carpet, but I do need to charge for the installation because matching the pattern will take extra time for the crew. And, if you like, you can make payments over time." He handed her the invoice, which showed a remarkably low number for the total.

Cami blinked rapidly so the tears that kept stinging her eyes wouldn't fall. "You'd do that for me?"

He smiled and nodded shyly. "Yes, indeed. For you and your grandmother."

Cami pulled a tissue out of the box on her desk and blew her nose. "Thank you so much! How can I ever repay you? A stay at the inn? Cooking lessons? Whatever you want."

He laughed. "How about a stay at the inn for me and the wife. She'd really love that."

"Deal," she said, grateful he'd allowed her to do something

nice for him in return for his generosity.

"I'll order the carpet. Let's get a date penciled in for delivery and installation," said Gene, checking the calendar on his phone.

They settled on a date at the end of January so the inn would be ready to receive guests for the week or so prior to the Valentine's Day rush.

Gene rose and said politely, "Thanks for the business."

Cami went to him and gave him a hug. "My grandmother and I thank you."

She walked him to the front door of the inn and stood there for a moment looking out over the rolling hills. They were a dull gray in the rain and fog that clung to the area. Even through the grayness, she felt as if a ray of sun was shining down on her. And in her mind, she could hear Nonnee say, "Be kind, Cami. It will be worth it in so many ways." Back then, she'd been dealing with a bullying classmate. Now, those very words had proved to be true because of her grandmother's kindness.

CHAPTER SIX

How did it go? Are we going to be able to afford new carpeting?" Becca asked after Gene had left.

"Are we ever!" exclaimed Cami, doing a little dance. "Listen to this!"

Cami told her about the deal and laughed when Becca gave her a high-five and began a dance of her own.

She gave Becca a quick hug and said. "New carpeting wasn't our only problem. I've called a couple of the painters in the area to see about their redoing the guest rooms, but they're already booked. One of them said he'd try to make it over to us toward the end of the month. We're not the only business in the area taking advantage of this slow time."

"All right. I'll do some investigating on my own," Becca said, serious now.

"Okay, in the meantime, I'll pick out some colors for the rooms," said Cami. "I have an idea I want to work on. I'm going over to Salem to the Home Depot. Can you handle things here for me?"

"Sure," Becca said. "I'll keep looking around for painting contractors."

Later that afternoon, Cami pulled the paint chips out of her pocket and held them up to the light from the window in her office. The colors, funky and different, would give the rooms an entirely unique look, but would still be compatible with the more traditional furniture and fabrics in the guest rooms.

Becca approached. "How did you do?"

"Very well," said Cami. "I want to check these paint chips against the fabrics in some of the rooms. I figure with six different colors, only four rooms will have walls the same color, though I plan to change the look of them by moving some of the soft goods and upholstered furniture around."

Cami and Becca studied the colors in several of the guest rooms, checking their tones with different lighting and how the colors blended with the different fabrics in the rooms.

"I love it!" said Becca. "With the new paint and carpet, plus rearranging some of the beds and furniture, everything will look brand new."

Cami let out a sigh of satisfaction. They could get away with spending little money and still accomplish what she wanted. She realized it couldn't have happened if Nonnee hadn't been the kind of person she was. She'd also wisely chosen high-quality case goods, like bureaus and chairs.

Cami was working at her desk the next morning when Drew and three other men entered her office.

"What's up?" she asked, staring at them with surprise.

"We heard you need painters, and we're here to offer our services," said Drew, grinning.

One of the men stepped forward. "Hi, Cami. I'm Dan Thurston, from Thurston Construction. My family has dealt with Lettie Chandler for years. My crew of two and I are here to help. Becca and Drew both told me of your situation, and we'd like to offer our painting services for free. Your grandmother and mine were friends, and Gram insisted we show our support. Besides, Becca would never forgive me if I didn't do this."

Cami laughed with the others. Becca had gushed to her

about her boyfriend. Cami understood why. Not only was Dan decidedly handsome with his brown, curly hair and sparkling blue eyes, he was kind.

She went over to the group. "Thank you so much for your help. I know Drew, of course, and now Dan, but who are you?" she asked the other two.

Matt Lincoln and Juan Molina smiled as they introduced themselves and shook her hand.

Cami stood back and beamed at them. "What a great crew. Thank you so much for your help. I'll see to ordering the paint right away."

"We can begin by preparing the rooms," Dan said.

"Wonderful. The carpeting is being removed now to be given to charity so we don't have to worry about that, but we'll need to tape the edges of the baseboards, the windows, and the crown molding. The ceilings themselves are fine as they are."

Becca joined them. After giving Dan a quick kiss, she turned to Cami with a smile. "They're good guys. They'll do a great job for you."

"Yes, I believe they will," said Cami, suddenly wanting to cry. She'd always loved the land, the vineyards, and the inn. But now she appreciated the people in the valley in a way she hadn't experienced before.

Drew stepped forward. "Want me to go to Home Depot with you? I can help you gather the supplies you're going to need, and we can load everything up in my truck."

"That would be great," she said, realizing how many cans of paint and the number of other things they would need.

"We've got several drop cloths, but you're probably going to need more if we're to make this a rush job," said Dan. "I figure with twenty-four rooms, we should be done within a week or so, depending on how much time we can give to it.

While you're gone, the other guys and I will start moving the furniture."

"I'll help them place mirrors, lamps, and paintings in one of the storage rooms, and the furniture in another," said Becca.

Again, Cami felt moved to tears but she wouldn't show any weakness in front of the men. She was the one in charge. "Okay, let's go!" She grabbed her purse, followed Drew outside to his truck, and got in.

Drew climbed behind the wheel and started the engine.

Cami watched his precise movements and was reminded of Rafe. In many ways, the two men were alike—both soft-spoken and self-contained, but well aware of what was going on around them.

"Got your colors all picked out?" Drew said.

"Yes. They're very different from what is on the walls now, but I think it's going to work nicely."

"Ah, that artist's touch, huh?"

She smiled at him. "There are so many beautiful colors in the world, why not use a few of them?" She pulled the chips out of her purse. "I'm going with different shades of these— Peach Blossom, Kombucha, Smoked Oyster, Mushroom, Strawberry Cream, Green Mint."

Drew grinned at her. "Wow! You must have been hungry when you chose those!"

She burst out laughing. "I hadn't thought of it, but you're right. I'd skipped lunch when I went to the store."

"I'd hate to think of the names you'd choose if you'd skipped dinner," he teased. "Steak Red, Mashed Potato White ..."

They chuckled together, and then a companionable silence followed.

"Thanks again for Christmas breakfast at your house," he

said, breaking into the quiet. "It meant a lot to me."

"I'm glad you could come. When Nonnee was alive, we used to love to fill the house with guests on Christmas Day. I'm still getting used to taking over for her, so it was nice to have you there. Next year, I'll recruit more people."

Drew pulled the truck to a stop in the Home Depot parking lot and turned to her. "I don't want this to be too awkward, but I'd like to get to know you better." His light-brown eyes bore into her, demanding honesty.

"I'd like that," she said simply. The quick kiss he'd given her at Christmas held the promise of something more. Remembering her dismal failure with Bernard, she added, "We could start out by simply being friends."

"Okay," he quickly agreed. "As I told you earlier, I'm not ready for anything more."

"Deal," she said, giving him a warm smile. Friendship was a fine idea.

Inside the store, while Cami worked with a store associate to get the proper quantities and colors of paint, Drew filled a cart with drop cloths, paint brushes, paint pans, blue painters' tape, rollers, and other equipment they would need.

An hour or so later, they were ready. Drew stacked paint cans in the bed of his truck and placed the bags of supplies in the backseat.

"Looks like a Christmas sleigh," said Cami, climbing into the passenger seat.

Drew laughed. "I'm glad Dan and his crew could help me. We'll get the job done as quickly as we can."

"Good. We have a couple of spring weddings coming up. A girl from California is getting married here. It's been on the books for almost a year. The bride and groom are coming here for Valentine's Day weekend to go over a final checklist."

"Owning the inn must be pretty exciting," Drew said.

She wasn't sure how to answer that. "In many ways it is, but what interests me most are growing grapes and making wine. I'm resigned to the fact that I can't devote much time to it until everything else is running smoothly. My grandmother was clear about that."

"It must be nice to have so much family," said Drew, his voice wistful. "Sam has been great to me, but I wonder what it might have been like if I'd had a regular family."

"Well, my family isn't exactly regular, but it's more standard than yours. Still, I wish I knew who my father is. That would fill a gap I've always felt."

Drew gave her a sympathetic look. "I understand."

The next morning, Cami put on an old pair of jeans, a sweatshirt, and sneakers and headed over to the inn. She'd accept only so much free help. She was skilled at painting in small, difficult areas and would be relieved to do something to help the painters.

When she went to the second level of the inn, she found rock music blaring and a busy scene as four men worked in two rooms. She approached Dan. "Hi! I'm here to help."

He looked surprised. "Okay, you can do the work in and around the shelves in the alcoves. We need someone with a careful touch to do it."

She grinned and saluted him. "Hand me a paint brush and a small roller, and I'll get to it."

Two hours later, her back sore, she sat with the guys in the corridor sipping a cup of hot coffee. Becca kept them well supplied with it and a selection of cold sodas.

Drew came over and sat down beside her. He smiled and swiped the top of her nose with a finger. "Got a dab of paint on you."

"Mushroom," Cami said, taking a painting cloth and rubbing her nose.

He laughed. "Here, you're making it worse. Let me do it."

Cami sat very still as he studied her face and then gently took a cloth to the smudges on her nose and cheeks. At his touch, heat raced through her and settled in her core.

"That's it. I've got it," he said, pulling away from her.

"Thanks. I'd better get back to work." She left the men in the hallway, but from inside the room she was painting she could hear Dan speaking in the hallway. "What was that about, Drew?"

"Nothing," he said with such conviction that, for a moment, her feelings were hurt. *Friends*, she reminded herself. *We're just friends.*

By the end of the week, Cami's body was stiff and sore, but she felt great about staying with the painting job until it was done. Now, the new carpet was being laid. The smell of fresh carpet, both satisfying and too pungent, was tickling her nose.

"Scott, Drew, and Dan will be here the day after tomorrow to help resettle the rooms," said Becca. "I just reconfirmed with them."

"Great. The carpet will all be laid and vacuumed by then." Cami put an arm around Becca's shoulder. "I appreciate your help. My grandmother had a friend like you. I hope we share that same kind of bond."

"You'll never know what it means to me that you're giving me an opportunity to participate in the inn's success."

"If we do well, it's only right for you to benefit with bonuses, profit sharing, and other rewards."

"For what it's worth, I'm going to work my butt off."

Cami chuckled. It's exactly what she had in mind when

she'd included those arrangements as part of her contract with Becca. She was a little younger than Cami, but Becca had a no-nonsense attitude about her that Cami guessed was her New England upbringing. Whatever it was, they clicked as friends and work partners.

Four days later, Becca and Cami inspected each of the refreshed rooms. "Wow! It looks spectacular," said Becca. "I don't know how you did it, but while each room is very different, they look as if they'd been designed this way."

Cami studied the effect of their work. The darker paint on the walls offset the prints in the bedspreads and the colors in the upholstered furniture. But rather than having the rooms overly color-coordinated, Cami had changed up that blandness for an edgier look by exchanging some of the furniture between rooms, adding new color to them. They'd even switched around the artwork and added new pieces from local artists. The effect was stunning.

"Jonathan should see the rooms now. He wouldn't believe it," said Becca. "I hear he's working at a hotel in Portland. Maybe I'll invite him down here for a look."

"Don't waste your time," scoffed Cami. "He reminds me of my old boyfriend. If he bothered to come, it would be only to criticize."

Becca gave her a steady look. "So, what was the deal between you two?"

Cami shrugged, trying to fight off the old hurt. "It turned out to be a one-sided relationship. At any rate, Bernard is in France, and I'm here."

"A Frenchman, eh?" Becca said, wiggling her eyebrows.

"I hope never to see him again," said Cami, meaning it. She hated that she'd wept in front of him when he refused to come to America with her when she'd needed him most.

"Well, don't look now, but Drew is heading our way." Becca gave her a sly look. "He's worth more than the other guy any day."

As Drew approached, Becca slipped away. He waved to Cami. "Hey there! I thought I might find you here. Everything looking okay?"

Cami smiled. "Better than I'd hoped."

He stepped to her side and looked into the room she'd been inspecting. "It looks great. Nice job, Ms. Artist. Say, I was wondering if you want to have dinner with me tonight. I'm hungry for some pasta at Nick's."

"Funny you should mention pasta. How about coming to my house instead? I've got pasta ready to go, and Darren has cooked up a crab sauce for it that is to die for."

"Sounds great," Drew said. "I'll bring a bottle of wine. Anything else?"

"No, we'll make it a nice, relaxing evening. We have guests coming to the inn later in the week, but we're pretty empty now."

"Okay, deal. What time do you want me there?"

Cami checked her watch, wanting to give herself time to take a shower and get dressed in something more sophisticated than blue jeans. "Let's say seven."

Drew tipped his head. "See you then."

Cami watched him walk away. His tall, erect figure moved with confidence without any sign of the swagger she'd sometimes seen in Bernard.

CHAPTER SEVEN

As soon as she could, Cami left the inn with the crab sauce Darren had packaged up for her, checked in at The Barn, and headed home. Even though they were just friends, Cami wanted to look nice for Drew. It had been a while since she'd had a date, and it felt good to have a man's interest, even as just a friend.

Sophie greeted her with howls of indignation that she'd not been allowed to accompany her to work. But with Sophie's curiosity and new paint and carpeting, Cami had decided not to take her.

She swept the dog up in her arms and crooned to her. Sophie gave her a mollified look and responded with warm, forgiving licks of her tongue on Cami's cheek.

"Okay. Time for us girls to look our best. First, you need to go outside."

Even though a staff member had taken Sophie for a walk at noon, Cami hurried Sophie out of the house. Cami had thought about putting in a doggie door but didn't like the idea of Sophie being alone outside and exposed to either birds of prey or other creatures who might find a miniature dachshund an edible treat.

Inside again, Cami fixed Sophie's dinner and then headed into her bedroom. Standing in front of her closet, she looked over her slacks and sweaters and decided on a pair of winter-white slacks and a black turtleneck. Black always brought out the color in her light-red hair.

She laid the clothes on her bed and went into the bathroom

to draw water into the large, deep tub. A nice soak would do wonders for the soreness that still lingered in her body from painting.

Sophie came into the room, jumped up onto the side of the tub, and looked in. "Not for you," Cami warned her. "Here, you lie down on the mat."

Stepping into the tub, Cami sighed. It felt great. She lay back against the tub and kept the warm water swishing around her with a stroke of her hand and the movement of her feet. She let her thoughts drift. She and Bernard used to share times like this in the deep tub in the apartment she'd rented. He was, she admitted, a good lover. She missed that in her life. As much as she was looking forward to an evening with Drew, she knew it was not a real date. How could it be? They'd promised one another to be only friends. Besides, being with a man right now would detract her from the important work she had to do.

Sighing with regret, Cami turned her thoughts to the upcoming visit from the bride and groom who'd booked a wedding in early May. She was counting on it being handled well and was relieved the guest rooms at the inn were now in order. The bridal party was renting all thirty rooms. The six in the main house would be for family only. The twenty-four rooms in the wing would be for the wedding guests.

The alarm she'd set on her phone sounded, startling her out of her reverie. She opened the drain on the tub, stood, and stepped onto the bathmat. Sophie scrambled to her feet and began licking Cami's toes. Laughing, she nudged the dog away. "Okay, little one. We can't waste any time. I need to get some things ready for our guest."

She went through her usual routine of moisturizing, spritzing perfume behind her ears, brushing her teeth and putting on eye makeup.

After she was dressed, she studied herself in the mirror. She'd thought about wearing the pendant Rafe had given her for Christmas and chose the diamond earrings instead. Go for simple, but elegant, she thought.

In the kitchen, Cami pulled out the wine glasses, assorted silverware, china, napkins, and placemats. She'd been taught from an early age that each was important. Nonnee used to tell her how when she first came to the inn, she knew how to set a basic table but wasn't sure where to place all the extra pieces of flatware—things like fish forks and cream soup spoons.

"I don't want that ever to happen to you," she'd told Cami.

Smiling at the memory, she carefully set each place for dinner. They'd have drinks by the fire in the living room and then eat in the kitchen. On a cold winter's night, it was the best of options. Warmer weather would find her preparing to eat out on the deck outside the kitchen, one of Nonnee's favorite spots, one that offered a full view that had captivated her from the beginning.

Cami stood a moment looking out at the barren winter land. It always amazed her how the bleak vineyard landscape on a day like this would transform into row after row of promising grapes come the warmer months. Turning the grapes into luscious red wines seemed another miracle.

The doorbell rang. Eager with anticipation, she rushed to answered it.

Drew stood on the porch. In his hands he carried a bottle of wine and a bouquet of pink roses.

"Come in," she said. "How did you know pink roses are my favorite?"

"They signify grace and beauty. I thought they were perfect for you." He grinned. "And Rafe said you liked them. In fact, he suggested I bring them to you."

"He did, did he?"

They smiled at one another.

She waved him inside, and he followed her into the kitchen.

"While I work with these lovely roses, would you like to open the wine to let it breathe?"

"Sure," he said agreeably.

"Perfect." She handed him a wine opener.

Cami trimmed off the ends of the stems and arranged the flowers in a glass bowl she brought out from a cupboard. Pink roses had been Kenton's choice of flowers for her grandmother's wedding. Nonnee had loved them ever since. Cami liked the idea that Drew had brought the same for her.

"Shall I pour the wine?" he asked, indicating the two glasses she'd already placed on the counter.

"That would be nice. I'm ready to relax," she responded, pleased. Drew was an incredibly handsome man who was as nice a guy as she'd met in some time.

He poured the wine and handed her a glass.

"Let's go sit by the fire. It's warmer there."

They walked into the living room and took a seat at either end of the couch facing the fire.

Cami patted the empty space beside her, and Sophie jumped up. "Hope you don't mind sharing space with Sophie."

He laughed and rubbed Sophie's ears. Sophie licked his hand and rolled over for a tummy rub.

Cami lifted her glass and smiled at him. "Here's to a nice friendship!"

"Yes," said Drew. "Good friends are hard to find."

"Where did you live before coming here?" she asked, eager to know more about him.

"In Napa. A couple of friends of mine and I shared an apartment. But I left in a hurry when the position opened up at Chandler Hill. I didn't realize at the time an opportunity with Rafe would be a possibility. I'm delighted I made the decision to come here."

"Rafe wouldn't ask you to train under him if he didn't believe in your abilities," said Cami. "I admit I'm a little jealous. My grandmother's wines and his were always considered among the best. Now you have the chance to continue with Rafe's, while I have to wait until the next harvest to work with our grapes."

"You said you were living in France when you got the call to come home. Were you working with grapes there?"

"Yes," said Cami. "I lived in the southern part of the Côtes du Rhône region. It was beautiful and the wines superb. Most of the grapes were grown on the eastern side of the Rhône between the river bank near the town of Orange, and the Vaucluse-Luberon chain of mountains. Such a pretty area."

"Tell me about the wine."

"The majority of wine is grenache noir, but other grapes such as syrah and mourvedre are pretty typical."

"How did you like working with different grapes and making white wines?" he asked.

"It took some time to get used to," she said. "I guess grapes are like children or dogs. You get used to their idiosyncrasies and do your best with them. They're all a little fussy in their own way. That's the fun of it, I suppose."

"Are you glad to be home?" He took a sip of wine and waited for her to speak.

"Yes and no, truthfully. I understand I've been given a great opportunity not many have, but the pressure of carrying on for my grandmother sometimes seems overwhelming. She was such a fantastic person. And the inn needs a lot of my attention. Jonathan Knight didn't really understand the charm of the inn. He wanted it to be something it's not. Glitz has its place in the resort world, but that's not us. I like to think of the Chandler Hill Inn as a resort that is quiet, classy, and traditional without being boring. Does that make sense?"

"It makes perfect sense. The last thing you want to do is to become something you're not. I appreciate that in people too."

"A bad experience?"

Drew let out a sigh and set down his wine glass. Staring into the fire in the fireplace he was quiet for a moment before turning to her. "My ex-girlfriend came from a rich family and was pretty used to getting her own way. She desperately wanted us to marry, but over the course of the relationship I realized I was never going to measure up to what she expected from a husband. First, it was because I hadn't traveled much. Then, I didn't earn enough money." Drew's voice became bitter. "You get the picture."

"Apparently, I wasn't good enough either. My boyfriend ditched me in a hurry when I had to come home quickly when Nonnee was terminally ill."

Drew poured a little more wine into their glasses. "Well, that's all behind me. I'm not going to get in a situation like that again. My uncle and I have always lived without a woman in the house telling us what to do. Believe me, it's a lot easier that way, or so I've learned."

"Someday you might change your mind."

He snorted, waking Sophie from her nap. "Doubtful."

Cami raised her glass. "Here's to easier days ahead." She clinked her glass to his. "Remember, you and I will be rivals when the winemaking begins."

"All right then, here's to Lettie's Creek Wines!"

"And Chandler Hill wines," Cami quickly amended, making Drew laugh.

She rose to her feet. "I'd better put our meal together. You can either relax here or join me in the kitchen."

"I'll come with you." His eyes sparkled with mischief. "I like to see a woman cooking in the kitchen like she should."

"Whaaat?" She threw a pillow at him.

Chuckling, he followed her into the kitchen.

Cami moved easily heating the sauce, cooking the pasta, and putting together a salad. Rafe was a great cook and had enjoyed teaching her many of his favorite recipes. It had been a wonderful way for them to bond when she'd first come to live with him and Nonnee. They still loved to cook together.

Later, as she and Drew sat together eating their meal, Cami experienced a sense of peace. It was nice to have a man in the house—a man she didn't have to worry about pleasing. A friend who accepted her for herself.

As they ate and later sipped after-dinner cups of coffee, they talked about some of their favorite films and moved on to other things. It was surprising how well their tastes meshed. She happened to glance at the clock on the microwave and was surprised that it showed eleven o'clock.

"Wow! I didn't realize I was keeping you so late," Cami said, rising to her feet. "I know how early you and Rafe start your day."

Drew rolled his eyes and grinned. "Rafe is an early riser, for sure." He carried his coffee cup over to the sink and set it down. "Delicious dinner. Thanks."

"This was an easy one. Sometime I'll show you a little of my more complicated cooking skills."

His face lit up. "I'd like that. It's been a great evening."

Cami walked him to the front door. "I've enjoyed the time together too." She handed him his jacket.

He put on his jacket and turned to her. "Thanks again." His golden eyes studied her with satisfaction, then he leaned over to kiss her.

Cami offered her cheek as she would have in France and

turned her face in time to feel his soft, warm lips on hers. Savoring the moment, she closed her eyes. When she opened them, he stepped away.

He looked startled and said, "I gotta go."

CHAPTER EIGHT

During the week, Cami spent some time talking on the phone with Laurel Newson. Laurel finally agreed that when she concluded her vacation in Palm Springs, she'd handle weddings and special events at the inn until she was bogged down with garden duties. With five days left before Valentine's Day, Cami wanted to be sure she had everything in order before meeting with the bride and groom about their May wedding. Justine Devon was quiet-spoken on the phone, but there was no mistaking that she wanted her wedding plans to be exactly right. Her fiancé, George Dickinson, was apparently willing to go along with anything she planned.

Cami met with Becca inside Chandler Hall, a separate building adjacent to the inn designed to accommodate special functions such as weddings, banquets, and other events. They stood in the middle of the hall surveying the area with a critical eye. Glass garage doors made up a large portion of the perimeter walls, giving groups the option of rolling them up for an outdoor event when weather permitted. Often wedding parties served food inside the building and then made the doors disappear to make the inside space and outside patios perfect for dancing. It worked well, especially at night when the sparkling stars in the sky matched the white mini-lights strung among the abundant, green rhododendrons and other foliage surrounding the building.

The interiors of the walls that didn't consist of the glass doors were paneled with a rich walnut that worked well for both casual functions like barbeques or dressier ones like weddings and wedding receptions. In the main hall, a massive stone fireplace was another functional feature that anchored one end of the room and sometimes served as a background for simple weddings. At the other end of the room, a large, modern kitchen provided a suitable workspace for food preparation and easy dining or buffet service.

Bathrooms and a special room where brides and their attendants could change their clothes completed the basic layout of the space. It was a simple design, but one that worked well.

"Someday I want to be married here," said Becca. "With the views to the outside, it's perfectly beautiful."

"It's one of my favorite places too. I used to come here with Nonnee to watch wedding celebrations." Cami smiled. "If I behaved, I usually got a piece of the wedding cake."

"What a life you must have had growing up here," said Becca. "And now all this is yours."

Though Cami returned Becca's smile, her stomach clenched. The inn wasn't a simple piece of property. It had become a destination resort where people expected the best. The Barn, the swimming pool, spa, and excellent food made it much more than the inn of long ago. Nonnee had grabbed hold of the opportunity given to her and made it so much better. Cami worried that she wouldn't be able to maintain what was already there, much less make it grow as they'd envisioned.

"I think we can do better with our wedding parties," said Cami. "I want to assign a special staff member to 'bird-dog' each group. He or she will need to be everywhere, responding to every request. Can you think of anyone for that job?"

"I wasn't going to say anything to you just yet, but one of my old college friends, Vanessa Duncan, thought she might like to try living on the west coast. She knows how happy I've been and has asked me if I could help her get a job in the area."

"Has she ever done anything like this?" Cami asked. "The hospitality business isn't as easy as people think. It can be very demanding."

"She's worked in an advertising agency in New York dealing with clients, but she's tired of doing that. People like her. She's outgoing, and she loves wine too."

Cami laughed. "I guess those are all admirable qualities to have. But living in Willamette Valley is a far cry from the hustle and bustle of New York. She might be bored."

"I don't think so. She usually finds something to keep her busy. I haven't seen her for a couple of years now, but she was generally a lot of fun."

"Okay," Cami said, shrugging. "Have her send me a resumé, and I'll take a look at it."

The setting sun sent streaks of color through the sky that were reflected by the glass doors of the building in striking shades of red and orange. Observing such natural beauty, Cami's sigh of appreciation met Becca's. At times like this, she could almost sense Nonnee here with her, admiring the sight of the hills painted with color from above.

"Dan and I are going out to dinner downtown. Want to join us?" said Becca, standing by as Cami locked the empty building.

"No thanks. I'm going to stay at home."

"You and Drew are both such homebodies. We can't get him to go out with us either," Becca complained.

Cami smiled to herself. She and Drew were going to have dinner at her house for the third time. The first two evenings together had been great—two friends just relaxing. Though they'd end up competing against each other in wine tastings, they loved to talk about wines and what was happening in the industry.

She and Becca walked together to the inn. Cami had left Sophie snoring beneath her desk. On cold winter days like this, the dog was content to stay inside.

A number of guests were at the inn taking advantage of the advertised February specials. When Cami walked into the main house, several people were enjoying happy hour in the library. She smiled and entered the room to speak to the guests, welcoming them, and finding out a little about each one, all part of her normal routine each evening.

She left a short time later and went to her office to get Sophie. She greeted the dog with several pats on the head, then grabbed her coat and purse.

"Where are you going in such a rush?" teased Becca.

"Home. See you later," Cami replied, avoiding further conversation as she hurried away. Sensing a race, Sophie yapped and charged ahead, her short legs moving as fast as they could.

At home, Cami lay back in the tub, loving the feel of warm water swirling around her. Relaxed now, she could think ahead to the evening. She enjoyed being with Drew. Even as he made no advances, he made her feel attractive. Though she had no intention of getting involved with anyone, she liked being in his company.

Sophie's head bobbed up and disappeared as she tried for the impossible leap that would get her into the tub. Cami laughed. "No, girl. One is enough."

Later, after she dried and dressed, she stood in front of the mirror brushing her curly, strawberry-blond hair into submission. She didn't mind that it was sometimes a struggle. The hair came from Nonnee, her dark eyes from her mother and Rafe.

When at last she felt ready, Cami headed to the kitchen. For this cold evening, she'd planned cheese fondue. It was one of her favorite, festive wintertime meals. The recipe, originally from the Swiss Embassy in Washington, D.C., was easy to make. That morning, she'd cubed a loaf of french bread and set the pieces on a tray to crispen. Now, she'd go ahead and shred the gruyère and emmentaler cheeses. Later would come the wine, garlic, a bit of kirsch, and a touch of nutmeg mixed together for a creamy blend. She set the ceramic fondue pot she'd bought in Switzerland next to the stove. It was one of her prized possessions.

She'd just finished whipping up a simple salad dressing of olive oil, balsamic vinegar, and a few spices, when the sound of the doorbell sent her hurrying to answer it.

Smiling, she opened the door with a flourish and then reeled away in shock. "Bernard! What are you doing here?"

His lips spread into a smile she'd once thought charming. "I'm here, just like you wanted. I had to get used to the idea. And when I understood what a big responsibility you have, I knew my place was with you."

"That's quite a speech," Cami said, facing him with her hands on her hips. She remembered the hurtful way he'd ended their relationship. A fun, summer romance he'd called it. Ending it in an email. Not even a call. Well, this was winter now.

"Aw, *ma chère*, aren't you going to welcome me?" He stepped forward and swept her up in his arms. His kiss, those soft lips of his, brought back memories of passionate days and nights in France. For a moment, she succumbed to his touch. Then she remembered how he'd treated her and abruptly straightened.

"Bernard, why are you here? What makes you think you can assume that everything will go back to what it once was before I discovered your true nature?"

"Because of this." He brought her closer and kissed her once more.

At the sound of Drew's truck entering the driveway, she stepped away. "No, Bernard. I can't do this. Besides, I'm expecting company for dinner."

They turned as Drew pulled to a stop and got out of his vehicle.

"So, this is how you missed me?" Bernard looked at her with hurtful surprise.

She waved to Drew, so happy to see him she wanted to run to him. Her emotions were doing cartwheels inside her, and she needed his steady friendship to help her.

"Hi, Cami." Drew's brow creased with concern as he stared from her to Bernard. "Am I interrupting anything?"

"No." Cami said firmly. "Bernard is an old friend from France. He just stopped by to say hello."

"*Chérie, ce n'est pas vrai.*"

"Yes, it's very true," said Cami. "We haven't spoken or had any kind of real, honest communication since just before my grandmother died. You should have called before coming to my house. Where are you staying?"

Bernard looked down and shuffled his feet. He lifted his handsome face to her and winked. "I thought I'd be staying with you."

Cami let out a sigh. That wasn't going to happen. At one time, it's what she'd prayed for. "I'll call and get you a room at the inn."

"Look," said Drew. "I can leave you two alone, come back another time."

"No!" Cami responded more sharply than she'd intended.

That message wasn't lost on either man. They studied one another. Bernard, tall and thin, seemed almost weak in comparison to Drew's broad shoulders and sturdy body of equal height.

"It's cold. Why don't you both come in while I call the inn to make arrangements for Bernard?"

She stepped back and waved them inside.

"*Très beau*," murmured Bernard, glancing around, a smile forming on his lips. "I had no idea the Chandler Hill property was so big, so beautiful."

"From all the stories I've heard, it's a successful operation that's been a labor of love," said Drew, earning a smile from Cami for his understanding.

"Yes, Nonnee made it seem that way. I know, though, how hard she worked to make it so."

"With my experience we can make it even better, *non*?" Bernard smiled at her.

Dismay took Cami's breath away. Was this why Bernard had come to visit her? "But you have an interest in a vineyard in France. Why would you come here to work?"

Bernard's shrug was telling. "I am not a part of it anymore. You know how unreasonable Jacques could be. It wasn't what I wanted."

Ah, thought Cami. *Bernard and Jacques were not able to settle their disagreement about how the vineyard should be run.* Brothers, they were as different as they could be. Jacques was a serious, hard-working man. Bernard was the schmoozer, the salesman.

She eyed her former boyfriend. Realizing how stupidly in love she'd been with Bernard, she knew she had a lot of soul searching to do before getting involved with anyone else. Her judgement in men was obviously lacking. It was a good thing she and Drew were merely friends.

Drew handed her a bottle of wine. "You said we'd need a white wine for dinner. I thought you'd like this pinot grigio.

It's from a California vineyard I like."

"Ah, but you need a wine from France," protested Bernard.

"Thank you, Drew," said Cami, accepting the bottle he offered her. "Give me a chance to call the inn."

She quickly placed the call and then turned to Bernard. "You're all set. I have a complimentary room for you, which includes dinner for tonight. I think you'll enjoy the food. Darren does a nice job." Cami walked to the front door to show him out. She knew she was being incredibly rude, but at the moment it suited her. Bernard had ended their relationship online.

At the door, Bernard kissed her on both cheeks in the French way and said, "I'll get you to change your mind about me. I promise. *À bientôt!*"

Cami saw him off silently. At one point in time, she'd given her heart to him. But now? How could he think it could happen again?

She shut the door and turned back to Drew. "Sorry about that."

"No problem. Like I said, I could've left you two alone and come back another day."

"I'm glad you didn't. I don't know about you, but I'm ready for a glass of wine," she said. "It's been a tough day." That, she told herself, was an understatement. It had been one hell of a ride.

She opened the bottle and handed it to Drew. "Why don't you pour while I serve up the canapés I brought over from the inn. Let's relax in the living room."

"Sounds good." He grabbed the bottle of wine and two glasses and carried them into the living room. Cami followed with the hors d'oeuvres.

They took seats on the couch facing the fireplace. The flames inside spread an orange glow that softened her mood.

Drew poured the wine and handed her a glass. Lifting his in the air, he said, "Here's to ... whatever makes you happy."

She smiled and clicked her glass against his. "And for you!"

They gazed comfortably at each other, took a sip of wine and settled back against the seat cushions, staring at the fire.

Into the quiet, he said, "So that was the guy from France you told me about? The one who broke up with you?"

She faced him. "The one and only."

"He seemed real sure of himself." He arched an eyebrow at her.

Warmth crept into her cheeks as she recalled that brief moment she'd wanted to welcome him back into her life. From the warning look Drew gave her, he knew it too.

He reached out and patted her arm. "My serious girlfriend and I broke up so many times I lost count. The thing I learned is that you can't go back. Doesn't mean you can't go forward, but it has to be something you both want to do."

"I'm sorry. That doesn't sound like fun." Cami vowed not to get caught up in a bad relationship. Bernard might think he could change her mind, but even though she knew him well enough to know he wouldn't give up trying, it wouldn't happen.

"My first priority now has to be to Rafe," said Drew. "He's spending a lot of his time teaching me how he wants things done at Taunton Estates."

"You like working for him?" Cami asked.

He grinned. "Yeah, he's the best. Someday, I'd like to have my own small winery, and I need to know all I can about running it. Classes in school are important, but it's the real-life stuff that makes a big difference."

Cami couldn't help her smile. He didn't know about Rafe's plan to give him some land of his own.

###

During the meal of fondue and nibbling on salad, conversation continued easily between them. After Drew told her more details about his mother taking off when he was a young age, Cami better understood Drew's devotion to both his uncle and to Rafe. She'd taken enough psych classes to know that trust of women might be an issue for him. She told Drew about Rafe coming to get her in Africa after her mother died and how Nonnee had always been a role model for her.

"Guess it proves there are many ways to have a home," she ended. "One thing missing for me is not knowing who my father is. I don't want to interfere in his life; I just want to know who he is."

"Yeah, I get it. I've sometimes wondered what I'd do if I met my mother. I don't remember anything about her, to be honest."

"I was six when my mother was killed, but I remember how beautiful she was, how much people liked her. I sometimes felt as if I were in her way, but then I had Karabo, who was much more than a housekeeper. She was a second mother to me, the one who told me stories and sang to me at night." Tears sprang to Cami's eyes. "Karabo's gone now. I went back to Africa to see her after I graduated from college. We had a lovely visit."

"Nice." Drew's smile was a bit sad, reminding her how lucky she was to have so many good people in her life.

She rose from the table. "Shall we finish our wine in the living room?"

"Sure." Drew followed her into the living room and sat in the brown-leather chair beside the fireplace.

"Dinner was delicious. Thanks for having me. It can't be a late night, though, I'm going over some PR plans with Rafe tomorrow morning." He paused. "And you know what an early riser Rafe is."

Cami laughed at the way he'd rolled his eyes. "I sure do. Living with him here, I learned that in a hurry. As he ages, he sleeps less. He tells me it's because Nonnee doesn't share his bed anymore." She sighed. "When the time is right, that's the kind of love I'm looking for."

"Theirs was a rare relationship." Drew took a sip of his wine.

"I know, but with the right guy, I believe it will happen." She chuckled. "A romantic's dream, I guess."

Drew studied her but didn't respond. "Rafe told me he's going to train you to accompany him to wine shows. Right?"

"Yes. Now that I've got the inn in order, it's time. He wants me to learn about the shows and to handle the online activity for both Chandler Hill and Taunton Estates. You're doing some of that, too, I guess."

"Yes, it's easier to do it than try to explain it to him."

They looked at each other and laughed. Newfangled things, as Rafe called them, remained a mystery to him.

CHAPTER NINE

The next morning, Cami awoke and stretched in bed recalling the evening with Drew. It felt great to be able to talk to him as a friend, to get a guy's perspective on things. Growing up, she'd been surrounded with plenty of Nonnee's female friends and workers. But aside from Rafe, who was so much older, she hadn't had the opportunity to learn things in the same way a girl might from a father, brother, or an uncle.

Her thoughts turned to Bernard. How arrogant he was! She hated confrontation, but she was going to make it clear their past relationship was over for good. And she'd tell him there was no work for him at Chandler Hill. She was sure Rafe would feel the same way about not hiring him, but, to be sure, she'd call him.

She lifted Sophie down from the bed. "C'mon, girl. It's a busy day and you need to go outside."

Sophie gave her an annoyed look at having her sleep disrupted.

Laughing, Cami rubbed Sophie's ears. "Let's go!"

Later, sipping coffee and gazing out the window at the rows of vines empty of grapes, Cami decided to call Rafe.

"Hi, sweetheart. What's up?" he said cheerfully.

She explained the situation with Bernard. "I'm going to tell him he can't work at Chandler Hill."

"As well you should. The guy's an ass. I don't want him working here either."

Cami let out a sigh. "I was hoping you'd say that. It would be uncomfortable for me if he were involved in any way with my business. He's a clever salesman, but it was his brother who ran the vineyard in France."

"That's an ironclad reason for me not to hire him. On another topic, I've been thinking of taking that river cruise Lettie planned for me sometime next fall. What do you think?"

"Nonnee would be very happy for you. She told me how disappointed she was she couldn't travel with you, that she wanted to give you the wings she could never find for herself."

"I wish we could have done it together."

"I do too. But it's the kind of trip that can be comfortable for a single person because of the group activities."

"I thought it would also be a great way to test how Drew runs the winery when I'm away," admitted Rafe. "I need to slow down."

"Are you okay?" Cami asked, her pulse racing at the idea that he might be sick.

"I'm fine. Just getting old and tired. Don't worry. I don't plan to leave you for a long time."

"I'm glad. I couldn't bear to lose you."

"I've got to go," said Rafe. "Drew's here. You know how early a riser he is."

Cami laughed. "Talk to you later."

Feeling better about how she'd handle Bernard, Cami finished getting ready for the day and headed out to the inn.

When she arrived, Imani and Becca greeted her and followed her into her office.

"What's going on?" Becca said. "I thought we were working together on the inn. Now, Bernard Arnaud is here, telling me how he's going to help us."

"He told me I need to dress differently, wear a uniform of some kind," said Imani. She brushed a hand over her brown slacks and straightened her print top.

Cami held up a hand. "Hold it! Bernard arrived

unexpectedly last night with the crazy idea we were going to get back together. That's not going to happen, and he's not going to work here at the inn or at Taunton Estates either. I haven't had that discussion with him, but I will."

"Whew!" Becca let out a long breath. "I thought I was going to have to deal with him on a daily basis. As much as I love Chandler Hill there's no way I could work for that egotistical prick." She gave Cami an apologetic look. "But I can see how you'd fall for him. He's handsome, and I'm sure that French accent of his can be seductive, especially when he's being charming."

Cami pressed her lips together. "Well, his charm is long gone. He was never this way in France except with his older brother. I should have paid better attention to that trait." She turned to Imani. "Will you try to find him and let him know that I need to see him?"

"Sure," Imani quickly responded.

"Thanks. By the way, your outfit is perfect."

Imani's smile brightened her face as she left the office.

Cami turned to Becca. "Has Bernard done any damage with our guests?"

"I don't know, but I'll check."

After Becca left, Cami sat down at her desk and made a list of items to be done that day. Justine Devon and her groom, George Dickinson, were scheduled to arrive that afternoon, and she wanted to put together a welcome package for them. All guests received one, but for a bride and her party additional things like soaps, lotions, and a Chandler Hill cookbook were added.

Cami was on the phone with one of the staff at The Barn when Bernard strode into the room.

"You wanted to see me?"

Cami held up a finger to stop him and continued her

conversation. Hanging up, she turned her attention to Bernard who was standing at the window looking outside to the garden.

"Bernard. We need to talk. Please sit down."

He grinned. "Change your mind already?"

Cami forced herself to speak calmly. "As a matter of fact, I have. After you left, I had time to settle my thoughts. You're not welcome here, either as a friend, a staff member, or a guest. You had one free night's stay as a matter of courtesy, but that's it."

"What? But you know I have a background in winemaking. I can help you." The look of shock on his face made Cami certain of her decision. The guy didn't get it.

"My staff is like family to me. Another valid reason for you to leave. Do you realize that the word 'sorry' hasn't been uttered by you since you've been here? Even then, saying the word and meaning it would never make up for the hurt you caused me. My grandmother, the person I loved most in the world, was dying, and you didn't care." Remembering the pain, Cami's stomach curled.

"*Mais, Chérie* ..."

Cami raised her hand to stop him. "Enough. I want you to leave now." She rose from behind her desk and indicated the door with a sweep of her hand.

A scowl crossed Bernard's face, changing it from handsome to ugly. "You'll be sorry."

"I am, believe me. I thought we had a special relationship. *Adieu*, Bernard."

Bernard slammed the door behind him.

Knees shaking, Cami took a seat at her desk and buried her face in her hands. She'd been so stupid not to realize how shallow he was. Had the wine, the cheese, the bread, and all the joy of being in France hidden that from her? She lifted her head with fresh determination to stay away from any serious relationships until she had a better sense of who she was and what she was looking for.

That afternoon Cami was going over the inventory sheets for The Barn when Imani buzzed her. "Justine Devon and George Dickinson are checking in."

"Thanks." Cami left her office and hurried to the reception area.

"Hello and welcome to the Chandler Hill Inn," she said, striding toward them. "I'm Cami Chandler."

Justine was a tall, attractive brunette with sparkling green eyes that stared at her with something like shock. "Oh, my word! For a moment I thought you were my friend Lulu with a different hairdo." She held out her hand, and they shook hands. "Hi, I'm Justine Devon and this is my fiancé, George Dickinson."

Shaking hands with George, Cami beamed at them both. "We're so happy to have you here. I think you'll find it's the perfect place for a May wedding." Cami reminded herself that if this wedding didn't go well, it might ruin their whole wedding season.

He grinned. "I'm just here for the ride. Justine is the one who knows how she wants things. All I have to do is show up and say 'I do.'"

The three of them laughed together.

Justine elbowed George. "Doesn't Cami look an awful lot like Lulu?"

George studied her and nodded, his blue-eyed gaze resting on her face. "Yeah. It's uncanny. But then there's that old saying that everyone has a twin somewhere."

"Lulu is my maid of honor," Justine explained. "Wait until

you meet her. She's a hoot!"

Justine and George grinned at each other. They were a cute couple. George, with his blond hair, blue eyes, and husky build looked like a college football player in contrast to Justine's appearance.

Cami decided she'd wait for a guy who looked at her like George was looking at Justine.

"Let me show you to your room, and then, whenever you're ready, I'll give you a tour of the property."

"Okay," said Justine. "I want to see how everything looks in the daylight."

"The grounds will naturally be a lot different in May, and so will the lighting. But we can talk about how you want things to look. And while you're here, be sure to check out the food and our spa."

"Can't wait!" said Justine.

George winked at her. "I can't wait for the cake tasting."

"You'll love all of them," said Cami with confidence. "Our pastry chef is a recent transplant from San Francisco, and his creations are spectacular."

Becca approached them. "Sorry, I'm late. I got tied up in a meeting."

Cami indicated Becca with a fond smile. "This is Becca Withers, my assistant manager."

Justine and George introduced themselves and listened while Becca assured them that if they needed anything, to please give her a call.

"Do you want to go ahead and take them to their room?" Cami said to her as she noticed Bernard coming through the entrance.

"Sure." As Becca led them away, Cami hurried to intercept Bernard. The scowl on his face was ominous.

He stormed over to her. "What do you think you're doing?"

"I don't know what you mean," Cami replied, her voice low so other guests wouldn't hear. "Come to my office. We can talk there."

He stood glaring at her.

"Please," she said, and walked away. When he followed her, she let out a sigh of relief. The last thing she wanted her guests to see was her arguing with him. He'd only get louder, angrier.

In her office, she closed the door, turned to him, and stood. "What's going on?"

"I went to Taunton Estates to see if I could find work there, and the old guy there practically threw me off his land. I know enough Spanish to know what he called me. What have you done? Told everyone not to hire me?"

"That old man is my grandfather, and as you might guess, there's no way he'd ever hire you after the way you hurt me. But, no, I haven't been talking about you to others."

"You'd better be telling the truth," he said, glaring at her.

"I am. But you're on your own. I still don't understand why you don't go back to France."

"It's Jacques ..." his voice trailed off.

In the past, Bernard had kept her laughing at the antics between him and his brother. "You and your brother are always fighting. Go back, say you're sorry, and take advantage of what you have there."

Bernard shook his head sadly. "I can't. Not after what I said to him. He kicked me off the property."

"I'm sorry. I'm not going to help you here, but neither am I going to step in your way. It's over between us, and that's how I want to keep it."

Bernard studied her. "You really mean it, don't you?"

Cami gave him a steady look and nodded.

His expression contrite, Bernard opened the office door and turned back to her. "I don't know who's the bigger fool.

You or me. Either way, I'm going to prove to you that I don't need you. I can be a success on my own."

The door closed softly behind him.

Cami walked to the window and gazed outside, her thoughts whirling. *In France, Bernard had been so attentive, so charming. Would things have been different if she hadn't been called home? Or would she have eventually seen this side of him?*

The phone rang, and as Cami went to answer it, she realized she'd never know.

CHAPTER TEN

As Cami showed Justine and George the property, she saw it with fresh eyes. Chandler Hill Inn offered many choices to the bride and groom who wanted to make a simple wedding, uniquely theirs. She saw how effectively her grandmother had placed several arbors, and had added colorful flowering foliage to different locations for beautiful wedding photos. Even in the cold of the winter, it was easy to see how nice everything would be come spring.

Inside Chandler Hall, staff was decorating it for the Valentine's Day Dance. Twinkling lights dangled from the open beams in the ceiling like snowflakes suspended in the sky.

A sound of delight escaped Justine's lips. She turned to Cami with a smile. "I want something like that for my wedding."

"I'll note it," said Cami, writing it down on a checklist she'd put together earlier. "Anything else?"

"Baskets of flowers everywhere. My small wedding party will be wearing pink, so I'd love to have the color of the flowers be compatible."

Cami was thankful that, before she left, Lisa had enlarged the flower garden for just this kind of use. "We'll take photos of what your arrangements might look like and send them to you for your approval ahead of time. I'll make that notation."

By the time the tour was over, Cami had a better idea of the work they needed to do. She spoke to Becca. "How long before Vanessa comes here? We need her sooner than I thought.

Justine's wedding is the first of the season, but we have several others planned through the summer and into the fall. I want her well trained before then."

"I spoke to her last night. She should be here by March 1st. She's going to share my apartment, though it will be more or less hers." A pretty pink washed over Becca's cheeks. "I'm moving in with Dan this weekend."

"Oh, nice. I'm happy that things are going well for you. I like Dan."

Becca beamed at her. "I'm not sure, but I think he's going to give me a ring for Valentine's Day."

"Wow! You guys move fast."

"It may seem that way, but I felt from the beginning we were meant to be together."

Cami could feel her eyebrows lift. "You did? How do you know?"

Becca shrugged. "You just do. Don't worry. It'll happen to you."

Cami wasn't sure it would ever be that way for her. She was not about to rush into any relationship.

The next two days grew busier as they completed final preparations for the Valentine's Day Dance.

All guests of the inn would receive invitations to the occasion, which included a gourmet buffet dinner. Other winegrowers in the valley would also attend and display bottles of wines from their different vineyards so guests could sample wines from places they hadn't crammed into their tasting tour schedules. It was Cami's favorite inn event.

"What are you wearing to the dance tonight? I can't decide what to choose," Becca said, taking a seat in Cami's office.

Something fun, and maybe a little fancy. It's a rare

opportunity to dress up," Cami replied. "I'm wearing a long red dress, but you'll see a bit of everything. Some of the men will be in tuxedos, others in sport coats."

"Thank you for inviting me," said Becca. "Jonathan didn't allow any of us to join him for this event."

Cami pressed her lips together. "Without you and Imani, I couldn't run the inn. It's only right for you to come to the party, enjoy yourselves and our guests, and meet the other winemakers in the valley. It's our way of thanking them for their support."

Becca rose to her feet and faced Cami. "I'll let Imani know what you told me. I don't know how I could be so lucky to be working here now. Believe me, with Jonathan running the show, I often thought of quitting."

"We're both lucky. We have a lot of work ahead of us, so get ready!"

"Aye, aye, Captain!" said Becca with a saucy mock salute that made Cami laugh.

Before she went home to change clothes for the party, Cami talked with Darren about timing, checked the arrangements in Chandler Hall, and called Rafe to make sure he was on schedule to help her host the event. In the past, he and Nonnee had greeted guests as they arrived.

"No problem, we'll be there," Rafe assured her.

"We?"

"Drew and I. He'll need to see how it's done if he's going to take over for me in the future."

"But ..."

"I'm not going to be around forever, sweet girl," he said softly.

Her stomach did a flip-flop. "Don't talk that way." Even as she said the words, tears stung her eyes.

"Don't worry, *cariño*, I'm not leaving you for a long time, but I am getting old enough that I sometimes need help."

"Of course. I understand. See you later."

Cami hung up the phone realizing that Drew was going to have to play a part in her life whether she was ready for him or not. The idea both excited and worried her. She'd been honest about wanting only to be friends, yet she was attracted to him.

At home, Sophie sat at Cami's feet, ears cocked, listening to what she was saying. Seeing her expressive face and alert eyes, Cami stopped talking to the dog about her worries, leaned down, and scratched her ears. "You know what? It'll all work out as it's supposed to be. At least, that's what Nonnee would say."

Later, Cami checked herself in the mirror, taming the curls as best she could, and slid the diamond earrings into her earlobes. Then she hooked the grapes necklace behind her neck and studied her reflection. The jewels on her ears and the necklace settling in the vee of her dress's neckline sparkled like Nonnee's smile, bestowing gracious wishes for a lovely evening.

Straightening, she told herself that she had business to take care of. This was her first big social event at the inn as owner and manager.

She left the house, drove to the inn, parked her car, and headed for Chandler Hall. The sparkling lights among shrubs outside the building looked like stars fallen to earth. A few red mini-lights twinkled among the many white ones.

Cami entered the building and stood a moment gazing at her surroundings. A welcoming fire glowed in the large, stone fireplace, soft mood music came through strategically placed speakers, and the buffet table looked inviting with its crisp white linen cloths, rows of chafing dishes, and stacks of serving plates. An ice carving of a heart backlit in red and small, flower bouquets added color and elegance. Around the perimeter of the room, round tables of six covered in black linen awaited the guests. The bar at the opposite end of the room from the fireplace had a number of wine bottles on display. Champagne and sparkling wines sat in ice buckets ready to be served. Carefully hidden spotlights highlighted key focal points. The serving staff, dressed in special, red knit shirts with the Chandler Hill logo, gathered in a group, talking softly as they waited for guests to appear.

A young staff member hurried over to her. "May I take your coat?"

She smiled as he helped her remove it. Service at every level was important.

Becca and Dan arrived a moment later.

"Wow!" Becca said to Cami. "You look beautiful! Love that dress."

"Thanks." She'd chosen to wear a sleeveless dress that followed the contours of her body and then fell to her ankles in gentle folds. The lines of the dress were simple, and the silky, deep-red material was the perfect background for showing off the grapes necklace and her creamy skin.

After removing her coat, Becca twirled in front of her. "Bought this dress for a friend's wedding. What do you think?"

"It's perfect!" The short black dress fit Becca beautifully. She complained that she was chunky, but Becca was fine just as she was. And by the looks of it, Dan thought so too as he wrapped an arm around her.

Cami turned as Imani and her date arrived.

Imani looked wonderful in a long-sleeved, ankle-length green dress. She was a striking woman with caramel-colored skin, sharply defined features, and dark eyes that sparkled. The man beside her, introduced as Hank Danvers, matched her appearance in size and quiet demeanor. A handsome couple, Cami thought. Better yet, Imani was a bright, capable assistant who was fast becoming a friend, along with Becca. "The Three Musketeers" Darren had once called them.

Rafe and Drew were the next to arrive.

Cami hurried over to greet them. She hugged Rafe and tweaked his bright red bowtie. "Looking mighty handsome!" she teased. In truth, he looked fabulous in his tux.

She stepped away from Rafe and smiled at Drew. "Glad you could make it. This is a fun party."

"Thanks." He pulled at the collar of his crisp, white tuxedo shirt. "Not used to wearing this, but Rafe insisted. All part of the deal." His tawny-colored eyes filled with humor.

Cami and Rafe exchanged amused glances. If Rafe was handsome in a tux, Drew was absolutely delicious.

"Hi, everyone." Rafe introduced himself to Hank and smiled at the group of staff. "This is an evening for fun, but remember you represent Chandler Hill, and Drew, here, represents Taunton Estates. Enjoy!"

As Rafe continued talking with the group, Cami went into the kitchen to check on things. A lot of the food had already been prepared in the inn's kitchen, but several items were being cooked here. Satisfied that everything was in order, Cami returned to join Rafe to greet the guests.

Fifteen minutes later, guests began to arrive in droves. For others, the fun would begin. But Cami and Rafe would spend most of the evening talking to guests and introducing winegrowers to her assistants. It was important for Becca and Imani to meet them. The success of the many different wineries in the valley depended on cooperation between the vineyards. It wasn't uncommon for a tractor man to work for more than one vineyard. And sometimes staff members of one vineyard were called upon to help with an over-abundant harvest at another.

Cami had just introduced Imani to Mark and Jean Pierce, fellow winegrowers, when Mark mumbled. "Here he comes. Can't stand the guy."

Sensing a commotion at the entrance, she turned to see Rod Mitchell and a voluptuous young woman enter the building. Cami froze when she realized the man behind them was Bernard.

Letting out a long sigh, Cami gathered herself and went over to greet them. Rod Mitchell was someone Nonnee and Rafe had always disliked. In his seventies, he, like Rafe, was a striking man who had managed to irritate almost every other winemaker in the valley by some act of rudeness or worse.

The young, voluptuous woman accompanying Rod looked to be about Cami's age, much too young for him.

"Hello, Rod," Cami said coolly. "Good evening. And this is?"

"Cookie McDonald." Rod smiled at her and waved Bernard forward. "And this is Bernard Arnaud, a French winemaker who is going to help me develop some new wines."

"I see," Cami said evenly willing herself not to laugh at the way Cookie was fluttering her eyelashes at Rod nor react to the triumphant look Bernard was giving her. Drawing upon years of being in situations like this beside her grandmother, she managed to say, "Welcome. Please come in. We have several tables set aside for winemakers. You'll see your name at one of them along the wall."

As she watched the trio head for the tables she'd indicated, Rafe came up beside her. "What bimbo is Rod with now? And what's the deal with Bernard?"

"Bernard is now working for Rod. What a pair they'll make."

"I'll keep my eye on them. I don't want anything to ruin this evening for you or our guests."

As the wine flowed and people became more comfortable with one another, the volume of noise increased. Cami didn't hear Bernard speak until he was right behind her.

"Thought you could get rid of me, huh? I'm going to prove to you what an excellent winemaker I am. Rod Mitchell has the resources to create a world-class vineyard, and I'm going to help him."

"Good for you," Cami said, edging away from him.

She started toward Rafe, but Bernard grabbed her arm, preventing her from walking away.

"What are you doing?" Cami asked, pulling her arm out of his grasp.

"I just want to talk to you, that's all." He gave her a pleading look. "I made a mistake letting you go. You've got to give me a second chance. I'll make it up to you."

Cami shook her head. "It's not going to happen. Now leave me alone."

She felt a presence beside her and turned to face Drew.

"Thought you and I would hit the dance floor. A few couples have already started."

"Thanks." Cami's smile couldn't begin to show her relief at his presence. Bernard must have had a few drinks before coming to the party. He hadn't wanted her months ago. She didn't believe he really wanted her now. For him, it was just a bruised ego.

Drew took her arm and led her onto the dance floor. A jazz band had arrived earlier and was now playing appropriate music for dancing. Slow numbers were scheduled during dinner, and then livelier music would happen.

In his arms, gazing up at him, Cami felt some of the tension leave her. "Thanks for rescuing me."

He grinned. "I'm always ready to help a damsel in distress."

Looking across the room at Bernard, Cami said, "He would

give any damsel distress."

Drew chuckled and pulled her closer.

When the music stopped, Cami stepped away and smiled. "Thanks. You're a great dancer." What she meant was simply "Wow!" She had felt so fabulous in his arms, protected from the likes of Bernard.

Becca hurried over to her. "Rafe asked me to tell you it's time for the annual speeches."

Cami said goodbye to Drew and made her way through the crowd milling about, sipping wine and chatting while they waited for the opening of the buffet.

On the small stage, Rafe waited for her. She climbed up next to him and accepted the hand microphone he offered.

He winked at her. "Ready?"

"All set. You first."

Rafe shook his head. "No, Nonnee always went first. Now it's your turn."

Cami clicked on her mic and said, "Good evening! Welcome to Chandler Hill Inn's tenth annual Valentine's Day Dinner Dance. We hope you're having a great time. The buffet will be open shortly, but before then, let's have a little fun. Which couples here have been married longer than twenty-five years? Please step forward."

Two couples walked through the crowd to come to the front.

"Now, which of you has been married longer than thirty years?"

Everyone clapped when Mark and Jean stepped to the stage and announced they'd been married forty-four years.

The other couple, from Canada if Cami remembered correctly, and looking much younger, applauded with the others. "Only twenty-six years for us," the gentleman said, and gave his wife a kiss.

Becca slipped Cami a note with the names of the couple Cami didn't know.

"Every Valentine's Day, we like to recognize those people who've made it through many years together. So, Mark and Jean Pierce, here's your prize!" Cami handed them an envelope. "And a special Happy Valentine's Day to Randy and Susie Bennett."

"Thank you so much," Mark said. And then as they'd done the last few years, Mark handed the envelope to Jean.

Jean smiled and handed the envelope to Susie Bennett. "We'd like you to have this prize to encourage you to stay together and be as happy as we are."

The applause grew louder.

"What is it?" someone asked.

Susie opened the envelope and let out a squeal of delight. "Airline coupons for two first-class tickets for anywhere in the U. S."

Rafe and Cami exchanged happy smiles. Nonnee had decided to give away airline tickets as the Valentine prize some time ago. She said it gave her pleasure to give others wings when she was unable to fly.

Cami introduced Rafe, who told the story of the love he and Nonnee had shared and how this celebration was a favorite of theirs. "When love and kindness so often seem to be lacking, we hope you enjoy this special evening with us." He lifted his wine glass. "Here's to you! All of you!"

When the response settled down, he announced, "The buffet is now open. Help yourself to our chef's delicious food."

As people hurried back to their tables and got into line, Cami went over to Mark and Jean. "Thank you for sharing the prize again this year."

Jean chuckled. "Lettie and I made a pact a few years ago. I'm a lot like her with my fear of flying. So, we made a game of

Mark's and my winning, knowing the prize would go to whomever was next in line."

"That's so kind." Cami gave her a quick kiss on the cheek.

She left them and went over to the buffet, making sure food was replenished in chafing dishes and on platters as needed, and all was going smoothly.

"Nice party," said Rod, coming over to her. "I didn't realize you knew the new guy I hired. I hope you don't mind he's now working for me."

Cami ignored the snide tone of his voice and gave him her best smile. "Not at all. Competition is good for everyone." Rod Mitchell's winery—Lone Creek Winery—was not that successful. It wouldn't hurt Chandler Hill one bit to have his wines become better.

Before he could engage her in further conversation, she turned away. Spying Imani and Hank waiting at the end of the line for the buffet, she went over to them.

"How's the evening going?"

"Great," said Imani. "Hank and I actually danced."

Hank laughed. "I don't dance to this kind of music, but for her, I tried."

Cami decided she liked him a lot.

After seeing that everyone else was served, she joined Rafe at the end of the line. He indicated the crowd with a nod of his head. "Looks like we hit another home run. Everyone is having an outstanding time, and Darren, Liz, and their staff have done a great job with the food."

"Nonnee would be proud," said Cami, enjoying the moment. The happy buzz of conversation filled the room as people ate and chatted with one another, pleasing her. Unless someone specifically reserved a whole table, guests were seated randomly with one another. If the music, food, and wine were excellent, it helped to make it work well.

"Rod Mitchell has set his hopes high on Bernard. They're both out to prove they're the best."

"It's a sorry combination," said Rafe, shaking his head. "But make no mistake, we'll have to watch them carefully. I don't trust either of them."

"I think you're right." Even as she helped herself to the food, her stomach curled at the idea of Bernard living next door. He seemed quite desperate to get back with her, and though it hurt, she knew it had a lot to do with Chandler Hill and her inheritance.

Later, after the guests had left, Rafe and Darren passed out glasses of champagne to those members of the staff who were of age. They offered the extra desserts as well.

"Here's to another successful Valentine's Day event. Thank you, everyone."

"Happy Valentine's Day!" came a loud response, and they all raised their glasses.

As talk continued, staff members shared stories of the evening. Cami studied them. They were a nice group of people. She thought of the changes she was making in The Barn and wondered how she could improve conditions for this crew working for her. It was more than money that made a staff member loyal.

She put aside her thoughts and turned her attention to Rafe, who was speaking.

"Good night, everyone! See you tomorrow."

Cami gave him a kiss on the cheek and stood awkwardly in front of Drew, who was preparing to leave with Rafe.

"Thanks for the dance."

He grinned. "Good night, Cami." He leaned over and gave her a quick kiss on the cheek.

Whistles and cat calls erupted from the onlookers.

"We're just friends," said Cami, blushing to the roots of her hair as she turned to face them.

"See you!" Drew called to everyone before hurrying to catch up to Rafe.

Becca took Cami aside. "You call that 'friends?' Girl, you've got a lot to learn."

"You know it can't be more than that. Not now when we have so much going on at the inn. Later, when I'm a little more comfortable with managing the place, and maybe after the bud break in late March or the buds bloom in May after the wedding, I can think about it. He wants us to be friends and I'm willing to leave it at that."

"Okay, okay. It's just that the two of you seem to sizzle. Drew and I didn't click, but you two do. Know what I mean?"

Uncomfortable, Cami turned the conversation around. "Talk about sizzling, has Dan proposed yet?"

Becca's lips turned down. She shook her head.

Dan came over to them. "Ready to go, Becca? I'm beat."

"See you tomorrow," Becca said.

Sensing Becca's disappointment, Cami gave her a hug. "Tomorrow."

Cami lay in bed thinking of the evening. She'd lied to Becca. She wanted to be more than friends with Drew. With him, she wanted what her grandparents had shared. The way she'd felt dancing in his arms, as if she'd always belonged there, was something she'd once dreamed of. She realized more than ever that her romance with Bernard had been infatuation. But there were problems. Drew had trust issues, and she hadn't lied to Becca about needing time to get her arms around the job of running the inn, The Barn, the vineyards, and the winery. She had people to help her, of course, but she needed to be confident about handling it all. The thought of someday adding Rafe's property to hers scared the hell out of her.

She rolled over and hugged her pillow. Life was so much simpler when she was just a college graduate working for someone else.

CHAPTER ELEVEN

The next morning, Cami and Becca stood in the office to say goodbye to Justine and George, who had signed the final contracts for their May wedding.

"Thank you again for everything," Justine said. "Our stay this weekend was perfect. The Valentine Party was fabulous, and the staff was great. I'm so happy to know my wedding will take place here."

"Yeah, and the food was delicious." George patted his stomach. "The Beef Wellington was out of sight. That, and the cake we've chosen."

"I'm going to tell Lulu about meeting you," Justine said. "You two really do look alike."

Cami lifted her notepad, curious about her apparent double. "What is her name again?"

"Louise, Lulu Kingsley. She and I went to prep school together and have been friends ever since. She's a lot of fun."

"Nice. Again, thank you for choosing Chandler Hill for your wedding. One last question, do you mind if we discreetly take photos of your wedding to be used in promotions? With your permission, of course."

"Oh, that would be nice," said Justine, glancing at George. "We don't mind sharing our happy day, do we?"

He shrugged. "It's okay by me."

"Thank you. It's going to be a gorgeous wedding. Let's hope the weather will cooperate. If not, we'll set things up nicely in Chandler Hall." Cami was planning to do some special promotions for weddings, and having visual proof of wedding successes was important. Especially after spending money on the changes and additions she'd either done or planned to do.

Justine gave Cami and Becca hugs. "See you in May. In the meantime, if anything comes up, I have your email addresses."

"Things will come up, I promise you," George said, laughing when Justine took a friendly swipe at him.

After they left, Cami and Becca smiled at each other. "I hope all our brides and grooms will be like that."

"They won't," said Cami, remembering the times when Nonnee had grumbled about it. She studied Becca's left hand. "No ring?"

"Nope. My mother told me I shouldn't be so anxious, but I know it's what I want. I'm certain he wants it too." Tears filled Becca's eyes.

Cami put her arm around her. "Anyone can tell Dan loves you. Maybe he's planning something special, something different from many other guys' proposing on Valentine's Day."

"I hope so. Because I've moved most of my stuff into his apartment. By the way, Vanessa will be here next week, a little earlier than I thought."

"Terrific. We're still going through changes in The Barn, and I want to develop a whole new wedding package. She needs to be part of the planning so she can handle the details once a wedding party is on site."

The days flew by as The Barn was reorganized. Cami worked with Gwen Chapman, the new manager, to make things go as smoothly as possible. She wanted to change up the merchandise a bit, add a few different offerings similar to things she'd seen in Europe, and offer a range of higher-priced items. It was a bit risky, but as long as everything was top quality, she thought it would work. That and artwork from local artists would add dimensions to the items for sale that she thought had been missing.

Checking over the bills for the new inventory, Cami hoped she was right, and the money would be recouped. If only Nonnee's money hadn't been lost.

Cami sat in her office going over ideas for a new questionnaire for brides and grooms. After talking to Justine and George, she realized the forms they used were inadequate. In reviewing notes of her conversations with them, she found the name of the girl, Lulu, who was supposed to look like her. Thinking of the father she didn't know, she wondered if there could be a connection. Heart pounding, she typed Louise Kingsley's name into Google and came up with information. Twenty-one, Louise Kingsley was the daughter of Edward Kingsley, a congressman in California. She was a substitute teacher in one of the private schools in an underprivileged area in L.A. Intrigued, Cami looked her up on Facebook and stared in shock at the features of the young woman who could've been her. But after studying that photo more closely and others posted on Facebook, she realized that some of Lulu's features were definitely not like hers. Certainly, her coloring was different. Lulu had chestnut hair and sparkling blue eyes. In all the photos, she was smiling in a way that didn't match Cami's.

Ready to dismiss her idea as folly, Cami looked up information on Edward Kingsley. At fifty-eight, he was a handsome, dark-haired man with hair graying at the temples in an attractive way like some men aged. According to the facts, he'd been married for twenty-three years and was a staunch supporter of the religious right. His body language in the photos showed him to be sure of himself. She studied the picture of his family. Standing beside a small, pretty blonde, he had a hand on Lulu's shoulder and another on the shoulder of a boy who appeared quite a bit younger than Lulu.

She studied his features, looking for any similarities. She couldn't be sure, but she thought the shape of her face, maybe their ears, and definitely their mouths were the same. She studied another photo and let out a gasp. His left earlobe was exactly like hers—shorter, less well-formed than the one on the right. Her heart pounded so hard she felt faint. She searched other photographs. Both of his earlobes were like that, not just the left one like hers.

Everyone had always told her that there was no mistaking Nonnee as her grandmother. In fact, many thought Nonnee was her mother. She'd liked that idea. But now, after all these years, she might know who her father was.

Cami studied the garden outside her office window. What if she was the congressman's daughter? Would it mean an end to his career? A betrayal of her mother's wishes to keep him unknown?

Cami stood and went over to the window. The sun warmed her face as she gazed out at the blue sky. She took a deep breath. If the congressman and his family came to the wedding, she was going to try to talk to him privately. If he was her father, she had a right to know, didn't she?

Two days later Vanessa Duncan arrived. The blond, blue-eyed girl was what Rafe called "a knockout". Bubbly and full of personality, Cami felt a little overwhelmed and then reminded herself not to be silly. Vanessa was perfect for the job she had in mind for her, even though her instincts told

Cami there was something worrisome about her.

One afternoon several days later, while Cami was working at her desk, Becca approached her. "I'm throwing a party Saturday night to welcome Vanessa. Please come."

"Sounds like fun. Like you said, she loves to have a good time."

Becca started to leave and turned back. "Vanessa and Drew are double dating with Dan and me tonight. I know you've said that you want to be only friends with him, but I wanted you to know."

"Thanks," Cami responded, managing to hide her dismay. If Vanessa was just a pretty girl, she wouldn't be worried about her dating Drew. But Vanessa was way more outgoing than she, way more fun. *Relax*, Cami told herself. *You got what you wanted from Drew. A friend.* But that didn't make her feel any better.

Saturday night, Cami climbed the stairs into Dan's apartment. In a nice complex, his unit was bigger than some, with two bedrooms and a large kitchen, which Becca had confided to her she hardly ever used.

The party was already in full swing when Cami walked into the apartment. Music was blaring and a crowd had gathered in the kitchen, where beer, wine, and sodas were set out. Chips and salsa, nuts, and pretzels were placed on available spaces throughout the living area.

Cami guessed there were twenty or so people there as she made her way to the kitchen.

Drew stopped her. "Glad you could make it."

"Yeah, me too." She moved on to the kitchen. A glass of an after-dinner wine might help soothe her jangled nerves. Earlier in the office, Vanessa had raved about her two dates with Drew. She even announced that she'd love to have a wedding of her own at the inn.

Vanessa was in the kitchen surrounded by a number of men, making them laugh with tales of her work in New York.

"And here is my boss," Vanessa exclaimed, her face flushed from alcohol. She wrapped an arm around Cami's shoulder. "She's the best!"

Cami smiled at the assembled group, realizing she didn't know many of them. Too much work at the inn, she decided. She poured herself a glass of wine and joined the gathering around Vanessa. She was, Cami thought, a natural entertainer. Soon, she was laughing at Vanessa's antics and her uncanny way of imitating people.

Drew came up beside Cami. "The pruning is almost done in the vineyards. Then we'll begin checking all the wiring on the trellises. It looks like it's going to be an amazing season."

She smiled at him. "I think so too. I can't wait to be a part of it. By the time the buds bloom in May, the wedding should be over and I can give a little more time to the grape growing."

Vanessa sidled up to them. "What are you two talking about?"

"The schedule for the grapes," Drew said. "You might want to know about it."

Vanessa beamed at him and slapped his arm playfully. "I just like to drink the end product. Or spend time with you."

He laughed. "It doesn't have to be one or the other. We can do it together."

Cami eased away from them and went to join the others in the living room. Seeing Drew and Vanessa together hurt.

She'd just taken a sip of her wine when Bernard showed up at the door. She worked hard to swallow without choking.

"Heard there was a party," Bernard said, grinning at the group.

One of the girls on the couch beside her said, "Wow! He can come to my party anytime."

Becca hurried over to him. "Hi, Bernard. What's up?"

He grinned. "I live in the next building. I thought I'd better come and check this out."

Cami noticed the unhappy look on Becca's face before indicating he could come inside.

As Bernard headed for the kitchen, Becca came over to her. "Sorry about Bernard. But what could I do?"

Cami waved away her concern. "Don't worry about it. It's time for me to go anyway. I'm having breakfast with Rafe, and you know what an early riser he is."

Becca laughed. "We all do."

Cami hugged Becca. "See you on Monday. Enjoy your day off."

Quietly, before anyone noticed, Cami slipped out the door. She needed time to sort through her feelings for Drew. He'd told her he didn't want any serious relationships, but he and Vanessa appeared to have moved fast to build one.

Cami sat with Rafe inside Sunny Up, a new restaurant in town known for their tasty breakfasts. Sipping gratefully on her coffee, she felt the hot liquid help get her ready for the day. Sundays were busy at the inn with people checking out and rooms being cleaned for the next wave of guests.

"Heard Becca and Dan had a great party last night. Drew called in to say he wouldn't be at the winery, that he'd stayed out way too late. It's no problem, of course, at this time of year. Did you go?"

Cami set down her coffee cup. "I went and left soon after Bernard arrived. I couldn't face a confrontation with him." She wasn't about to tell him she couldn't stand to see how

Drew and Vanessa were acting after only a couple of dates.

He studied her. "You can't let Bernard interfere with your friendships, any more than you can allow him to interfere with business."

"I know. I know. You're right. He just seems to be everywhere."

Their omelets were served, and after taking a bite of his, Rafe said, "I've chosen dates for the river cruise. With Drew handling things at the vineyard, I'm going to take advantage of having the time to do it. I've decided on early September before picking and crush take place. Sound okay?"

Cami smiled and clasped his hand. "It sounds perfect. Nonnee really wanted you to do this." She paused, took a deep breath, and blurted, "I need to talk to you about something. What would you say if I tell you I think I've found my father?"

Rafe's eyebrows shot up. "What are you talking about?"

Cami told him how Justine and George had agreed she looked like their friend Lulu Kingsley. "I didn't think much about it as we finalized their wedding plans. But later, when I saw my note with her name on it, I did a little investigation on my own. I looked up both her and her father, a congressman from California, online." Cami tugged on her left ear. "You know how I've always hated the way this ear looks. Edward Kingsley has one just like it. Two in fact. And, Rafe, I do look an awful lot like Lulu, his daughter."

He set down his fork and leaned back in his chair, studying her. "I know how important it is to know who your parents are. It was always a big disappointment that your grandmother never knew either one of hers. Be careful, *cariño*. Poking into another person's business can end up hurting you. Your mother never wanted us to know. I believe she kept it from us for a good reason."

"She might have told me when I was older, but she never

got the chance."

Rafe shook his head sadly. "She died way too young, just when I was beginning to form a relationship with her as my daughter."

"But I have a right to know, don't I?" Cami persisted.

"Yes, but one person's right could be another person's trouble. Just be careful. That's all I'm saying."

Silence reigned as they continued eating.

Rafe was too protective of her, Cami thought. She was a big girl; she could handle this situation on her own. When the wedding party arrived at Chandler Hill, she was going to find a way to talk to Lulu or her father.

CHAPTER TWELVE

The bud break happened in early April and was as exciting as it was any other year. It always seemed a miracle to Cami when leaves emerged, changing the rows of stark vines into a pattern of green beginnings. At this time each year, Rafe invited fellow grape growers to his vineyard for an evening of celebration. The owners of vineyards were a compatible group for the most part. Rafe felt it was very important to keep on good terms with everyone, which is why he'd invited Rod Mitchell, even though neither he nor Cami wanted him there.

Rafe's winery layout was quite simple. A large open room with log walls and a wooden floor resembled a cabin in style, with a tasting bar at one end, tables where guests could sit, and a small hidden kitchen. A basement below held three enormous, stainless-steel tanks for holding crushed grapes before the wine was transferred to a number of nearby oak barrels for aging.

Cami stood with him and Drew at the entrance to the winery welcoming his guests. Inside, two staff members walked through the gathering with hot hors d'oeuvres provided by Chandler Hill Inn. Bottles of wine, along with beer and sodas, were set out on the bar with plenty of glasses and more appetizers.

Talk among the guests was that it was going to be an excellent year.

Drew turned to Cami. "A nice crowd."

"Yes, it usually is. Everyone likes Rafe. His family has been in the valley for a couple of generations."

Drew studied her a moment with a wistful look. "I've missed our dinners."

Me, too," said Cami. "But I know you're busy here with Rafe and dating Vanessa. I'm busy too with the inn and the vineyard."

Drew's gaze lingered. "You aren't upset with me for being with Vanessa, are you?"

"No," she said striving to be fair. It wasn't his fault she'd told him she wanted just friendship and had changed her mind. "Vanessa's a lot of fun. I'm sure you two have a great time together."

"We do. By the way, Vanessa really likes working for you and the inn."

"She's doing a good job," Vanessa was creative and eager.

"Great." He stopped talking when a gentleman approached and asked him a question.

With the promise of another growing season, the valley seemed to come alive. Everyone at the inn became excited about the busier months ahead. Cami was pleased that Vanessa's old job had been in advertising. They worked together to develop a better website presentation of wedding information and created an online marketing plan.

At The Barn, a nook offered books on such topics as cooking, winemaking, home gardening, and similar interests and held comfortable chairs for readers. Artists displayed a number of paintings and other forms of artwork for sale throughout the store downstairs as well as the tasting room on the second floor. The merchandise that Cami wanted to ease out of inventory was on sale in a special corner. Standing back, surveying the area, Cami and Gwen smiled with satisfaction. Their ideas were compatible. More than that,

Gwen was a whiz at analyzing merchandise turnover and forecasting inventory needs. For the time being, Cami was overseeing website sales, but she hoped to hand that task over to Becca after the end of the season.

As she was working at her desk going over employee performance reviews, her phone rang.

"Hi, Cami? This is Jamison. I just wanted to let you know that I've made reservations for Wynton and me to spend next weekend at Chandler Hill. We'll arrive on Thursday and leave on Sunday. While we're there, I'd love the opportunity to have dinner with you."

Cami warmed with affection. When Jamison had come to the inn to handle the legal issues with Jonathan, they'd formed a quick, easy friendship.

"I can't wait to see you again and to meet Wynton. As I told you earlier, I studied his work in one of my art classes. I even used some of his paintings as examples of artwork for an essay. Can I make a reservation for you for the spa? I don't want to intrude, but perhaps you'd like to come to my house for dinner and a special tasting of some of the local wines. I'm sure Rafe will join us."

"How about your Prince in Shining Armor, the man who we decided was definitely not a frog?"

Cami smiled at the memory of Drew helping to chase Jonathan off the property. "Unfortunately, he'll probably be out with his girlfriend, but I'll ask him. He's working closely with Rafe."

"A time at the spa sounds wonderful," Jamison said. "I'm excited to have the opportunity to get away. The girls will be out of town with their school class trip."

"I'll be happy to see you," Cami said.

As soon as she ended the call, she phoned the reception desk. "Mr. and Mrs. Winkler are arriving this Thursday and leaving on Sunday. Please mark their reservation as VIP Guests and compliment the account." She could never repay Jamison for the quick way she'd taken Jonathan down and off the property.

On Thursday, when the call from Reception came through, Cami rushed out to the lobby to greet the Winklers.

Jamison looked even tinier standing next to a tall, broad-shouldered man. Jamison's short blond hair was in place, and her trim body was dressed in wool slacks and blazer as if she was going into court. Wynton's long, loose brown hair and unshaven cheeks matched the casual blue jeans and long-sleeved T-shirt he wore.

Intrigued by their differences, Cami stepped forward. "Welcome to Chandler Hill Inn. I'm so happy you're here."

Jamison gave her a strong hug. "It's nice to see you again. Come meet your hero and mine." She indicated Wynton, who smiled somewhat shyly at her.

Cami shook his hand. "I've studied your paintings for an art class of mine. I'm honored to have you here. I don't know if you brought paints and supplies with you, but if you did, I think you'll find interesting material amid these rolling hills and all they contain."

He glanced at Jamison and smiled. "As a matter of fact, while Jami is getting pampered, I'm going to do a little wandering on my own."

"Wynn and I agreed on that beforehand," said Jamison.

"While you're here, I'm hoping to discuss something with you," Cami said to Jamison.

Her eyebrows rose. "More problems with the inn?"

"Something personal," Cami responded, hoping she was right and Jamison could guide her on talking to the congressman who just might be her father.

Friday morning, Jamison tapped on Cami's half-open office door. "May I come in?"

Cami jumped to her feet. "Wynton's off on his own?"

"Yes. He took a sketch pad and a camera with him." Jamison sat in the chair Cami indicated for her. "What's up?"

"Before we get started, would you like coffee? Tea?" Cami asked her.

"Coffee, black, sounds great. I don't know which is better, the first cup of coffee or the second. I like them both so much."

Cami called the kitchen. Moments later a staff member carried in a tray with two cups of coffee and a small plate of cookies and handed them out.

"Now that's service," said Jamison, happily taking a homemade butterscotch cookie and lifting her cup of coffee to her lips.

"Thank you," Cami said to the staff member, ushering her to the door and closing it behind her.

After sitting down at her desk, she faced Jamison. "Let me give you a little family history first."

Jamison listened intently to the story of Cami's birth, how her mother had always refused to tell anyone who her father was, and her recent encounter with Justine Devon.

"After doing some investigation of Lulu Kingsley and her father, I think he might very well be my father too. We have the same earlobes. I know that may sound silly, but Lulu and I really do look alike. So, when they're here for Justine's wedding, I want to speak to him."

"And exactly what would you say?" Jamison asked quietly.

"Well, I'm not sure. I hoped you might help me. Rafe told me I should leave things as they are, but I want, no, *need* to know if he's my father."

Jamison gazed out the window for a moment. When she turned back to Cami her expression was serious. "I know how much it would mean to you to discover him, but I think you have to go about it with caution. You can't accuse someone of being your father, especially someone in the public eye. That could be a dangerous situation if he retaliated against you, and, frankly, it might hurt the inn and winery. The repercussions from the exposure could hurt everyone."

"But I'm not accusing. I'm just asking."

"I understand, but I would advise you not to get your hopes up. You'll have a chance to meet Lulu and her father at the wedding. See how approachable they are, study their features, see if there's a way to make conversation without being direct about your interest in them. You already have an entrée into the conversation because you've been told by her friends that you look like Lulu." Jamison gave her a steady look. "My advice is to go slowly and cautiously. You've had a nice life here, one you say you're grateful for. Think about that too."

Cami wanted to cry. Her grandparents had acted as her parents for most of her life, and while they were wonderful, she wanted to know her real parents too.

"Thank you for the invitation to dinner tonight. You say you want us at your house at six o'clock?" Jamison said, deftly moving the conversation to another topic.

Cami brightened. "Yes. I can't wait to have you. Rafe will be there, too, along with Drew, who is taking on more and more of the work at the Taunton Estates Vineyards, Rafe's property."

"Whatever happened to frog boy?" Jamison asked playfully.

Cami couldn't help the groan that came from her mouth. "You're not going to believe it, but Bernard showed up on my doorstep expecting me to take him back. He's now living here in the valley. I made it clear he would never work here or at Taunton Estates. He found a job with Rod Mitchell at the vineyard next door. Rod is the least liked, least respected grower in the valley. It's not a good combination. Rafe and I agree we have to keep an eye on them."

"Wise move," said Jamison. Her brow furrowed. "You have an awful lot to handle for someone your age. You let me know anytime I can be of assistance to you."

"Thanks," said Cami, hoping she would never have to call on her for help with that issue.

That evening, Cami dressed in a long, flowy skirt in turquoise and a creamy silk top. She hooked the grape pendant necklace around her neck, where it rested in the V of the shirt's collar. Letting her hair have its way, Cami liked how it fell in soft red curls around her face. She gave herself a second look in the mirror and left the bathroom thinking it might be time for her to make another visit to the spa.

Rafe and Drew showed up as promised a short while later as she was completing the table settings. She'd ordered flowers and the main course from the inn so that appetizers, salad, and dessert were the only things she had to make.

She kissed Rafe and turned to Drew. "Glad you're here. It should be a nice evening."

"Something smells great already!" said Drew following her into the kitchen. "What are you cooking tonight?"

"Just the appetizers. The main course is coming from the inn. I took the lazy way out."

"The smell of cheese and garlic doesn't seem lazy. More like delicious."

"I think you'll like dessert too. A lemon sponge cake that is a favorite of Rafe's." Cami smiled at Drew. She loved his enthusiasm for her cooking. Maybe he was just hungry. She'd heard Vanessa complain that she didn't know how to cook.

Rafe opened a couple bottles of wine and placed them on the sideboard in the dining room. "A nice, hearty cabernet sauvignon for dinner."

"Thanks." She turned as the doorbell rang. "I'll get it. Make yourselves comfortable in the living room."

Cami went to the door and opened it. Jamison and Wynton stood on the porch. Jamison held a bouquet in her hands, and Wynton carried a brown-leather portfolio.

"So glad you're here," said Cami, accepting the bouquet of pink roses from Jamison. "Please come in. Rafe and Drew are already here."

Wynton followed Jamison inside and set his case by the door.

Cami made the introductions and then headed to the kitchen with the bouquet, quickly deciding to set aside the flowers she'd brought from the hotel.

Jamison entered the kitchen. "I hope you didn't go to much trouble for us. Wynton and I are pretty easy to please. Need any help with anything?"

"I've got everything set. Let me get the flowers arranged, and we can sit in the living room. Thank you again for these roses. I love them."

Jamison winked at her. "I heard they're a family favorite."

Cami laughed. "Guess everyone knows Nonnee loved them, and I do too."

On her way to the living room, she exchanged the flowers she'd set on the table with the ones Jamison had brought.

"Now, let's join the others."

Conversation was comfortable as the five of them chatted about their jobs. Cami was pleased by the way both Rafe and

Drew related stories of Taunton Estates wines. Interested in what others had to say, Wynton was quiet about himself.

"Cami, another reason Wynton and I chose to come here was business," said Jamison. "I'll let Wynton tell you about it."

Wynton looked at Cami. "Jami said you liked my work, and that you'd told her how you used it for a class study. I happened to mention it to my agent, and she urged me to talk to you about perhaps setting up an art show here. She's also started to have prints made of some of my pieces. Not all, of course, but enough to give you a nice inventory."

Cami's jaw dropped. She clasped her hands. "Really? That would be awesome! I'm trying to bring more of the arts to The Barn. I've already started to get in touch with a number of authors to do lectures and book signings here. This could be sort of the same thing—an opportunity for people to meet you and for you to showcase your work."

"I'm not doing any marketing like Thomas Kinkade, but I like the idea that prints give people who like my work the opportunity to have it in a way they can afford."

Cami was surprised by his modesty. He was famous. People loved the contemporary mixed media pieces he did. "It would be an honor to work with you. A dream come true for me, actually."

Jamison beamed at her. "I told him your guests appear to be people who enjoy the finer things in life, and this might be an excellent way for him to test the market, so to speak."

"I'm thrilled to be a part of it," Cami said, realizing they'd have to rearrange an area of The Barn just for his work. Even as talk turned to other things when they went on to dinner, Cami's pulse raced with excitement over this new project.

After their meal was over, they congregated in the living room once more for coffee and after-dinner drinks.

Rafe was the first to get to his feet. "Everything's been

fabulous, *cariño*, but I must go. I have an early day tomorrow.'

Cami and Drew exchanged wry looks. Rafe and his early days were a joke among the staff.

"Time for me to leave too," said Drew, joining him.

After shaking hands and murmuring goodbyes, the two of them headed for the door.

"Thanks for coming," Cami said, following them.

At the door, she gave Rafe a hug.

Drew surprised her by leaning over and kissing her cheek. "Love your dinners. Thanks."

When Cami returned to the living room, Jamison winked at her. "He does have shiny armor."

Cami knew exactly who Jamison was talking about and felt a hot flush creep up her cheeks.

CHAPTER THIRTEEN

As excited as Cami was about working on her art and author projects, she was anxious about the upcoming wedding. Justine had written to tell her that many of her friends were considering holding their weddings at Chandler Hill. And with the new promos on the website, reservations were filling fast.

With a little encouragement, most brides were willing to make a commitment for all thirty rooms. Some even had Chandler Hill Inn find overflow rooms at other properties. It became a juggling act to figure out how a wedding could be held and still allow room for the inn's regular guests. Sometimes, if rooms were available during a wedding, special discounts were offered to other guests. In all cases, Cami worked hard to accommodate regular guests the best way she knew how. They were the ones who kept the property going throughout the year.

Becca had come up with a presentation package for brides' families and guests, offering them room discounts in the future and providing a specially designed flyer showing a number of gifts from The Barn they could purchase to commemorate the occasion. Pewter picture frames with the Chandler Hill logo discreetly placed at the bottom and terry robes with the Chandler Hill logo were available along with simpler things like bride or groom T-shirts, mugs, cups, and wine glasses. And of course, the winery offered special case discounts for wine to members of wedding parties.

#

Justine's parents were scheduled to arrive two days before the wedding. A cold snap had come and gone, and the weather predicted for the wedding weekend was doable with warm temperatures and showers on Sunday, the day most of the wedding guests would leave.

Cami, Becca, and Vanessa went together to greet Justine's parents upon arrival.

"Welcome to the Chandler Hill Inn," Cami said. "Becca Withers is my assistant manager, and Vanessa Duncan is overseeing weddings for us. We want your stay here to be everything you wished, so please be in touch with any of us with any requests you might have."

"Lovely," responded Justine's mother, Olivia. Tall and thin, she was elegantly dressed in a St. John suit in soft blue that went well with her blond hair and blue eyes. Jewels winked on her fingers and in her earlobes. She took the hand Cami offered and shook it gently. She studied Cami a moment. "Justine mentioned you look like Lulu Kingsley. She's right, you do."

"Hello, I'm David." Justine's father shook hands with her. He was a pleasant-faced man whose brown eyes behind his glasses seemed to take in everything at once as he looked around and then settled on her with interest. "Nice place."

"Of course, it is, darling. We wouldn't do anything less for our Justine," said Olivia, all but cooing.

David gave Cami a sheepish grin. "Our princess is spoiled, but we love her."

"She's delightful," Cami assured them. She'd liked Justine from the beginning. "As arranged, all the rooms in the main house here are reserved for family. Vanessa will show you to your room. Join us here in the living area for cocktails at five.

The spa and the tasting room in The Barn are open for your pleasure."

"Can't wait," said Olivia. "I intend to make good use of the spa while I'm here."

"Great. And I understand your friends Lillie and Bud Tucker are arriving later today and will join you for dinner downtown."

"Yes, most of the wedding party is arriving late tonight, so it'll be a pleasant break before all the activity takes place."

"We'll be here for them. Now, Vanessa will show you to your room, and if you'd like, she can make a reservation at the spa for you."

Vanessa took her cue. "Come this way. We'll have your bags sent to your room. I'm sure you'll like it. It's one of my favorites."

Cami and Becca watched them leave.

"This is it," said Becca. "Everything we've been working for. Let's hope it all goes well." Her lips curved. "This wedding makes me excited for my own."

"Still no idea when Dan might propose?"

Becca shook her head. "No, and I've decided not even to hint at it anymore. My mother says I'm going to scare him off."

"I don't think so. I 've seen the way he is with you. Maybe he's waiting for a June wedding."

"Maybe he's waiting because he's not sure," Becca said glumly.

Cami laughed and slung an arm around Becca's shoulder. "No way."

The rest of the day passed quickly. Cami and Becca worked on a new purchase order system with their IT guy, Ben Bachman, a student at Oregon State University. After the mess with Jonathan and his kickbacks scheme, Cami wanted the whole system updated with a few protections added.

At the end of the day, almost numb from numbers and the terms Ben had thrown around, Cami called to Sophie and headed home for a quiet dinner. There wouldn't be another chance to relax for the next couple of days.

She planned to return to the inn later when the registration desk called to say Justine and her friends had arrived. But as the evening went on, she realized she was too tired, that it was one of the duties Vanessa was being paid for. Vanessa was a night owl; she was not.

When Cami awoke, the first thing she thought of was Lulu Kingsley. Maybe today she'd be able to strike up a casual conversation with her and make strides toward finding out about any relationship with her and her father. Everyone had told her to go slowly, so she'd leave it at that. Later, she'd work in more opportunities to talk to her alone.

It was a clear and sunny, perfect pre-wedding day. As she drove from her house to the inn, Cami gazed at the vineyards with satisfaction. By the end of the month, the buds would bloom. Small flower clusters would appear on the tips of the young shoots looking like buttons. A few weeks after the initial clusters appeared, the flowers would start to grow in size, and then pollination would take place. She loved that nature took care to follow the steps that helped her and other grape growers produce the best grapes for a lovely wine. Nature and man, sometimes at odds, could do wonderful things together.

When she arrived at the inn, Becca rushed over to greet her. "May I introduce you to the future Mrs. Daniel Thurston?" Beaming, her eyes liquid with tears of happiness, she held out her left hand to Cami. A solitaire diamond twinkled at her from a wide, platinum band.

"You're engaged!" Cami squealed and pulled Becca into a warm embrace. "I'm so happy for you."

"It was the sweetest thing ever," gushed Becca. "We were sitting on the couch and I was telling him how excited I was about our first big wedding this year. He gave me a funny look and said 'I hope you're not more excited about that one than you'll be about our wedding.' Then he got down on one knee and asked me to marry him." She dabbed at her eyes with a tissue. "He said he couldn't live without me."

"Awww, that's so sweet. The two of you are great together."

"Will you be my maid of honor?" Becca asked hopefully.

"I'd be proud to be your maid of honor," Cami said, touched by the request. In the last several months they'd formed not only an excellent working relationship, but a very strong friendship.

They walked toward Cami's office. "Have you seen Vanessa?"

"No. She called in to say she'll be in later. Justine and her friends didn't get here until close to midnight. They're all sleeping in this morning but will be ready for brunch at noon. The spa is reserved for them for tomorrow morning, and Lynn at Hair Styles downtown has agreed to come here to do their hair. She's the best."

"Fantastic! I'd better go check with Darren to see how he's doing with everything. He hired some temporary workers, and I need to make sure they understand how we pride ourselves on excellent, discreet service."

Cami left Becca and went into the kitchen. Darren and his wife, Liz, were there overseeing prep work. They were an interesting couple. Both were graduates of the Culinary Institute and were superb cooks, but Liz preferred to let Darren take the lead in the kitchen. Outside the kitchen, not so much.

Darren Bullard was a big man—tall, broad, and husky. Liz was of medium height, and though she was curvy, she wasn't heavy. As a rule, the two of them quietly bickered in the kitchen, then filled it with shared laughter. It was this openness that the kitchen staff loved. There were no tirades, no throwing of dishes. Moments of foul language occurred, and then it was over. Seldom was anger directed at staff, though a private conversation later wasn't uncommon. Best of all, the guests loved their food.

Cami watched as a team worked under Liz preparing fruit compotes, and Darren put the finishing touches on an egg and cheese casserole. One of the prep staff was mixing Darren's homemade sausage and then forming it into patties.

"Hi, Cami," said Liz, coming over to her. "How are things on your end?"

"Fine. The wedding party is here and will be ready for brunch at noon. Other guests will arrive throughout the day, so I want to make sure we have plenty of light snacks for them. We're offering fruit, cookies, cheese and crackers, and tea sandwiches. Correct?"

"You got it," Liz said.

"We'll meet next week after the wedding to discuss any new ideas any of us has about how best to handle weddings. With all the advertising we're doing, we're starting to get bookings."

Satisfied things were under control, Cami slipped out of the kitchen. If luck were with her, Lulu Kingsley would be up and about.

When she walked into the living room, Cami looked for her, but the main part of the inn was quiet, and no one from the wedding party was in sight.

Cami went into her office and went to work on the financials. Now that the slow months were past, she needed to reevaluate line items in the budget.

Vanessa showed up in the office mid-morning. "How are things going?"

Cami returned her smile. "Great. I hear you had a late night. Ready to do that all over again?"

"Sure. I'm aware the evening will continue after dinner with more celebrations. I understand a certain bar downtown is where they're headed. I'll be here to make sure everyone gets back safely."

"Great. The rest of us will be up early tomorrow for the Bride's Breakfast and the day's other activities." The wedding was planned for six o'clock, allowing daylight for photos and dinner, and the cloak of darkness for dancing under the stars.

Vanessa beamed at Cami. "Did you see Becca's ring? It's so beautiful! I can't wait to get mine!"

"You're getting that serious with Drew?" Cami asked, unable to hide her surprise. They'd been together less than three months.

Vanessa gave her a sly smile. "He doesn't know it yet, but I want a summer wedding right here."

Cami told herself it was none of her business and remained quiet, but inside she filled with dismay. She'd thought Drew wasn't ready for commitment.

Becca came into the office. "The wedding party is awake and up. You wanted me to alert you."

Cami rose to her feet. "Yes. Thank you. I'll go introduce myself to them." Her heart pounded as she left her office. Was she about to meet her half-sister?

Chatter and laughter were mixed in a loud chorus as Cami entered the living room. In addition to the bride and maid of honor, three young women made up the wedding party. As Cami walked toward them, she observed they looked alike with long blond or brown hair and trim bodies clothed in varying shades of color. Their assured manner as they casually lounged on the couches teasing one another indicated a background of money and privilege. Cami tried not to keep her gaze on Lulu, who appeared to be the leader of the group.

Cami walked over to Justine. "Good morning! It's a beautiful day today, and tomorrow is supposed to be the same for your wedding."

Justine gave her a quick hug. "Everything looks lovely. I peeked into Chandler Hall, and I think it's going to be exactly like I wanted. Thank you." She turned to the others. "Hey, you all, this is Cami Chandler, the owner of the inn."

Talk quieted.

"Welcome to the Chandler Hill Inn," Cami said, the words rolling off her tongue with familiarity. "We're looking forward to providing you with a special weekend. Let us know if we can do anything for you. We want this to be a memorable time for Justine and all of you."

"When does the spa open? I need a little recovery treatment from last night," said a pretty girl with blond hair. "Too many margaritas."

The other girls laughed.

Cami smiled. "The spa is open to all of you. Just call and schedule the times you want. Justine also has hired a limousine to take you to various wineries for tastings, so you might want to put the spa off until later."

More laughter.

Cami's gaze landed on Lulu. The similarities between them were shocking, even after her research. Pictures didn't do them justice. Even though the color of their hair was different, and Lulu was much taller, they shared eyes that rounded in the same way, a similar nose, and the shape of their lips. Cami tried to check Lulu's ears but they were covered by her long, dark hair.

Cami went over to her. "Hi! You must be Lulu. Justine said we look alike—almost like sisters."

Lulu's eyes glazed with frost and her facial features froze. She gave Cami a hard look. "I wouldn't say that. I had one brother, but he died. And I have no sisters at all."

Stung, Cami lifted her shoulders in what she hoped was a casual shrug. "I'm sorry for your loss. They say everyone has a twin in the world. Maybe you're mine."

"Maybe not," Lulu said. She turned to Justine. "After brunch, let's head out to the wineries."

Justine sent Cami a look of apology before nodding to Lulu. "Fine. Everyone else wants to do the same."

As she headed to the kitchen, Cami wondered at Lulu's treatment of her. Before she reached the door, she heard someone say, "Lulu, what's going on? You and Cami look so much alike ..."

Cami halted her steps, waiting for a reply.

"Stop it! All of you, stop! She's no relation to me."

Justine's soothing voice said, "No need to get upset, Lulu. I thought it was fun to find someone looking so much like you. That's all."

"Well, I've had enough."

The silence that followed was filled with tension.

Becca approached her. "Wow! It's true! Lulu Kingsley looks an awful lot like you."

"I know, but she sure doesn't like it,"

"Maybe you two are secret sisters or something like that," Becca said, giving her an impish smile, unaware they might be.

Cami didn't respond, unsure how she felt about that.

CHAPTER FOURTEEN

Cami stood at the doorway to the dining room. In addition to the girls in the wedding party, Justine's parents and their friends, and George and three of his friends were sharing the meal. It seemed a congenial group. George's parents were due to arrive from San Francisco soon, and if they were as nice as Justine's, it should be an easy wedding.

"So far, so good," said Vanessa quietly, coming up beside her.

Cami turned to her with a smile. "I spoke to the florist. Cynthia said they're still waiting for some of the flowers, but they'll get them from the Flower Market in Portland this afternoon."

"Fabulous Florals does such a great job. I think I'll use them for my wedding too."

Cami arched an eyebrow. "And when is that going to be?"

"Sooner than Drew knows," Vanessa said with a laugh. "Shhh. Don't tell him!"

Cami played along, but she was aghast. Drew must have fallen faster and farther than she'd once imagined. But then Vanessa was very attractive. "A looker," Rafe had called her.

Later, with the brunch a huge success, their guests headed outdoors to the three limos waiting to take them on a tour of wineries.

Watching them leave, Cami turned to Becca. "Cleaning crew ready to go?"

"Yes. I've added two more to our usual crew, as we discussed."

"Very good. I want the room for Congressman Kingsley and his wife to look especially fresh."

Becca frowned and shook her head. "Guess you didn't hear. They've cancelled their reservations. Something about his wife becoming ill."

Cami sagged with disappointment. Lulu might not want to discuss how or why they might look alike, but she'd hoped to corner her father privately to have a chat with him.

People were returning from the wine tour when George's parents arrived. Cami was on hand to greet them. Katherine Dickinson, tall and aristocratic, was dressed in a navy suit and heels. Her husband, Howard, a large man with a gray fringe of hair around his bald head, was wearing tan slacks, a small-checked sport coat, and a frown.

"Welcome to Chandler Hill Inn for your son's wedding weekend," Cami said, trying not to react to the way Katherine was giving the living room a disparaging look.

"Would've been much simpler to do something in San Francisco," grumped Howard. "Probably should have hired the company jet. The drive from Portland was not easy."

Cami bit her tongue and then said, "Well, now that you're here, why don't you relax? We have a nice welcome gift ready in your room, and we're here to take care of anything you might need. If you like, I can arrange an appointment at the spa for either of you."

Before they could respond, George entered the inn and hurried over to them. "Ah! You made it. Isn't this place great?"

Katherine's lips thinned. "You know I wanted you to have your wedding in San Francisco where many of my friends could join us. Our club would have been perfect."

"Your club, not mine," said George firmly. "This is what

Justine and I wanted all along—something quiet with people we care about."

Justine hurried to George's side, grabbed hold of his hand, and turned to his parents with a wide smile. "I'm so glad you're finally here. After you get unpacked and relax a bit, join us in the library for cocktails. Thank you for hosting the Rehearsal Dinner." She laughed softly. "It won't take us long to practice. Wait until you see how everything is set up in the garden. It's going to be beautiful."

Katherine's expression softened momentarily and then hardened into her usual judgmental manner.

Watching the interchange, Cami curled her fingers. No one was going to ruin this wedding. Not even the groom's parents.

"We have limousines lined up to take you into town for the dinner, so you won't have to worry about driving these country roads in the dark," Cami assured them.

"That will be fine," said Howard. "Lots of winding roads."

"A bunch of us are going swimming in the pool. Want to join us?" Justine said with a note of desperation.

Katherine's lips curved into a smile and straightened again in such a short time Cami wasn't quite certain it had actually happened. "No, thank you, dear."

"See you later," George said. He turned and, still holding hands with Justine, walked away, his head bent low to Justine's.

"After all the trouble we went through to get here, he just walks away?" said Howard.

Katherine shook her head. "Come, dear, let's get to our room. You can rest there. Maybe he'll come join us."

Maybe not, Cami thought, wondering at the way George's parents had treated him. Families could be so difficult to deal with—too many expectations, too many agendas to please everyone. A wedding often brought out the worst in people.

Justine's parents waved from across the room and came over to them.

"Hello, Katherine, Howard." Olivia gave Katherine a quick hug and the men shook hands.

Olivia beamed at them. "I'm so happy you made it in plenty of time to relax before dinner. I've heard many nice things about Rudy's, the restaurant you chose for the Rehearsal Dinner. It should be a lovely evening."

"Not too much choice," said Howard.

Cami fought the urge to roll her eyes. "I think you're going to be very happy with the restaurant. We recommend it to our guests all the time."

"And tomorrow's wedding dinner will be delicious too. The food here is terrific," said Olivia with a pleasant calmness Cami admired.

Vanessa entered the room and joined them. Cami introduced her to George's parents. "Vanessa will take care of handling anything you need." Cami turned to her. "Why don't you lead Mr. and Mrs. Dickinson to their room?"

"Are we close to Congressman Kingsley's room?" asked Katherine.

"No, unfortunately he had to cancel at the last minute. Something unexpected came up," said Cami, unable to hide her disappointment.

Katherine made a face. "What a shame. I'm in charge of several charities and wanted his participation in one of them. Now, I'll have to call him."

As Vanessa led Katherine and Howard away, Cami couldn't help exhaling a sigh. She glanced at Olivia.

"We've tried our best to keep things pleasant between us for the kids' sakes," said Olivia. "Not to worry. As one might say, their barks are worse than their bites."

Cami smiled, thinking of Katherine as a snippy terrier and

Howard as a great dane with a deep-throated growl.

The next morning was as beautiful as predicted. Blue skies and sunshine complemented the burgeoning vines with a promise of a nice day. Cami uttered a thanks to the heavens and headed to the inn. She and Becca would oversee the wedding party until later in the morning when Vanessa would relieve them. Vanessa didn't mind the "late shift" with their guests, something for which Cami was grateful. By the end of the day, she needed a break from the inn. She remembered how trapped Nonnee sometimes had felt about having the responsibility of the inn and vineyards. Cami understood why. Owning them sometimes seemed as if she were dealing with a temperamental two-year-old clinging to her, demanding more and more of her energy.

But on this day, Cami was determined to enjoy as much as she could while making sure the wedding went off well. Some of the people in the wedding group had daughters wanting to get married at the inn too. She couldn't avoid the cost of extra staff for the event and additional purchases of furnishings for Chandler Hall and the outdoor gardens. As worried as she was about expenses, she realized it was excellent PR and could mean a lot of future business. She hoped so, anyway.

Cami drove to the inn, parked her car, and walked into the building. All was quiet. A good sign, she thought, aware of the fabulous time the wedding party must have had last night. After dinner at Rudy's, most of the group had planned to go to the hotel downtown and party. Vanessa had sent a text message that some of the group didn't get back to the inn until well after one o'clock.

Cami went into the dining room to check on the breakfast arrangements and was surprised to see Howard sitting at the table alone, sipping a cup of coffee.

"Good morning. Nice day for a wedding," she said, smiling at him.

"We lucked out on the weather." He studied her. "So, you own this place?"

"Yes. I inherited it from my grandmother. Why?"

"Pretty big load for a young woman like you. You're about the same age as George and Justine."

"I grew up here and always knew it would become mine. I just didn't think it would happen this soon," she replied, wondering where he was going with the conversation.

"One of my clients is a man named Rod Mitchell, a neighbor of yours. You know him, of course."

Cami nodded and waited for him to continue.

"He's thinking of selling his property. Says living here is like being part of a television show called Hicksville, USA. His words, not mine."

Not willing to be caught up in the conversation about Rod Mitchell, whom she detested, Cami said cheerfully, "I hope you're able to find a buyer soon—someone who is truly interested in growing grapes and making excellent wine. It's a lot of work, but for someone who is committed, it can be very rewarding."

"I've tasted Chandler Hill wines, of course. They're fantastic. You must be proud of them."

Cami relaxed. "I am. After a season at the helm of the inn, I'll be able to spend more time on that aspect of the business."

He squinted as he studied her. "Very interesting. I'm glad I've talked to you. I feel better about advising Rod on any sale."

"Oh?"

Howard shook his head. "He'd be better off hiring reliable help and making it a very profitable year before he puts the property up for sale. What do you think about the coming season?"

"If the weather holds, it's predicted to be an excellent one." She didn't tell him that no matter what the weather held, Rod's crops and his wine would never be at the top. They never had been. Some people thought it was because Rod was too stubborn to listen to advice, but Cami felt there was a nastiness about Rod that affected his grapes. And Bernard would only add to their sourness.

The day that had begun so quietly erupted into one filled with the noises of a happy gathering. Even Katherine seemed to mellow in the sun as she sat outside reading a book apart from the others.

The girls of the wedding party chattered with excitement as they got their nails and hair done. Observing them, a streak of regret flashed through Cami. It wasn't that long ago that she'd had images of herself preparing to wed Bernard. Life, as cruel as it could sometimes seem, had rescued her from making a foolish decision. Now, if she were honest with herself, any thoughts of romance and weddings included a friend named Drew. A friend who apparently had plans of his own.

Cami unobtrusively studied Lulu. With her hair pulled away from her face, Lulu's earlobes were shown to be slightly misshapen like hers. What were the odds of that happening with just anybody?

Lulu noticed Cami looking at her and turned away.

Not wanting to ruin the wedding, Cami decided to let it go for now. In weeks to come, she hoped to follow up with her or her father.

As the time for the wedding neared, Cami filled with

anticipation. It was a beautiful day, a lovely setting. What could go wrong? The minister would arrive any minute for final instructions, and then it was only a matter of a few minutes more before the ceremony took place.

Cami checked the parking lot. She'd instructed the minister from a local church to park right in front of the inn to alert the wedding party that he'd arrived. Observing the still-vacant parking spot, worry threaded through her. She quickly called him.

"Sorry," he said above the noise of his car's engine. "I've been delayed at another wedding. I'm on my way and will get there in about ten minutes."

Cami had just hung up the phone when Olivia approached her. "The minister's late. Have you heard from him?"

"I just spoke with him and he's on his way."

"All right," sighed Olivia. "Who knew weddings would be so stressful?"

Cami's felt her eyes widen. "Is anything wrong? Have you needed something from me or my staff? Everything seems to be in order, but if we've fallen down, please let me know."

Olivia smiled. "Oh, sweetie, it's not that. I've been designated to entertain Katherine, and I'm about worn out. We love George, but it breaks my heart that my daughter will have such a difficult woman for a mother-in-law."

Cami hadn't gotten that far in her relationship with Bernard, but she realized how important that could be. "Perhaps time will change things. And seeing how much in love they are, Katherine might soften. George is an only child. Surely, she won't want to ruin her relationship with him."

"That remains to be seen. Don't worry. Everything here has been terrific."

Cami went into the living room and found George and his groomsmen dressed and ready to go. They looked handsome in Navy blazers, tan slacks, and pink ties that matched the color scheme of the wedding.

Katherine entered the room and stopped in front of George. "What? You're getting married in a sport coat?"

George made a face. "Mom! I told you we were having a casual wedding. No tux, no silly stuff."

"Well," she huffed, "I hope you're not thinking of marriage as casual, a faithful church-goer like you."

George took hold of his mother's elbow. "C'mon. Let's go find Dad." As they left the room, he turned back and rolled his eyes at the sympathetic group.

At that moment, the minister arrived. Looking harried, his dark hair hung at his shoulders, his white shirt was a bit wrinkled, and he held a gray tie in his hands. Cami had heard of James Bliss, but had never met him. He was young, full of energy, and well-liked among more open groups in the community. But she was pretty sure Katherine would find fault with him.

Cami approached him and introduced herself.

He shook her hand in a firm grip and gazed at her with warm brown eyes. "Sorry to be late. There was no way I could leave before the receiving line was over, and I could make a proper exit."

She returned his smile, charmed by his down-to-earth manner. "No worries. We're ready to go anytime you are. Take a few moments, and then I'll show you where the ceremony is to be held. We had a rehearsal of sorts last evening, but your part simply requires you to stand behind the temporary altar that's been set up in the garden."

"Easy enough for me," he said agreeably.

George entered the room and came right over to them. "Jim, glad you made it. Guess I can't back out now."

"Afraid not," Jim said, playing along. "Don't worry. Like

you wanted, we'll make the ceremony short and sweet. Got your vows memorized?"

George pulled a small card out of his jacket pocket. "In case I forget."

Jim clapped George on the back. "I have a feeling you'll have no trouble. When I met with you and Justine, you both seemed really in tune with one another. Now, let's get this show on the road."

Chuckling, the three of them headed to the garden. Cami took a moment to study the scene. With some wedding guests staying at other properties, the number of guests for the ceremony totaled seventy-five, a nice number for the flat expanse of lawn.

White wooden chairs were lined up in several rows. A white cloth covered the back of each chair, softening the look of the wood. At the end of each short row on either side of the aisle, small wicker baskets filled with assorted pink and white flowers were tied to the chair with a pink bow. The same kinds of flowers, arranged in a large, rectangular, white-wicker basket, sat atop the temporary altar, along with two tall, wide white candles. The effect was stunning in its simplicity.

A harpist had already set up her instrument near the altar. Her fingers played over the strings, emitting lilting sounds that Cami always considered angelic. She thought of Nonnee and wished she could see how beautiful the setting was with their recent improvements to the landscaping.

Vanessa approached them. "Guests have gathered in the living room. We're ready to have the ushers escort them, if everything is ready here."

"Let's do it."

The harpist began playing a different song in earnest, and Jim took his place at the altar. George stood beside him.

Cami hurried to the side of the garden and waited for the

first guests to walk into the garden. With three young men doing their jobs as ushers, guests were quickly seated.

Then it was Katherine and Howard's turn to walk down the aisle. He wore tan slacks and a navy blazer as requested. Cami's eyes widened. Looking straight ahead with little expression, Katherine wore a white, ankle-length, sleeveless dress that made her look more like a bride than mother-of-the-groom. A wrist corsage of wildflowers rested on her arm.

Olivia followed in a short, rose-colored, silk sheath whose simple lines fit her thin body perfectly. Even though her eyes were glazed with tears, a happy smile lit her features. She clutched the wrist corsage in her hands like a tiny bouquet.

One by one the two bridesmaids followed, each stunning in ankle-length, pink dresses in different styles. One was sleeveless with a boat neckline; the other dress was a V-neck with capped sleeves. Lulu, the maid of honor, entered the garden. Dressed like the others in pink, her dress was sleeveless with a sweetheart neckline. Even from where she was standing alongside the group, Cami noticed the large, solitaire diamond pendant she wore around her neck. Lulu's smile as she gazed out at the audience was bright. When she noticed Cami watching, her smile wavered then turned bright again as she looked away.

The music changed to Pachelbel's "Canon in D."

Cami turned with the others to watch the bride's entrance. Justine's dark-brown hair was pulled back away from her face into a flowing gathering of curls into which wild flowers had been woven. Dressed in a long, sleeveless lace dress, Justine was the most beautiful bride Cami had ever seen. And knowing how compatible she and George were together, they were, in her mind, the perfect couple. Justine's father, David, walking at her side, was unable to hide the tears that escaped his eyes and slid down his cheeks.

A sharp pang cut through Cami. She would never know the joy of having a man she knew as her father walk her down the aisle. In time, if Rafe were still alive, the honor would be his.

When they reached the altar, David kissed his daughter and went to his wife's side.

The ceremony was as short and sweet as the minister had promised. Both George and Justine recited their vows to each other, and after a quick exchange of rings, Reverend Bliss said a few concluding words and pronounced them man and wife.

As they kissed, applause rang out, and then the happy couple stood and talked to their friends before heading to the reception festivities.

Cami hurried over to Chandler Hall to alert the staff that the crowd was on its way. She entered the building through the opened doors, and stood a moment surveying the room. It was exactly as Justine had wanted. Crisp pink tablecloths covered the rounds of eight. Pink flowers in small, white-wicker baskets sat on top of the tables and perched wherever there was a space for them. Mini-lights sparkled in the rafters, making it seem as if stars were twinkling above the colorful, tasteful hall.

As guests flowed inside, Cami stood aside and listened to fragments of conversation as everyone waited for the bride and groom to appear. After having their pictures taken, George's parents arrived.

Cami overheard Katherine tell her sister, "Hardly seems like a wedding. The minister, the service was awful."

"Katherine, it was a very lovely wedding. I know you wanted it to be held at the gallery in San Francisco, but this is even better," her sister replied with impatience. "If you ask me, George is a very lucky man to have found someone like Justine."

"But you don't understand ..." Katherine's voice trailed off as her sister marched away.

Good for you! She'd liked Katherine's sister when they'd first met and liked her even more now.

Katherine turned and noticed Cami. "Such a different wedding."

"Just as Justine and George wanted. Very sweet."

The arrival of the wedding party caused an outbreak of applause. Laughing, George picked up Justine and swung her around crying, "We're married!"

After he set her down, they walked over to Justine's parents, who were beaming at them. As Justine and George exchanged hugs and handshakes with them, Cami heard a sigh come from Katherine.

Cami turned to her with an encouraging smile. "Such a nice couple."

Katherine's pursed lips morphed into a small smile. "Yes, yes."

While dinner dishes were being cleared away, Cami went into the bathroom. Lulu was standing at the sink washing her hands. No one else was in the room.

"Hi," Cami said pleasantly. "I need to talk to you."

Lulu's lips thinned. "What do you want from me? Or is it something from my father that you're after? Need him to do a favor for you? Money? What?"

"I'd simply like the opportunity to talk to him," Cami said in a calm, controlled manner, though her insides had squeezed tight.

Lulu placed her hands on her hips and glared at Cami. "I know what you're thinking. We look alike, but that doesn't mean anything. My father is a pillar in our community, our church, in the state, in the nation. He's going to run for president one day. Stay out of our lives."

Cami took a step backward and stared at her, startled by the venom in Lulu's voice. "It might mean something important. Important to both of us."

"Leave me alone! Understand?" Lulu tossed the hand cloth into the wicker basket by the sink and stomped out of the room.

Shocked, Cami watched her go.

CHAPTER FIFTEEN

Sunday morning, the wedding party was slow to rise, and then the inn burst with activity as people prepared to leave to catch flights or to make the long drive home. By three-thirty in the afternoon, the only guests left were Justine's parents, who'd decided at the last minute to stay an extra day.

Though a change in the weather was due in the next couple of days, the sun shone bright in a sea of blue, filling the air with a welcome warmth. Cami joined Justine's parents in the small garden between the main house and the guest wing. It was one of her favorite spots. She and Nonnee used to sit and talk there.

"It was such a lovely wedding weekend," said Olivia. "We want to thank you again for everything you and your staff did to make it special."

"Believe me, it was our pleasure," Cami replied. "Can I bring you anything now? Coffee? Tea? A glass of wine?"

Olivia glanced at David and turned to Cami with a smile. "A glass of wine and some of those little cheese puffs that you served in the library would be delightful. It's a little early in the day, but a nice, quiet celebration of our own is called for." Her eyes filled. "Our little girl is on her own now, and it's both sad and satisfying."

Sitting in a chair next to her, David reached over and clasped her hand. "Olivia's suffering a bit from the empty-nest syndrome."

"Why don't I have the kitchen staff put together a special tray for you?"

David shot her a grateful look. "That would be superb."

Cami hurried to the kitchen to make sure Olivia and David would be taken care of. This, she reminded herself, is the kind of thing Nonnee had impressed upon her—doing the extra little things for guests that made a difference to them. That was true hospitality.

After seeing that Becca had the housekeepers under control and Darren was prepared to handle the dinner crowd, Cami hurried home for a break. A couple of hours with a book and Sophie curled up next to her on the couch seemed the perfect way to end the afternoon. She'd return to the hotel to greet their happy hour guests and then hopefully have an early evening at home. Tomorrow, she'd do a recap of the weekend with Becca, Imani, and Vanessa to determine any improvements they needed to make to handle the slew of upcoming weddings. She, Gwen, and Laurel would also analyze the sales of wedding-related gifts to determine if they'd expand or delete the program. Not every group would be as well-heeled as this one.

Cami was into a good book by one of her favorite authors when the doorbell rang. She reluctantly set the book down. The heroine and hero were finally getting together after several misunderstandings.

Her irritation at the disruption fled when she saw Drew on the porch. She opened the door. "Hello! What brings you here on a sunny afternoon?"

"Are you up for a talk with a friend?" he asked. "Maybe even a glass of wine?"

"How about a cup of coffee instead? I've got to handle the pre-dinner cocktail hour at the inn."

"Sure. I need the talk more than anything else."

Wondering at the worry reflected in his eyes, Cami waved him inside.

They headed into the kitchen. Sophie eagerly followed them, vying for Drew's attention. He sat at the kitchen table and stroked the dog's black and tan head. Sophie wagged her tail and licked his hand in appreciation.

"What is it about you and girls?" Cami teased, carrying a mug of coffee to him.

Drew laughed and then straightened in his chair. "I've been totally honest with you about my feelings about family, marriage, and my goals in life. I wish others understood that I don't play games."

Cami retrieved her coffee mug from the kitchen counter and took a seat opposite him. "What's going on, Drew?"

"It's Vanessa. She's in a real hurry to get married. I tried to tell her it was too soon, and now she's mad at me."

"You've been dating only a few months," said Cami, struggling to hide her alarm. Drew looked as disheveled and unhappy as she'd ever seen him.

"I know," said Drew. "But what do you do when you think you've found someone you see possibilities with for the future? Do you take a chance and let her go?"

"I thought you and Vanessa had already talked about marriage," Cami said. Vanessa had already spoken to her about marrying Drew.

Drew's cheeks grew pink. "I told her I cared for her, that's all. It's too soon for anything else."

Cami's emotions were so mixed, she knew she couldn't help him. Not really. Not when she'd changed her mind about having him as only a friend. Even now, disappointment tore at her insides like the talons of a hungry hawk. It was too late for her to say anything about her feelings for him. Even though he said he didn't want to marry Vanessa, he sounded as if he really cared for her enough to think about the possibility of a future together.

"Drew, I think you and Vanessa need to talk it over with a professional, maybe someone like a life coach."

Drew slumped in his chair. "Maybe you're right. I knew I could count on you to steer me in the right direction. I like that honesty about you, Cami. It means a lot to me."

She felt like a fraud. But if she said the words that nudged her throat, she might hurt both Drew and Vanessa by adding to their problems.

"Can I ask you something else?" Drew said, studying her a moment.

She nodded, dreading another question.

"When I saw Lulu and how much she looks like you, I got to wondering if there might be a real connection between the two of you. I know enough of your family history to think of it. Do you believe there might be more to it than a mere coincidence?"

Cami pushed her coffee mug away and faced him. "I do. I tried talking to Lulu about it, but she became very angry. She thinks I'm after money, but all I want is the truth from her father. Lulu claims he's a pillar of their church and may even run for president one day. She told me to stay away from her family in a very threatening tone. I'm not sure what to do about the circumstances. But I'm asking you not to discuss this with anyone else."

"I understand," said Drew. "Getting into the middle of that family might be a huge mistake. He's a powerful man, and I can't imagine he'd be happy with questions from you. Be careful, Cami."

"But I need to know the truth," Cami said, stubbornly. However, the thought of Edward Kingsley's being her father wasn't turning out to be what she'd once hoped for.

Drew got to his feet. "Thanks for being here for me. It's nice to know I have a friend like you."

Cami rose. "Of course."

He pulled her close and gave her a kiss on the cheek.

His soft lips and warm breath sent goosepimples racing down her body. She stepped away and gazed at him, confused by the way his arms around her had felt so right. Had he felt it too? That magical connection?

"See you later," said Drew turning and leaving the kitchen. "Becca and Dan are throwing a party next Friday to celebrate their engagement. Maybe I'll see you there."

"Sure," said Cami, wondering if she could arrange to be too busy to attend. The thought of seeing him with Vanessa was painful.

After Drew left, Cami plopped herself down on the couch and pushed the book aside. She needed to deal with the real issues that faced her, not some made-up story that almost surely would bring about a happy ending.

When Cami arrived at the inn, she was pleased to see a number of dinner guests had already arrived and were enjoying refreshments in the library. The restaurant was open every night but Monday, when Darren took a well-deserved night off. Having locals and guests of other properties come to the restaurant was an important factor in maintaining visibility and spreading news of the hotel by mouth. Cami sometimes got tired of the responsibility of being around for this time every evening, but she tried to make it as often as she could. It had paid off many times, allowing people to get to know her and to arrange special events. The inn was small but served many purposes for assorted groups and individuals.

Cami was making her rounds, visiting with everyone, when

Bernard appeared and headed right for her. Uneasy about confronting him in front of other guests, Cami looked for a graceful way to make an exit.

"I need to talk to you," said Bernard, rushing up to her. "I understand you've told your staff that they are not to recommend wines from Lone Creek Winery. How dare you? Rod Mitchell's wines are as good as anyone else's in the valley."

She forced a fake smile and led him out of the room. "Let's go someplace else to discuss this."

Cami led Bernard into her office and stood behind the desk. "I'm not sure where you heard such a thing, but it isn't true. We did a recent wine tasting here at the hotel for our staff and purposely included Rod's wines."

"That's right. That's when your staff was told not to recommend them," said Bernard. "That's what I heard, anyway."

Her lips thinned. "Who told you this?"

"Someone who worked the wedding over the weekend. Rod sent me over to give you a warning. He says that if you keep up this kind of thing, he'll run a smear campaign against you and the inn that you won't believe."

"Bernard, you can tell Rod that Chandler Hill has never done business this way and I don't intend to start now. His wines speak for themselves." Though she spoke calmly, she was unable to keep the irritation out of her voice. Dealing with Rod was bad enough, but now Bernard was doing his dirty work for him.

His manner changed. He smiled at her. "You know the big party on Friday night for Becca and Dan? I've offered to host it, being new neighbors and all. You coming?"

"I don't know yet," Cami replied.

"Hope to see you there." His eyes lingered on her. "I haven't given up on us yet, *chérie.*"

"You know it's over between us," said Cami firmly. "I won't change my mind."

Bernard studied her with genuine surprise. "But we'd make such a great team."

"No, we were never a team. Not then. Not now." She checked her watch. "I have to get back to my guests. Remember to tell Rod what I said. I have no desire for bad feelings between us."

"You're being stubborn. You'll regret your decision about us. I promise you."

Cami felt a momentary flutter of fear as Bernard stormed out of her office. Why did some men get so angry when they were spurned? And he was hosting the party for Becca and Dan? How did that happen?

CHAPTER SIXTEEN

The days flew by as Cami worked with her staff to come up with better ways to handle weddings at the inn based on their experiences over the weekend. Stories were shared about different guests and comments overheard. During that discussion, it came out that Vanessa had been drinking with the guests and had even met them at the bar downtown. Fighting back her annoyance, Cami calmly reinforced to everyone on her staff that socializing with the guests was not allowed beyond their assigned jobs. Vanessa's cheeks turned bright red and her lips formed a pout, but she kept quiet as the others indicated their agreement.

After more discussion, the consensus of the group was that Justine and George's wedding would be the one they'd strive to duplicate. With the addition of extra hired help, things had generally gone smoothly. Most weddings were planned for weekends, but a couple had scheduled their wedding in the fall during the middle of the week so the wedding party could enjoy time before and after the wedding to visit wineries.

Satisfied that things were moving in the right direction, Cami devoted some time to the outdoors. She walked the land, stopping to kneel and sift the soil through her fingers, remembering all she'd been taught. The soil consisted of marine sedimentary deposits and volcanic rock and appeared light in color because of the clay and the naturally crushed rock. The pulverized rock provided good drainage which was important because grapes didn't do well in poorly drained soils. The composition of the soil was the reason why most of the vineyards were located in the hills and not in the valley below.

Cami was sitting among the vines one afternoon when she heard her name called. She turned to find Rafe walking toward her. She lifted a hand in a wave and came to her feet.

"Taking advantage of a beautiful day?" he said, joining her with a smile.

Her lips curved. "Just checking on the vines. Things look fine, thanks to Drew and his crew."

"Yes, he does a great job," said Rafe. "You can teach someone the fundamentals of growing grapes and making wine, but unless they love the land and have a good palate, they'll produce only ordinary wines." His eyes glazed with memories. "Your grandmother had a sensitive palate. The first time I met her she tasted wines with Kenton and me, and we knew it then."

"I hope I can do as well," Cami said, in awe of all her grandmother had done with both the inn and the vineyard.

He placed a gentle hand on her cheek and looked at her with both love and admiration. "You will. You're like her in so many ways."

Tears unexpectedly filled her eyes. Nonnee and Rafe had been such encouraging figures in her life. But as grateful as she was to them for all they'd done for her, she wanted to know more about her mother and father's relationship.

"Uh-oh. Why the troubled look?" asked Rafe, stepping away and studying her with those dark eyes of his that missed nothing. "Does it have anything to do with the wedding and the girl who looks like you?"

Cami nodded. "Lulu Kingsley made it very clear that I was to stay away from her father. She even told me he's considering running for president. In the past, you've told me that my mother would never name him because of how it might hurt him and his family. Her reaction makes me believe even more that he might be my father."

"Ah, *cariño*, sometimes it's better to be happy for what you have than to seek something more. Unlike a gift inside a gaily wrapped package, revealing a secret that's been boxed up for years can be devastating. Your mother might have been a stubborn woman, but she was smart too. I say respect her wishes. Nonnee and I have. Perhaps you should too."

She turned away from him, afraid he'd see the unwavering determination she couldn't hide.

He placed a hand on her shoulder. "Leave it alone. Now, come with me. We need to talk, and I know just the place to do it."

Cami drew a deep breath and turned to him, forcing back her disappointment at his response to the need that dwelled and grew inside her.

As they walked, she lifted her face to the sun. Its warmth caressed her cheeks like a kiss from above, and she felt some of the tension leave her shoulders.

"You know, way back when Rex Chandler started this vineyard, he studied organic farming and set this place up to be sustainable," said Rafe. "Even today, using only natural products for fertilization has made such a difference. I swear the grapes love it."

She studied the straight rows of grapes marching in a north/south direction. Seeing them now, like soldiers in parade formation, a sense of pride filled her. She might be young, she might need to learn a lot, but she was both a Chandler and a Lopez with winemaking in her blood.

Out of the corner of her eye, she studied Rafe. Still handsome in his seventies, he'd lost the spring in his step that her grandmother Lettie had given him. In fact, the limp that had plagued him from youth was much more noticeable. She realized with a start how frail Rafe had become since Nonnee's death. Sadness tugged at her heart, snatching a beat of it. She loved him so much.

He stumbled, and she quickly grabbed his arm.

"Damn leg," he grumbled. "It kept me out of the war when my best friend was called to serve."

"You mean Kenton Chandler?"

"Yes. Funny, we didn't know one another for a long time, but he was and always will be the one friend I hold closest to me."

She looked at him with surprise. He'd never been so poetic.

He gave her a sheepish smile. "Guess I'm sounding like the old, sentimental man I've become. Truth is, I'm looking forward to the time when I'm with him and Lettie again."

Cami gave his hand a squeeze. "But I'm not ready to let you go," she said softly.

He gave her a loving smile. "I know."

They walked in silence to the destination that was on their minds.

Some people might have thought it odd that both she and Rafe sometimes sat in the small grove of trees on the property where the ashes of the Chandler men, Lettie, and her mother had been scattered and buried. It wasn't a maudlin act. The grove was a peaceful place where memories and new ideas for the inn and vineyard came alive. Cami had always found it a great source of inspiration for both personal and professional reasons.

Rafe, with a courtly gesture, invited her to sit on the stone bench that had been placed there many years ago. He lowered himself beside her.

"As you know," he began, "I'm taking the river cruise in September. Before she died, Lettie told me she had a surprise for me. As ill as she was, she was excited about it. So, as much as I don't want to leave the vineyard at that time, I'll do as she wanted and go. My heart isn't in it, but without her nothing is the same."

Cami clasped his hand. "I miss her too."

He looked out at the scenery, his expression reflecting the sadness he felt. He turned back to her. "I'm glad you came home. It meant so much to both your grandmother and me for you to do as she'd asked."

"Of course. I promised her," Cami replied, wondering where this conversation was heading.

"I'm sure you've noticed that it's harder and harder for me to move around. My arthritis is kicking in, and I have other old-age issues."

"Yes ..."

"The point is that Drew is handling most of the fieldwork himself, along with overseeing the winemaking. I think instead of giving him just a section of the vineyard, I should divide the whole property between you and him. Would you be willing to share my land with him, maybe work together on Taunton Estates wines? Realistically, that's the only way to keep my business going, which is to take nothing away from you, my darling. I see what you have done and are doing for Chandler Hill, and I think Lettie would like nothing to deter you from your success. You know how much I love both of you."

"Yes, I do." Cami drew a deep breath. His idea made sense. She'd been worried about struggling with the additional responsibility of Rafe's business after he died. Still, it meant she'd be tied to Drew Farley for the future. It would be especially difficult to work with him if he was married to someone else.

She drew another breath and told herself it was too soon to worry about any of that. Rafe might be aging and slow moving, but he was basically in good health. She'd see to it he stayed that way. And maybe she could get past the notion she and Drew could be more than friends.

"Well?" Rafe asked, giving her a worried look.

"It's the smart thing to do," she admitted, pushing away her personal concerns. "You've built Taunton Estates Winery and your wines into a highly successful and respected business. It's right that you make arrangements to keep it that way. I have my hands full with Chandler Hill but not too full to contribute time and energy to Taunton, too."

He smiled and exhaled a long breath. "I thought you'd see it that way, but I needed to be sure before I changed things once more. You're the most important person in the world to me. And I respect what you've done and are doing with the responsibility Lettie left to you. Together, you and Drew should be able to grow my business. You have talents he doesn't and vice versa. The two of you will be a superb team."

"Don't worry. Neither one of us would ever let you down. Drew talks about you all the time and everything you've done for him."

He held up a finger of warning. "He knows nothing about this. And I don't want him to. We have a great working relationship and a personal one, too. I don't want that to change. If he should indicate that he wants to leave the valley, we'll have to address that issue then."

"Okay, I promise I won't say anything about it to him."

Rafe smiled with satisfaction. "That's settled then." He leaned over and kissed her cheek. "I love you, little one. You're my greatest gift—-a surprise to be sure, and one that has filled my heart and soul."

When he pulled away, Cami saw the tears that had leaked from his eyes.

Not bothering to wipe his cheeks, he smiled at her. "Such a

weepy old man I've become."

"A dear one," she replied, praying they'd have many more years together.

CHAPTER SEVENTEEN

Friday afternoon, Cami realized there was no way she could gracefully skip the engagement party for Becca and Dan. Besides, she was thrilled for them and wanted to share in their joy. Though they wouldn't marry for a year or so, Becca was full of ideas about how she wanted her wedding at Chandler Hill and had talked all week about it. Vanessa, Cami noted, held onto every suggestion Becca made, adopting Becca's ideas for her own wedding.

Listening to her, Cami doubted Drew knew Vanessa was still making plans.

As Cami prepared to leave the inn, Becca knocked on the door to her office. "Be sure and come a little early. Dan and I are sharing a special toast with you and a few others before we go on to the party. You *are* coming, right? Bernard told Dan this afternoon that you probably wouldn't make it."

Cami gritted her teeth. She'd stewed all week about Bernard hosting the party for her best friend, placing her in an awkward situation socially. Now, it seemed he was baiting her. "He knows I wouldn't let you down."

Becca beamed at her. "That's what I told Dan. I don't know what he sees in Bernard, but they've become friends of sorts. Just good neighbors, as Bernard says. I personally don't like him, especially after knowing what a slime he was to you. But, as Dan says, our community is a small one, and we need to get along with everybody." She gave Cami a hug. "Even so, I'll always be there for you."

Grateful for her friendship, Cami hugged her back.

###

That night as Cami was dressing for the party, Sophie stared up at her from her place on the floor.

"What do you think, Soph? The red or the black top?" She held up a red silk shirt and a light-weight, black knit sweater with a low V-neck.

Sophie barked when Cami showed her the black knit top.

Cami laughed. "Okay, then, I'll go for this one." She slid it over her head and studied herself in the mirror. The sweater called for something to offset its starkness. She lifted the grape necklace and hooked it around her neck. Staring at the sparkling diamonds mounted on the grape leaf, she liked the reminder of the woman who had worn it and the man who'd given it to her.

She said goodbye to Sophie and left the house determined Bernard wouldn't ruin the party for her.

Becca greeted her with a smile. "Drew and Vanessa are already here. We're going to have a quick toast with champagne and then head over to Bernard's apartment."

"Best wishes," Cami said, handing Becca the small package she'd prepared and wrapped earlier.

"What's this?" Becca asked, grinning as she held up the package and shook it.

Dan approached. "Hi, Cami! I'm glad you could make it."

Becca handed him the package. "Cami has given us a gift. May I open it?"

Dan chuckled with his usual kind nature. "Sure. Go ahead. I'll watch."

Becca untied the gold silk ribbon and ripped off the silver paper. She lifted the lid of the plain white box and let out a whoop of excitement as she held up a gold key.

"Really? We get to stay in the Presidential Suite for two

nights this summer? Wow! Thank you!"

Cami smiled. "I thought you'd like a special time there to practice for your wedding."

Dan wiggled his eyebrows at Becca. "See? I keep telling you practice makes perfect."

Becca's cheeks colored when she realized everyone else knew what he was really talking about, and then she joined the laughter.

"Time for a little champagne, I think." An impish grin remained on Dan's face.

Drew and Cami smiled at each other. Vanessa took his arm and they all followed Dan into the kitchen.

"I borrowed the tulip glasses from the hotel," Becca confessed as Dan made a show of popping the cork from the bottle of champagne.

"Any time," Cami said. "And you and Vanessa can purchase things like that through the hotel for your trousseaus."

"That would be fantastic," gushed Vanessa.

"How about me, for my apartment?" Drew said. "I'm working on getting it spruced up."

"Yes, I told him if I'm going to live there, it has to be nicer." Vanessa smiled at Drew and lifted on her toes to give him a kiss on the cheek.

The frown that creased Drew's brow was a contrast to the smile on Vanessa's face. Drew glanced at Cami and looked away.

Cami accepted champagne from Becca and waited until they each held a flute.

"Here's to Dan and Becca!" said Drew. "May they be happy together."

Careful to avoid looking Drew's way, Cami lifted her glass in salute, wondering where the next few months would take all of them.

Dan poured out the last of the champagne. "When we finish this, I guess we'd better head over to Bernard's place. I told him we wouldn't be late."

"What's with you and Bernard, anyway?" Drew asked. "I've met the guy, and he's an ass."

Dan shrugged. "I know he's been a pain to some people but he's trying to fit in. I'm ready to see if he means what he says."

"He's very handsome," said Vanessa. "And that accent of his would make any woman swoon."

Cami let out a soft sigh and told herself not to worry about Bernard, but to simply enjoy tonight. She was getting to know some of the other people her age in the valley and was anxious to see them again.

Bernard greeted them at the door to his second-floor apartment. He gave Becca a kiss on both cheeks. "*Chérie,* you look lovely." He turned to Vanessa with shining eyes and a broad smile. "And you? Ooh, la la!"

Cami stood back and watched with fascination as Vanessa fluttered her eyelashes and beamed at him. "*Merci.*" She elbowed Drew. "See? I know French."

Drew remained quiet. Cami could see how irritated he was by the way his lips thinned, but Vanessa didn't seem to notice as she turned to Bernard. "*Bonjour, monsieur.*"

"*Bonsoir,*" responded Bernard with amusement. "It is evening after all." He turned to Cami with a smile. "And you, Cami, are the picture of perfection."

His words felt oily on her skin. She'd once fallen for that charm of his but she wouldn't again.

Dan shook hands with Bernard. "Thanks for doing this party for us. Becca and I are real grateful to you."

"Bah! It is nothing. Come in."

Cami didn't know what to expect, but when she stepped into the living room, she stopped and stared at the sophisticated glamour of the space. A leather couch, upholstered chairs and glass-topped end tables looked like they'd come out of a decorator's magazine. Cami wondered where Bernard got that kind of money. Then it hit her. Jacques must have paid him to leave the vineyard. Rod Mitchell wasn't known in the valley for paying his employees well.

"You like my place?" Bernard said, coming to stand beside her. "No cheap stuff for me. I deserve the best, as do you. I think we should talk some more."

Drew came over to them, making a response unnecessary.

"What can I get you to drink?" Drew asked her, barely looking at Bernard.

Cami smiled at him with relief. "I'll go with you and choose. Thanks."

As she walked away, Cami could feel Bernard's stare, like sharp-edged knives entering her back.

"Thanks for the rescue," Cami said softly.

"Not a problem. I don't like the guy any better than you do."

Sipping her wine, Cami studied the crowd. There was a nice mix of people from throughout the valley. As busy as she was with the inn, she knew how important it was to be active socially with others in the community. Besides, she'd found since coming home, they were a fine group of hardworking people, who liked to have a good time. And she needed that.

She was deep in conversation with a worker from Yamhill Wineries when shouts erupted from the balcony off the living room. She looked up in time to see Vanessa running to the bathroom in the hallway, tears streaming down her face.

Drew stormed after Vanessa and came to a sudden stop when she slammed the door in his face.

Drew slumped against the wall and took several deep breaths.

Cami went over to him. "What's going on? Anything I can do to help?"

He let out a sound of disgust. "No. Yes. Will you see that Vanessa gets home? I'm leaving."

She studied him. "Do you want me to try and talk to her?"

He shook his head. "Naw. I'm outta here."

Cami sighed. "Okay, if you're sure that's what you want, I'll drop her off at her house."

Drew narrowed his eyes at the closed bathroom door, then turned to her. "Thanks." He left the apartment without talking to anyone else.

Becca came over to her. "What's with Drew?"

"I don't know what he and Vanessa were fighting about, but he's really upset. He asked me to take her home."

Becca clucked her tongue. "Vanessa's had too much to drink. She and Bernard have been flirting all evening. I don't know why she keeps pushing for marriage, not when she's behaving like this. She and Drew haven't been together for very long. Drew's a nice guy, but I can't imagine any woman pushing him around."

"Neither can I," Cami sighed. "I guess I'd better go check on her."

She knocked on the bathroom door. "Vanessa? It's me, Cami. Open up."

Vanessa opened the door. Her cheeks were still wet with tears, and her blue eyes filled with more. Even in this state of disarray, she was beautiful.

"Drew asked me to take you home," Cami said. "I promised I would."

Vanessa's eyes flashed with anger. "He did, did he? Well I'm not ready to go home. In fact, I just might stay here all night. I'm sure Bernard won't mind. Not after the way he's been looking at me all evening."

"Oh, hon," said Cami, genuinely concerned. "You don't want to do anything foolish."

"What do you care?" said Vanessa. "I've noticed how Drew is with you."

Cami's eyes widened. "I don't know what you're talking about. Drew and I are friends. That's all."

"Well, I don't care. I'm tired of trying to work things out with him." A smile transformed Vanessa's face. "I can speak a little French. Maybe Bernard will teach me more."

Rather than argue with her, Cami said, "Remember, I'm taking you home."

"We'll see," said Vanessa, tossing her blond hair.

Cami walked away, wondering how she could've misjudged Vanessa. If she was that desperate for a relationship and marriage, Cami wasn't sure she wanted Vanessa around wedding parties at the inn. A wedding was the perfect place for hook-ups.

"Everything all right?" asked Becca.

"I'm not sure. Let's talk tomorrow."

Cami decided it was time to leave the party. She'd spoken to most of the people there, and she was due at the inn early the next morning. She went in search of Vanessa.

When Cami couldn't find her in the living room, on the balcony, or on the back lawn where a small group had gathered, she climbed the stairs to the apartment once more.

As she walked down the hallway to the bathroom, she heard sounds coming from behind the closed door of one of the two bedrooms. She leaned closer and heard a male voice and the high-pitched voice of a woman. She paused, not sure what to do when Bernard and Vanessa opened the door and stepped into the hallway, looking somewhat disheveled.

Hiding her consternation, Cami said coolly, "There you are, Vanessa. Time for me to take you home."

Vanessa gave her a triumphant smile. "I'm not going home. Bernard has asked me to stay. Right, *mon chère?*

He wrapped an arm around her. "*Oui.*" He winked at Cami. "Vanessa appreciates everything, I mean everything I can offer her."

Cami knew he was baiting her and remained quiet. Though her stomach grew sour at the idea of the two of them together, she continued to hold back words. Neither Vanessa nor Bernard was about to listen to anything she might want to say.

Turning on her heel, Cami went to find Becca. Maybe Becca would be able to talk some sense into Vanessa.

After bringing Becca up-to-date on the situation, Cami left, dreading the idea of informing Drew that Vanessa intended to stay the night with Bernard. As much as she hated doing it, she would tell him the truth. She owed him that much.

CHAPTER EIGHTEEN

Monday morning, Cami was sitting at her desk talking to Becca when Vanessa came into the office. "Am I missing something?" Vanessa's gaze swung from Cami to Becca.

"Please sit down," said Cami. "There's an issue we want to discuss with you."

Vanessa scowled and took a seat next to Becca. "This isn't about Friday night, is it?"

"Not exactly," said Cami. "It's about your drinking both here at the inn and off-duty."

"Look, I may have had too much to drink Friday night, but I was very careful the night of the Bachelor Party," Vanessa protested.

"You shouldn't have been drinking at the inn. We've been friends since college," said Becca. "I care about you and would hate for anything bad to happen."

"The drinking is something you need to be able to control while you perform your duties here helping to oversee weddings," said Cami kindly. Initially, she'd been impressed with Vanessa's attitude and her work. But being around food and alcohol all the time could become problematic for some. It now appeared that Vanessa might be one of these people.

"We'll help you in any way we can," Becca said. "But the decision will be yours as to whether or not you can perform your job the way we need you to do."

"Why are you two against me?" said Vanessa. "It won't happen again. I promise."

"All right. We'll leave that up to you," said Cami. "But with so many weddings booked, at the first sign of a problem again, we'll need to let you go. The inn's reputation cannot be jeopardized by one of our employees. I hope you understand."

Vanessa drew a deep breath and glared at Cami. "Rod Mitchell is building a function facility like Chandler Hall, and Bernard wants me to run it for them. I told him no, but I can always change my mind."

Cami wouldn't be drawn into an argument. "I can't force you to stay, but after all the training we've given you, it would be the fair thing to do," she said quietly.

"I know you and Bernard were dating in France," said Vanessa. "He told me all about it."

Cami remained in control.

"Just so you know, I'm going to move in with him this week. He's a fascinating man who owns a vineyard in France and is very talented with grapes. So now, Cami, Drew is yours."

"Whoa," said Cami. "Whoa! What are you talking about? We're just friends."

"Vanessa, you really hurt Drew. You owe him better than that," said Becca. "You were talking about marriage, for God's sake."

Vanessa stared into space and sighed. "That's the problem. *He* wasn't ever talking marriage. Not really. *I* was talking about marriage. Drew wanted to wait before any such decision was made. But Bernard is a totally different kind of guy— someone sensitive to my needs, a wonderful lover ..." She stopped and covered her mouth with her hand. "I'm sorry, Cami, I shouldn't have said that." She cut Cami a triumphant look as she got to her feet. "I'd better go and see what requests have come in on the computer."

Vanessa hurried out of the room.

"That was awkward," said Becca, shifting uneasily in her chair.

"Yes, it was." Cami had no wish to hear any of the details of Vanessa's time with Bernard. And she was pretty sure Bernard *had* owned part of a vineyard, but no longer did.

Cami awoke from a dream in which she'd been running after a stranger who ignored her calls for his help. Lying against her pillow she stared out through the blinds. It didn't take much analyzing to realize the dream related to her desire to talk to Edward Kingsley.

Rosy streaks of dawn fingered the sky, beckoning her to rise. She got out of bed, lifted Sophie into her arms, and headed outside with her. The sun was rising in the sky above the low-lying fog that clung to the ground, softening the landscape for a few moments before it would lift and evaporate in the warmth of the fresh June morning.

Standing on the deck of her house, watching Sophie romp in the grass below her, Cami gazed at the landscape. She thought of her father. His identity seemed as obscured as the ground covered by the gray mist of the fog. Maybe, she thought, instead of trying to talk to Edward Kingsley, she'd write a discreet comment on his blog, forcing him to pay attention to her.

She called to Sophie and went inside, pleased with her decision. It was only fair. Without knowing who her father was, she didn't have a true idea of her background and who her people were.

Cami poured herself a cup of hot coffee and returned to the deck with a notepad and pen. Looking out over the rows of grapes and the distant grove of trees for inspiration, she began writing. She knew she'd have to be careful how she phrased her note, but if he was the man her mother had been with in Africa, he'd know the meaning behind her words.

After many attempts, she looked at the final version and was satisfied:

> "Dear Congressman Kingsley – I understand you visited Africa in the past as a young student in the 1990s. Africa has always been of interest to me, especially knowing that my mother, Autumn Chandler, spent several years there during that period helping in Zaire and then in South Africa. Would you be willing to share some of your experiences with me? I'm working on a study of student life there for a project of mine. Thank you so much. Signed, Camilla Chandler."

Pleased, she patted the pad of paper and got to her feet. Before she could chicken out, she went into her computer, added her comment to his blog, and clicked send.

CHAPTER NINETEEN

When Cami stepped out of the shower, she heard her phone ringing. She wrapped a towel around herself and hurried to answer it.

"Got a minute?" Drew said. "I'm just swinging by your place on my morning run and thought I'd stop by for a cup of coffee."

"Great. Give me a chance to get dressed and I'll get our coffee ready. How about a cinnamon biscuit too?"

"Thanks. I'll be there in a few."

Cami remembered the hurt in Drew's voice when she'd told him about Vanessa's unwillingness to go home and how she planned to spend the night with Bernard. He'd been pretty quiet since that night ten days ago. Vanessa and she hadn't spoken about it either since that Monday morning. Not that Cami would. She wanted no part in Vanessa's life outside her work at the inn. Vanessa had handled the latest wedding very nicely, maintaining a friendly yet professional relationship with the bride and groom and their wedding party.

Thinking about her now, Cami wondered how much longer Vanessa would stay at Chandler Hill. Word in the valley was that Rod was cutting prices for events and was now paying staff above the going rate in order to get people to work for him.

Cami had just slid a couple of biscuits into the oven to warm when she heard Drew call out, "Hello!"

She turned and smiled at him. Even with sweat streaming down his face and glistening on his torso, he looked delectable. It was a very nice body. His golden-brown hair was pushed away from his face, and the high color in his cheeks matched the brightness in his tawny-colored eyes.

"Looks like you've had a nice run. Why don't you go on out to the deck and relax? I'll bring the coffee and biscuits out. I know you like your black coffee strong."

He grinned and headed out to the deck.

When Cami went outside, Drew was sitting back in a chair, his legs stretched out in front of him, his face tilted toward the sun.

"Ahhh, this feels fantastic," he said when she approached him. He took the mug of coffee she offered and grabbed one of the biscuits the inn was famous for.

Cami set the tray down and picked up the other mug of coffee. She'd decided that on slow days at the inn, she'd spend a little more time at home with Sophie. This being a Tuesday morning, there were no unusual situations that required her attention.

They sipped and ate in quiet contentment for a while. Then Cami asked, "How are you doing?"

Drew let out a long sigh. "I've learned a lesson or two in the past couple of weeks. Until I can work on a couple of issues on my own, I'm not dating. Growing up with only an uncle for my family has always made me wonder what it would be like to be married to someone smart and beautiful, have a houseful of kids and all that goes with it. I need someone who wants to be with me forever. Even though Vanessa made me believe that's what she wanted, I think it was the idea of marriage, not me, that she was interested in."

There was so much Cami wanted to say. She hesitated, choosing her words carefully. "You'll be happy with a family of your own someday. I'm sure of it."

"Thanks. Funny, isn't it, how old family issues reappear

just when you think you've put them behind you."

"Yes, I know. I'm still struggling with a few things of my own. I went ahead and sent in a comment on Congressman Kingsley's blog. No one else will think anything of it, but if he is my father he will get the meaning behind the message."

Drew frowned. "Do you think that's wise?"

"Maybe not, but I had to try."

He lifted his shoulders and let them drop in a sympathetic shrug. "I get it. I really do. I just don't want anything bad to come out of it. And I know Rafe is worried about it, too."

"I won't do anything more at this time. I promise both of you. No one else but Jamison and the two of you know about it."

"Okay." He took a last sip of coffee and rose. "Guess I'd better run," he said, his eyes twinkling with humor at the pun.

She laughed. "I can drive you home if you want."

"No, I need to run off a few pounds. Vanessa liked to go out to eat and party, and I've gained a few pounds." As he patted his perfectly acceptable stomach, Cami's body reacted. Mortified, she quickly looked away.

"See you later," said Drew, oblivious of her reaction to him. He kissed her cheek lightly and walked into the house, leaving her on the deck wondering at the sudden heat wave. From below, Sophie barked, and she turned her attention to the dog, happy for the distraction.

When Cami got to the inn, things were fairly quiet. She entered her office hopeful that she could work on some new ad campaigns. She opened her computer and lifted the written notes she'd made the day before. As she was reading them a knock sounded on her door.

"Come in," she called out, surprised to see Vanessa. It was

her day off.

Cami grinned. "Hi, there! Couldn't stand to stay away?"

"Just the opposite," said Vanessa, plopping down in one of the chairs in front of Cami's desk. "We need to talk."

Cami's pulse stuttered. She knew from the expression on Vanessa's face that it wasn't good news. Still, she waited for Vanessa to say the words.

"I'm taking the job at Rod's winery. He's offered me so much money I can't turn it down. And, besides, Bernard really wants me there."

Cami remembered when she would have done almost anything to please Bernard. She wanted to warn Vanessa about him, but, of course, she couldn't ... wouldn't.

"When is this going to happen?" she said, wondering who she could hire quickly to replace Vanessa. The wedding and tourist season was about to pop open.

"I normally would give a two-week notice, but Rod wants me on the job right away. We have a wedding coming up in two weeks."

"I see. I'm sorry that it's come to this, Vanessa. I was hoping we could work things out." She lifted the phone. "Becca, will you please come here? I need you right away."

Cheeks flushed from hurrying, Becca entered the office in a rush. "Is everything all right?"

Cami indicated Vanessa. "Vanessa has resigned as of this moment. I need you to walk her out of the inn. We'll box up her personal belongings in her office and give them to her at a later time."

Vanessa jumped to her feet. "Wait a minute! What about all that advertising work I did with you? I told Rod I'd have it ready for him this week."

Controlling her anger, Cami rose and spoke as calmly as she could. "That's proprietary information. It stays here, as does your computer and all your office supplies. I'm sorry you didn't choose to make a smoother transition, but we'll work things out with you the best way we can."

Vanessa shook a finger at them. "Wait and see, both of you, I'm going to be better there than I ever could be here."

"Good luck, Vanessa," said Becca. "C'mon. I'll walk you out."

"I can leave by myself," snapped Vanessa.

"No, I'll walk with you," Becca said with unmistakable anger.

Cami watched them go and then hurried into Vanessa's office. Fortunately, she knew Vanessa's password to the computer and quickly changed it. She'd have their IT guy come in and take care of the rest of it.

Sinking down into Vanessa's chair, she went through the desk, searching for any other information she'd have to protect. The idea of a wedding already taking place at Rod's winery was upsetting, to say the least. She hadn't thought they'd be able to move so fast. But then, Chandler Hill had given them a successful blueprint for building the business, especially with Vanessa's apparent secret input.

Cami cleared out all the drawers and checked the files, setting aside personal items for Vanessa to get at a later date.

Together, she and Becca went over Vanessa's computer and looked through the spreadsheet that listed inquiries for weddings and follow-through actions.

Susannah Grant had asked for the weekend Vanessa had mentioned. Vanessa had responded, and then had made a phone call. No further action was taken.

"I'm going to call my friend at the flower shop and see if she's helping with the wedding and if so, what the bride's name is," said Becca, her eyes flashing with anger. "I bet it's the same name. Now I know why Vanessa insisted on handling the list herself."

Cami's stomach twisted. "We'd better get in touch with everyone on this list to see if there's anything we can do to help them make a decision to have their wedding here."

"Imani and I will get right on it," said Becca.

"And I'll work on it too. We're counting on a decent percentage of those wedding information requests to come to fruition," said Cami grimly. She'd spent as little as she could with the new landscaping, the renovation of rooms, and the new carpeting throughout. She needed to recoup that cost.

After talking to two different prospective brides, Cami hung up the phone so angry she pounded the desk with her fist and shouted into the room, "How could she?"

She placed a call to Jamison Winkler, the lawyer who'd been so helpful to her.

"Hello?" chirped Jamison. "How are you? Wynton and I were thinking of making another trip to Chandler Hill sometime in the near future."

"You'd better make a reservation soon. I've got a big problem," Cami said. She launched into the details of her struggle with Vanessa and Rod Mitchell's new wedding business.

"Mm, sorry to hear that," Jamison commiserated. "From what you've told me, there is little you can do about it. We could try a Cease and Desist order, but the fact is there is little involved here except hearsay, nothing in writing."

"I haven't found any," Cami replied. "But what can we do about it?"

"You're doing the right thing by contacting the women involved and checking in with them without referring to Rod Mitchell or his winery at all. I'm sorry this happened to you. Doing business in a market like yours can be difficult but, Cami, I don't believe Rod Mitchell and Vanessa will be able to compete effectively. Your property, your staff, your facilities are incomparable."

Cami drew in a deep breath and gazed out the window at the little garden she loved. Emitting a long sigh, Cami knew Jamison was right. Chandler Hill was a first-class operation. People would get what they paid for, and undercutting her prices would get Vanessa, Bernard, and Rod nowhere in the long run.

"Thanks, Jamison. I needed to hear that. Let me know when you and Wynton want to come, and I'll make arrangements for you."

Cami exchanged a few more pleasantries with Jamison and hung up determined to follow up with every prospective bride.

Later, when Becca reported that one of their staff had been approached by Vanessa to come and work for her, Cami decided to call a staff meeting.

She asked the kitchen staff to put together some sweets and coffee and was able to arrange for her staff to leave their posts for a short while that afternoon to attend the meeting.

Standing in front of her staff, a few of whom she'd known since she was a young girl, Cami's eyes misted. They were like extended family to her.

Seeing how emotional she was, Becca came to her side. "Let's all give a round of applause for Cami, our leader."

As applause broke out, the tears that Cami had held back rolled down her cheeks. She dabbed at her eyes with a tissue and straightened. "Thank you so much. I became overwhelmed when I realized how so many of you have seen Chandler Hill grow and evolve from my grandmother's time to my own. We owe you a debt of gratitude."

After the murmuring in the room stopped, Cami

continued. "Unfortunately, we lost one of our employees today. Vanessa Duncan has left us to work at the Lone Creek Winery handling weddings and other functions for them. It is with regret that I inform you that she has apparently been working for them on the side for weeks now, undermining everything we've trained her to do here."

Cami paused as more murmuring broke out. "I understand that at least one of you has been approached by her to leave here to work for her. Of course, you're free to do as you wish, but as I consider you a member of the Chandler Hill family, I ask that you please talk to me first."

"I wouldn't leave here for anything," said Imani, rising from her seat among the others. "You've given me a chance to grow at my job, days off when I've needed them, and a healthy benefits package."

"Yes," came another from the crowd. "My brother worked for Rod Mitchell for less than a month. He couldn't take his treatment."

Cami held up her hand. "This isn't a vendetta against the Lone Creek Winery. I'm merely offering my counsel, should any of you be tempted to leave. I need you, I care about you, and I want to be able to continue working with you for a long time."

A young woman on the waitstaff raised her hand.

"Yes, Rosie?"

"We *are* able to defend Chandler Hill against those people spreading rumors about Chandler Hill, aren't we?"

Cami's heart bumped to a stop and raced ahead in panicky beats. *People were saying bad things about Chandler Hill?* She straightened her shoulders and steadied herself on her feet. "Chandler Hill is proud of our reputation and of the work everyone does here. If anything needs to come to my attention, please let me know. Lettie Chandler supported many a valley resident, and I will continue to do so."

"That's right!" cried Becca, coming to Cami's side. After the applause died down, she began to speak. "I'm here to talk with you as a staff member. If any of you are unhappy with your job, please come and see me. My office is always open to you. This is a perfect opportunity to make suggestions and to simply talk about things. The summer months are busy for us, but we always have time for you." She smiled at Cami.

"And now, let's have some refreshments," said Cami. "We'll cover for you as long as we can while you enjoy them."

As planned, Cami left the room so the staff members would feel freer to talk. Becca and Imani had agreed to represent her.

Cami hurried to the front desk to answer the phone and help guests check in.

Wearing his black-checked pants and white chef's jacket, Darren walked over to her.

"Hi, Cami. I heard what you said in the meeting. I wasn't going to say anything to you, but Bernard approached me a couple of days ago about working on functions for him. I didn't think too much of it at the time because people from Portland, Seattle, and other places are always asking me to go to work for them. It's nothing serious, just a compliment to a worthy chef."

"What did you tell Bernard?" Cami asked in what she hoped was a calm manner, even though her pulse seemed to be running a marathon.

Darren grinned. "I told him to fuck off, that I'd never work for Rod Mitchell or him."

"Great response." Cami couldn't help the smile that crossed her face.

Laughter erupted from Darren, a deep, rewarding sound to Cami's ears. "Liz and I love it here. We're not about to change our minds. In fact, I haven't said anything to anybody else, but

Liz is expecting."

"She is?" Cami couldn't hide her surprise. Liz was over fifty.

Darren gave her an impish grin. "She's getting a dachshund puppy. After having Sophie around so much, Liz informed me she has to have one of her own."

Cami clasped her hands. "Terrific! It will be such fun to have them play together."

"Liz is pretty excited. We're picking up the puppy in a couple of weeks." Darren checked his watch. "Better get back to work. Talk to you later." He turned to go, then stopped and turned around. "Cami, I've heard many nice things about your grandmother, but you're great, too. Everybody loves working here. At least those of us who've been here for a while. Some of the younger kids don't know what a fabulous deal this is."

"Thanks." As she watched him walk away toward the kitchen, Cami thought of his words. The young, temporary staff people were the most likely to leave. If that was true, the situation wasn't as bad as she'd thought. Maybe.

CHAPTER TWENTY

As suspected, some of the younger staff people, lured by money, chose to leave and work for Rod Mitchell. But the key members of Chandler Hill's staff opted to stay. Several of the older group were angry that Vanessa tried to lure them away with what they knew would become empty promises. Lone Creek Winery had a reputation for treating people poorly.

With the vacancy left by Vanessa, Cami spoke to Laurel Newson. A widow in her late forties, Laurel was the picture of elegance. Her frosted brown hair was carefully tied in back of her head, her blue eyes sparkled with humor, and a smile curved her lips as if life hadn't shattered her dreams. Cami had always admired her outlook.

"You did such a lovely job in advising us about wedding photo venues outside and supervising the gardening staff that I'm wondering if you'd consider handling the details of our weddings and overseeing each one."

Laurel's smile brightened her face. "I would love that challenge. My days seem longer and lonelier as time goes on."

"I was sorry to hear about your husband's death a year ago," said Cami. "He was well liked in the valley."

"A good man." Laurel's lips curved, and a pink flush colored her cheeks. "The love of my life."

"It's that kind of feeling I want our weddings to have," Cami said. "I think you can bring that to them."

"Thank you. I'd like to try."

Cami studied Laurel, pleased with her response. She

realized it had been a big mistake to put someone like Vanessa in charge. She wanted a quieter, more refined person to oversee weddings at Chandler Hill.

Cami was even more impressed when Laurel pointed out several items on the bride's questionnaire Vanessa had drawn up and suggested changes to them—things like specific likes and dislikes of decorative colors, flowers, and food, and filling in ideas of their dream wedding. Sometimes it was only a word or two, but it made a big difference in trying to discover what a bride really wanted.

Laurel fit easily into the position, and by the time the next wedding party was due to arrive in June, Cami was excited to anticipate how things would go under Laurel's direction.

Content to let her handle that wedding, Cami concentrated on the local artisans show set for the Fourth of July weekend. With no weddings scheduled for that Sunday, Chandler Hill was opening Chandler Hall and adjacent lawns for the show. The event had captured the attention of several artists throughout the Northwest. A jury of local artists limited the number of entrants to fifty. The entrance fees for the juried show would cover the cost of extra help needed to park cars and direct people around the property. Chandler Hill wines would be offered, of course, along with appetizers from Darren's kitchen. The first of its kind in the valley, the show was getting a lot of early attention. Wynton Winkler had agreed to participate by providing prints of three of his latest works. If everything worked out well, Cami wanted to make the art show an annual affair.

Cami met with the local board of artists to help determine placement of the tents on the grounds. The Wedding Garden was off-limits, but most of the other lawn space would be available.

She was deep in discussion with two members of the board,

when one of women cried, "Hey, Josh! Just in time. Come meet Cami Chandler, owner of the Chandler Hill Inn and Winery. She's here to help us design the layout of the tents on her property."

Smiling, Josh strode over to them and held out a hand. "Hi. I'm Joshua Evans."

When his callused fingers curled around hers, Cami's eyes widened with recognition. "Oh, you're the artist who sells those beautiful metal sculptures. I love the one you did in copper for the art museum in Portland. 'Girl in Rain,' I think you called it."

Beneath his straight, dark hair, his brown eyes lit up. "Everyone likes that one."

"Hey, Josh," said a watercolorist, coming up to him. "I thought you were a no-show. Glad you're here."

Amused, Cami watched the pretty red-head bat her eyelashes at him.

Josh smiled over her head at Cami and rolled his eyes.

Choking down a laugh, Cami turned away. She didn't blame the young woman for flirting. Joshua Evans was one hot guy.

After the final plan was made, Cami rose to leave. "Thank you for being so cooperative. We want this event to be comfortable for everyone, including our hotel guests."

Josh got to his feet. "Are you heading to the Chandler Hill Inn? If so, could I have a ride? I'm staying there for the weekend."

"I'll be glad to take you. I'm going there now."

"Thanks. Let me grab my bag and I'll join you out front." Josh left the room.

Outside, Cami pulled her SUV up to the front door just as Josh emerged from the building. He threw his bag in the backseat and climbed in beside her.

"Thanks again. I've heard so much about the inn I wanted to see it for myself. Hard to believe someone your age owns it and the winery, too."

"I inherited it from my grandmother. It's a bit of a challenge, but I like the business," admitted Cami, at ease with him.

"It's great you found something you like. For me, it's been a struggle to convince my family that I don't want to take over my father's accounting firm." He chuckled. "Can you see someone like me wearing a suit and pushing numbers all day? God! I'd be so bad at it."

"You're very good at what you do," said Cami. "I've seen pictures of some of your sculptures, and the art museum has several. I particularly like your artwork made of both metal and found pieces."

He turned to her with interest. "Do you? They're my favorite too because much of it depends on those things I've found among nature—sticks, stones, bird feathers, anything I can uncover."

"While you're at Chandler Hill, I hope you'll walk the land with me. There's lots to be found. In fact, why don't I show you around later this afternoon?"

Josh beamed at her. "That would be great. I can make something special for you and your guests."

"Perfect," said Cami, pulling up to the front of the inn. "I'll drop you off now. How about meeting up right here for our walk at about four o'clock?"

"Sounds great." Josh got his bag out of the car and walked toward the entrance.

Cami watched him go, admiring the way he strode with an easy confidence. She looked forward to meeting him later. He was easy to talk to and very easy to look at.

At four that afternoon Cami met Josh at the inn. "I have my walking shoes on and my dog, Sophie, with me." At the mention of her name, Sophie barked and wiggled for attention.

Josh leaned down and patted her on the head. When she rolled over for a tummy rub, Josh laughed and obliged her.

"She's a little spoiled," said Cami.

"Why not? My dog, Spike, is pampered too. He's a golden retriever and too big to do much traveling with me. Right now, he's back home in Santa Fe."

"Ah, Santa Fe. Such a pretty place."

"It's been a great place for me to live and work," said Josh. "Very spiritual overtones, if you're into that kind of thing."

Cami smiled and wondered what he'd think if she told him that she often talked to her grandmother, trying to get a sense of what she'd do in certain business situations.

"Let's head out. There are a lot of things I want to show you," she said.

They walked into the vineyards. They hadn't gone far when Cami knelt on the ground and sifted the dirt in her hands. Josh knelt beside her and listened while she explained about the composition of the soil, why grapevines were planted in it, and why the rows of vines were placed in a north/south direction.

"Pretty basic stuff," said Cami, "but I thought it might be helpful to you in designing a new piece of art."

"Very nice," said Josh. He picked up a string of vine that had been cut away from a plant and held it up to the sun.

They walked on, chatting easily. Cami was proud to show the vineyards to him. He noticed a number of different items and placed them in a small canvas bag he'd brought along.

After an hour or so, Cami said, "How about coming to my house for a drink before you head back to the inn? It's right here on the property."

"Sounds good. It's the perfect time of day to relax." He studied her a moment. "I know this is going to sound corny as hell, but could I photograph you one day? Though I'm more well-known for my metal sculptures and pieces, I still do photography."

Flattered, Cami laughed. "I should warn you that I don't take good pictures."

"Then you've never had the right photographer. The next time I come here I'll bring my camera."

They'd reached the long driveway to Cami's house when Drew's truck pulled up. "Hi, what's up?" he asked, looking from Cami to Josh and back again at Cami.

"Hi, Drew. This is Joshua Evans, an artist who's exhibiting at the art show next weekend." She turned to Josh. "Drew Farley is a friend of mine."

She faced Drew. "We're about to have a drink. Want to join us?"

Drew shook his head. "Thought we'd have dinner, my treat, but I guess not. I'll see you later." He turned his truck around and left.

"A friend?" said Josh. "More like a boyfriend. My boyfriend gets jealous too."

"You're gay?" Cami couldn't hide her surprise.

He laughed. "Yeah. Who knew?"

She grinned at him. "Who's the lucky guy?"

"Bruce Patterson. He owns an art gallery in Santa Fe and is a great cook. We've been together for ten years now and married for two."

"You're so lucky. Ten years is a long time. I hope I find someone special."

"Are you sure you're not overlooking someone?" He tilted his head in the direction of Drew's truck.

"We're just friends," said Cami. "That's how he wants it."

Josh shook his head. "I don't think so. But then it's none of my business. How about that drink?"

"Oh, yes. I could use a nice glass of pinot noir," said Cami. "I've got the perfect wine for you."

As they walked to the house, Cami wondered why everyone but Drew thought they should be more than friends. He'd made a choice to date Vanessa and then had come to her, his friend, when things weren't working out. And he'd told her he wasn't doing any dating for a while, so he obviously didn't consider her a date. He'd hurt her feelings more than once because of his decisions, but after the mess with Bernard, she wasn't going to say anything about it. She'd learned to let things fall into place on their own, rather than make a fool of herself over a man.

Following the uncertainty of a gray, cloudy start, the day of the art show turned out to be a glorious one with blue skies, bright sun, and a soft breeze to keep the attendees cool. The crowd was still celebrating the Fourth of July, as evidenced by the red, white, and blue color theme of their clothing. Watching people mill comfortably through the artists' tents and over the lawns, Cami filled with satisfaction.

Cami saw Drew and waved to him. He grinned and walked toward her. "I was talking to Josh. He does some really cool stuff."

"Yes, I love his work," said Cami.

"Uh ... I didn't realize he was gay. I'm ,,, uh ... sorry about running off the other night. Uh ... what do you say we go out sometime?"

Cami's eyes widened. "Are you asking me to go on a date with you?"

A pink color crept into Drew's cheeks. "Yeah, that's what I was thinking."

She hid her amusement. "I bet you and Josh talked about more than his artwork."

"I was going to ask you out anyway," said Drew, looking so uncomfortable Cami relented.

"I'd love to go out with you, even if it's not your own idea."

He held up a hand in protest. "But it is. I promise. We were just talking. That's all." In the silence that followed, Drew said, "How about Tuesday when all this excitement is over. I'll pick you up at six o'clock."

"Better make it 6:30," said Cami.

She and Drew smiled at each other.

"What's going on with you two?" Imani said, joining them. "Looks pretty interesting."

"Nothing," Cami and Drew said together, and then laughed.

Imani fanned herself. "Whatever this 'nothing' is, it's pretty hot." Chuckling, she walked away.

"Guess I'd better go check on things," Cami said, gripping the clipboard she'd been carrying. It was just a date. Right?

"See you later." Drew gave her a little salute and disappeared inside Chandler Hall.

When Cami caught up with Josh, she said, "Guess you talked to Drew, huh?"

Josh shook his head. "Poor guy is so lost when it comes to you. He didn't want to scare you off. But I set him straight."

"Thanks," said Cami, meaning it with all her heart. She'd tried to put aside ideas of being with Drew, but she could never stop wishing it would happen. Now she'd find out if those dreams had been foolish, after all.

CHAPTER TWENTY-ONE

Sunday evening, Cami sat on the couch, bare feet up on the coffee table, holding onto a glass of red wine. Sophie snuggled beside her, exhausted from the day's activity. Cami let out a sigh of relief. The art show had met her expectations and more. The artists were happy, and her staff was pleased with their cooperation in keeping the inn running smoothly while crowds of people wandered through the property. Next year, they'd extend the show to two days. A knock sounded at the door. "C'mon in, Rafe! We're just resting."

"It's not Rafe," said a deep familiar voice Cami knew. She whirled around. "Drew! What are you doing here?"

He walked over and stood in front of her. "You know that date I asked you about?"

Cami held her breath. Had he changed his mind?

His lips curved. "Can we make it tonight instead? I don't think I can wait that long."

Delight bubbled out of her in a chuckle. "Well, I think I can arrange that. Have a seat and I'll get you a glass of wine."

"No, no! Stay right there. You don't have to wait on me. I've brought some things with me."

She watched as he went to the front door and returned with a picnic basket. He set it down in front of her and held up a bottle of Taunton Estates wine. From the picnic basket, he carefully pulled out a fruit and cheese tray and a leafy green salad topped with shrimp and set it on the coffee table.

"Nice, you've thought of everything!" Cami said, pleased by his gesture.

"Almost everything." He lifted out a plate that held a huge slice of chocolate cream cake, her favorite, and placed it next to the other things.

She clapped her hands. "Perfect!"

They grinned at each other.

The moment Drew sat down on the couch, Sophie climbed into his lap and smothered his cheeks with kisses, which is exactly what Cami felt like doing.

"Yeah, I figured you'd be tired from the show, and waiting for another day to actually have a date with you seemed like an awfully long time."

"I'm glad you're here. I need to talk with a friend," said Cami, slipping into their old routine.

"Hold it! I have no intention of being just your friend. I want more than that." He set Sophie down on the floor and reached for her.

She happily went into his arms, remembering the times she'd dreamed of such a moment. When his lips, warm and full, pressed down on hers, her body reacted predictably. She knew then they'd both waited for this moment.

When they finally pulled apart, Cami gazed into Drew's eyes and saw the wonder she felt.

"How hungry are you?" he asked softly. "Let's ..."

She pulled him close, knowing where this was going.

"God! I've wanted you for so long," Drew murmured before lowering his lips to hers once more.

"Me too," she responded softly.

Drew pulled away and studied her. "But you made it plain you weren't ready for dating, not after your breakup with Bernard. And who could blame you? What an ass!"

"Yeah, and Vanessa turned out to be a mess," countered Cami.

"Can you believe I thought she was almost perfect? God!

I'm such a fool."

Cami cupped his cheeks in her hands. "You're no fool. You're a really nice guy."

He gave her a sexy grin. "Not always."

She laughed. They'd been friends long enough for her to know that deep down he was the nicest, the sweetest, the best guy she knew. She held out her hand.

After taking the food to the kitchen to keep it safe from Sophie, they walked to her bedroom and shut the door to keep Sophie out. Inside the room, Cami left the drapes open. No one could see inside the sliding door onto the private deck overlooking the scenery below. And on this summer's evening, she wanted to enjoy being with Drew as the sky filled with the colors of the setting sun, colors that were already highlighting the interior of her room.

Lying together on her bed, she and Drew began an exploration of one another, delighted by each response. Drawing out the anticipation each felt was both tantalizing and unendurable. When they finally came together, it was such an ultimate moment of sharing that Cami knew she'd never really made love before. With Drew, it was a spiritual act. Her heart filled with such emotion she couldn't hold back tears.

"Oh my God! Did I hurt you?" Drew asked, thumbing the tears at the corners of her eyes.

"No," whispered Cami. "I've never felt this way with anyone else."

He smiled. "I love you, you know. I have from the first moment I met you."

"When you rescued me from Jonathan?" She remembered how she and Jamison had called upon Drew to escort Jonathan Knight out of the inn after firing him.

"Ahhh," he said. "You remember it too."

"A damsel in distress always remembers her knight in shining armor," she replied playfully.

He grinned. "Come here, you gorgeous damsel."

She laughed and went into his arms again.

Much later, they sat in the kitchen together, sharing the contents of his picnic basket. Cami glanced over at Drew from time to time, seeing him in a whole new light. He was a friend and would stay a friend. But he was also her lover, and she welcomed that.

"Tomorrow night, I'll take you to dinner, if you'd like," he said, munching on a piece of cheese.

"I thought this was our date," said Cami.

"No, this is our predate." His expression grew serious. "I'd like to take you somewhere, show you off."

"That's so sweet, but, Drew, being here with you is enough."

He smiled at her. "Do you know how nice that sounds? But, someday, I'll surprise you with something different."

"I thought this date was pretty spectacular," she teased.

He grinned. "The best ever." Reaching across the table, he stroked her cheek. "I knew you were special. And, Cami, I trust you."

A warm feeling pulsed through Cami. Though she'd been given love and encouragement through the years by Nonnee and Rafe, a piece of her had been missing. Now she knew it as the part that loving Drew had fulfilled in her. She wasn't sure what the future would hold for them, but she knew she'd stand beside him for as long as he wanted.

The next summer days filled with cobalt-blue skies made Cami feel as if she was floating in a sea of happiness. Gone were the days of longing for someone she couldn't have. Drew was present in her thoughts and in her life, even as the inn remained busy.

Cami was working on inventory figures when Becca burst into her office. "Quick! Turn on the television!"

Surprised by Becca's wide-eyed look of excitement, Cami lifted the control off her desk and clicked it. "What's going on?"

"You'll see." Becca gave her a look of concern.

The picture popped into view. A news broadcast announcer stood in front of a large photograph of Edward Kingsley. "Several women who claim he assaulted them have banded together to hire one of the top lawyers in the country, who handles cases involving sexual assault."

The screen showed five women of varying ages. None, Cami noted, was auburn-haired like her mother, but all were women with light eyes and blond hair.

"Congressman Kingsley's office has announced that he adamantly denies such actions and will fight to protect his good name."

A picture of Edward, his wife, and Lulu was displayed on the screen, showing a perfect, happy family.

"Many years ago, the congressman and his wife suffered a heart-breaking loss when their ten-year-old son drowned. JoAnn Kingsley has been pretty much of a recluse since then except for her volunteer work to help organizations in their fights against cancer. All attempts to get any response from her regarding these allegations have been futile. But others are only too willing to come forward with new information about the congressman's behavior."

A video clip of the congressman leaving his Washington, D.C. condo appeared next. "No comment," was all he said as reporters clamored to get to him, shouting questions at him one after the other.

"I'm sure this is just the beginning of a long, troubled road for Congressman Kingsley," said the male announcer with enough regret in his voice to make Cami angry.

She slammed her fist down on her desk. "The bastard! Do you think that's what happened to my mother, and she was too ashamed to admit it?" Becca now knew the story about her father.

"I don't know," said Becca. "But he's got to be scared for the future. Lulu told you he wanted to run for president one day."

"That's not happening now," said Cami. "At least I hope not."

Throughout the day, the local TV stations pre-empted some of the regular programming to cover this salacious news. Cami was sickened each time she saw Edward Kingsley's face on the screen.

At the end of the work day, Cami left the inn and went to find Rafe.

He was returning to the cabin from his vineyard when she met up with him.

She got out of the car and ran over to him, feeling like a child again, needing her grandfather's protective arms around her.

"You heard the news?" Rafe said, patting her on the back.

She pulled away and looked up at him. "Do you think he raped my mother like those other women?"

"Come on inside," he said. "We'll talk there."

He led her inside to the kitchen. "I'll pour us each a glass of wine. Something I've wanted you to try. Then I'll tell you what I think."

It seemed to take forever for Rafe to wash his hands, get out a bowl of crackers, open a bottle of wine, and pour it into two glasses.

He handed her a glass of wine and the crackers. Groaning softly, he took a seat opposite her.

"Are you all right?" she asked.

He nodded. "These old bones get sore from time to time."

"I've thought about my mother ever since I heard about Edward Kingsley's trouble with women. Do you think she was one of his victims? That I was the result of something like that? The thought makes me sick to my stomach."

Rafe lifted a hand to stop her. "Hold on! Don't jump to conclusions about any of it. Even though some signs are pointing to his possibly being your father, I don't believe your mother was assaulted by him. I think she wouldn't tell us who your father was to protect him, like she said. And she clearly loved you, Cami."

"But she was young ... maybe she didn't want anyone to know she'd been taken advantage of ...." Cami's voice trailed off. Even she knew that didn't sound like the woman they both had known.

"I didn't tell you before, but I sent Edward Kingsley a message on his blog. I haven't heard a word from him and probably won't now. I was only asking him for information about his experiences in Africa. I used my mother's name. If he's my father, he'll put it together. Otherwise, it'll probably get ignored. Especially now, with all that's going on with him."

Rafe sighed. "I know how much you want answers. If you're meant to know, it'll happen. And if it doesn't, you still have more knowledge than your grandmother had about her family."

"That's why everyone loved her so much. She made them feel like family."

His eyes grew shiny. "Lettie Chandler was a very special person. You're a lot like her, Cami. Be happy for that."

"I know I have a lot to be thankful for."

A smile spread across his face, erasing the sadness that had filled it an instant earlier. "I understand you and Drew are what was called 'an item' in my time. I'm happy for you both. In fact, it's something I'd been hoping for—a union between two of my favorite young people. Drew's a fine man."

"Good enough for me?" She arched an eyebrow at him. He'd always teased about chasing off any young man who came courting her.

He laughed. "I trust the two of you to treat each other right."

Cami excused herself and came back to the table holding two framed photographs. She set them down on the table and stood by Rafe's chair to study them.

She picked up the first one—a picture of her mother smiling at the camera, holding Cami.

"She was so pretty," Cami said sadly. With a finger she traced her mother's auburn hair, dark eyes, and the cleft chin that came from Rafe.

"A very beautiful young woman," he agreed. "And very determined to do good work in Africa. She never wanted an active role in running Chandler Hill, in part, I think, because while growing up, she resented the time Lettie took with it." He smiled at her. "But Lettie and I knew you'd be up to the job."

"I still have so much to learn. And even though I adore Drew, I'm not going to let him beat me in any wine contests. Adam Kurey and I are going to work together on some new varietals."

He laughed. "That's my girl."

Cami studied the other photograph. In it, Lettie was smiling up at Rafe as they stood together near the cluster of trees in the family grove. The look of love between them lent a special glow to the picture that was unmistakable. Cami hoped that she and Drew would have an enduring love together like her grandparents. Right now, everything between them was new and tender and exciting. She smiled as she thought of Drew taking her to Nick's for dinner. But the best part would be later, at her house.

CHAPTER TWENTY-TWO

Cami took a last look at herself in her mirror. Her strawberry blond curls were in disarray, but that's how Drew said he liked them. Her face, browned by the sun, wore a happy expression that had been missing after her breakup with Bernard and the death of her beloved grandmother. Life wasn't really about plans, she thought. It was about opportunities for growth when those plans went awry. And sometimes, like now, life seemed good.

When she heard someone at the door, Cami hurried to meet him.

When Drew saw her in her new, floral-print blouse and white jeans, he let out a low whistle. "Wow! You look great!"

A warm feeling lifted the corners of her lips. She'd ordered the multi-colored top online, and it fit her perfectly. And if the neckline was cut a little lower than she normally wore, that was fine. Drew made her feel sexy.

He'd made a special effort to look nice too. His butterscotch-brown hair, still wet from his shower, was slicked away from his face, showcasing his classic features and strong jaw. He wore what looked like a new golf shirt in a dark shade of green that brought out the tawny color of his eyes. Clean blue jeans fit his well-shaped body—a body that was perfect for her.

They drove into town. At this time of year and even on a midweek night, there was a lot of activity. Drew found a parking spot a couple blocks away, and they walked to Nick's restaurant hand in hand. Cami was aware that once people saw Drew and her together, the news would be all over the valley, but she didn't care. She trusted Drew not to do anything to hurt her.

Rafe's youngest sister, Rose, was the hostess. She greeted them with a broad grin. "Good evening. I've saved a special table for you in the back corner where you'll have all the privacy you want. Rafe told me Drew made reservations here."

Cami and Drew glanced at each other, pleased.

Rose leaned toward them and in a soft voice said, "He's very fond of the two of you,"

and then she led them to the back of the restaurant.

They scanned the menus she handed them and, familiar with the restaurant, quickly ordered.

As they sipped wine while they waited for their entrees, conversation between them was easy. The table Rose had chosen for them turned out to be perfect. They had a view of the other tables in the restaurant but were not easily visible to other patrons.

As Cami finished her game hen, Bernard and Vanessa came into the restaurant. Cami tensed. She had no desire to talk to them. At the art show, she knew Bernard had approached many of the artists about doing a bigger, better show at Rod Mitchell's place next year. It was surprising to her to see how blatantly aggressive he'd become about taking business away from her. Vanessa was no better. Cami had lost a bid for a wedding to her just last week. It was frustrating, but Cami couldn't jeopardize future weddings and her business by cutting costs to a break-even level.

When Bernard spotted them, instead of sitting where Rose indicated, he remained standing. Pointing in their direction, he said loudly, "I want a table over there, next to them."

"I'm sorry –" Rose began and then stopped when Bernard marched right past her to the table next to Drew and Cami.

Vanessa followed him, giving her a little wave.

Bernard took a seat at the table and gestured to Vanessa to take a seat.

Rose hurried over to them.

"We'll sit here," Bernard announced.

Rose gave Cami an apologetic look and handed menus to them.

Bernard smiled at them. "I thought it would be nice to sit together. It gives me an opportunity to talk to you about a plan I have to do some joint advertising with the two of you."

Cami, who'd just taken a sip of water, choked.

Drew frowned at Bernard. "What do you mean by joint advertising? Why would we want to do something like that?"

"Actually, it was my idea," corrected Vanessa. "With the three wineries so close together, I thought we could advertise them as a group of places to go for excellent wines, weddings, and special events."

"I'm not interested," Cami said firmly. Who knew what kind of games Vanessa and Bernard would play? She didn't trust either one of these people. Perhaps Lone Creek Winery wasn't doing as well as everyone thought.

"I'm not interested either. The reputation for Taunton Estates wines is stellar," said Drew. "Frankly, we don't need to team up with anyone else."

The look Bernard shot him wasn't pleasant. He turned to her, giving her a smile that she now detested. "Cami, surely you see how beneficial working together would be."

"For you, maybe," she replied. "But as Drew says, Chandler Hill can stand on its own reputation."

"Are you upset because we're taking away some of your business?" Vanessa shook her head. "I'm surprised you don't see the benefit to everyone involved in the venture. It's a mistake not to work with us. You'll regret it."

"Yes. You'll be sorry," said Bernard in an ominous tone that sent a shiver through Cami. She wasn't sure what was going on at Lone Creek Winery, but she'd ask Becca to follow up.

As Bernard and Vanessa placed their orders, Drew said quietly, "Let's get out of here. Shall we go to your place?"

Her appetite gone, she nodded.

After taking orders from Bernard and Vanessa, Rose turned to them. "What else can we get you?"

"The check, please," Drew said.

"I'm sorry your private dinner has been interrupted," Rose said softly. "Rafe has already taken care of the bill. You're free to go."

"How nice. Thanks, Rose." Cami picked up her purse.

Drew held the chair for her, and they walked out of the restaurant together.

On the sidewalk, Drew turned to her. "Joint advertising? What was that all about? Do they think we're crazy? Lone Creek Winery has a terrible reputation."

"Rod is trying to build his business before he turns around and sells it. I don't think he's doing well, even though Vanessa has stolen a few weddings from me. One bad wedding will hurt the others, and I don't see how she can do what she promises at the prices she's offering."

"I'll talk to Rafe about it, but I know he'll agree with us." Drew put his arm around her. "I hope the evening hasn't been ruined."

She smiled up at him. "It's just about to begin."

Cami decided to look at the figures and results of the advertising campaign for Chandler Hill. Vanessa had suggested new social media ads, and some of them had turned out to be very rewarding. With the website updated and valuable relationships at both local newspapers and travel magazines, the numbers were looking more than satisfactory.

Sitting back in her chair, gazing out at a sparrow taking a dip in the fountain in the garden, Cami wondered what her grandmother would think of the many updates she'd made to the business and the inn itself. It was so easy to get the word out to everyone today. That's why she knew she was right not to share advertising with Lone Creek Winery. One misstep in social media meant a huge effort to change opinions again. That cost money, and she didn't have any extra. Activity had increased, as had the need for additional staff.

When the phone rang, she picked it up and said in her professional, cheery voice, "Cami Chandler! May I help you?"

"I think you can," said a deep, male voice. "I'm Paul Gardener. I work for Congressman Kingsley as his assistant. You sent him a message recently regarding his time in Africa. May I ask why?"

Cami's heartbeat galloped. She gripped the phone so tightly her knuckles turned white. "My mother did a lot of work there, and I believe she knew him. I'm trying to put together some family history about her and thought that perhaps he could help."

After a long pause, the man said, "Are you aware of all the recent publicity regarding the congressman? The allegations and the women coming forward with untrue claims?"

Cami forced her voice to be strong. "Yes, I am aware of that, sir. But it has nothing to do with me. I'm not interested in anything like that."

"I see. I'll report back to the congressman, and we'll get back to you with a response. Thank you." He clicked off the call before she could ask any questions.

Hope, like a burning blaze, spread through her. Maybe she'd get some answers after all. She decided not to mention the call to anyone else, especially Rafe and Drew. They wouldn't want to see her hurt.

Hugging the secret of the phone call to herself, Cami went about her business for the next several days. The wedding of one of Justine's bridesmaids was about to take place, and she wanted everything to be perfect. From a modest family, Samantha Eldridge had approached Cami hesitantly about having her wedding at Chandler Hill. She explained how small her budget was and asked Cami if she could work within those limits . Cami's heart went out to her.

They planned a small, mid-week wedding for twelve people. Samantha's parents were divorced and had been for a long time. Sam's uncle on her mother's side was stepping in for her father. The rest of the wedding party would consist of Justine and George, one other bridesmaid from Justine's wedding and her boyfriend, her fiancé, Curt Thompson's, parents, and his two younger brothers.

When the front desk clerk alerted Cami that Samantha's mother and uncle had arrived, Cami hurried out of her office to greet them. At a distance, she could tell from their dazzled expressions they were impressed with their surroundings and made a silent vow to make this a memorable experience for them. "Hello, welcome to the Chandler Hill Inn," Cami said, brightly.

"Such a beautiful place," commented Samantha's mother, Irene, a small, attractive woman with short brown hair. "I'm so happy that Samantha could have the small, intimate wedding she's always wanted. She told me I have you to thank for it."

"It's my pleasure to welcome you to what I'm sure will be a lovely event. Samantha was very clear on what she wanted."

"A headstrong girl. Always has been," said her uncle. He held out his hand. "Patrick O'Hare. Pleased to meet you."

His blue eyes rested on her as they shook hands. Dark hair was swept away from a face that was pleasant though not handsome.

"I understand that you will act as father of the bride."

Patrick's lips thinned. "Yes, the sonofabitch doesn't even have the decency to attend his own daughter's wedding."

"It's for the best," Irene interceded, placing a hand on his arm. "He would've ruined it for everyone."

"Got a drinking problem and a loud mouth," explained Patrick.

Laurel approached them. After Cami introduced her to Samantha's mother and uncle, she said, "You'll be in capable hands with Laurel. She's here to see that your every wish is met."

"Ah, a fairy godmother," said Patrick, giving Laurel a wink that made her laugh.

Satisfied that things were off to a good start, Cami said, "I'll see you later. Enjoy the afternoon."

Cami left them to go to her office. Thinking about her own situation, she wondered when the time came for her wedding, who would walk her down the aisle? Would it be Edward Kingsley? Even if he turned out to be her father, would he be willing to do such a thing? Would she want him to? With the many stories, rumors, and news reports about him lately, she didn't like him all that much.

Her thoughts turned to Rafe. He would be proud, no doubt, to be asked to do such duty. He'd always been there for her with advice, help, and a tender but fierce love that came from discovering she was his granddaughter.

Later that afternoon, Justine and George arrived with her friend, Kerry Moser, and Kerry's boyfriend, Rob Tuley.

Cami hurried to greet them. As beautiful as ever, Justine waved at her.

"Justine! I'm so happy to see you again! How are you?"

Justine beamed at Cami and threw her arms around her. "I'm great. George and I are enjoying married life."

"As much as we can before grad school," said George, grinning.

Justine reintroduced Kerry and Rob. While they were exchanging greetings, Samantha walked in with Curt.

Cami stepped back while group hugs took place.

Samantha, a small, attractive woman like her mother, had a presence about her that made her seem bigger than she was. Maybe, Cami thought, it was the constant smile lighting her features, or, perhaps, it was her sense of fun that drew attention to her.

Samantha's blue eyes sparkled as she stood beside her fiancé. "Thank you, everyone, for coming. I'm happy I'll able to share this special time with you tomorrow. Curt and I really appreciate it."

"I wouldn't miss it for the world," Justine said. "Especially here at the Chandler Hill Inn." She turned to Cami with a smile. "My wedding was perfect."

"My wedding is going to be very different," said Samantha. "But I'm thrilled with the plans."

Kerry gave Samantha a quick hug. "Thanks for having me."

Curt, broad-shouldered and husky, gazed at Samantha adoringly. Cami knew from meeting him earlier that he was an easy-going guy who wanted to please his prospective bride. With his light-brown hair and round, button-like dark eyes, he'd always seemed like a cuddly teddy bear to Cami.

He turned to her now. "I'm supposed to tell you that my family will be a little late. Their flight from Denver was delayed."

"That's not a problem. We'll be ready for them any time they get here."

Laurel and Becca arrived to greet the group. Leaving them, Cami went into the kitchen to see Darren about the special dinner they were serving the wedding party tomorrow.

In the planning stage, Samantha and Curt had shyly approached Cami and Darren with the idea of fried chicken, salad and cake. "I think that's all I can afford," Samantha said. "We're paying for the wedding ourselves."

"Let's work on some ideas and get back to you. We'll keep within your budget, I promise," Cami had assured them. What she didn't tell them was that the inn would absorb any additional costs in order to present a beautiful meal for the occasion.

At first, Darren had been dismayed by the simplicity of the menu, but then he'd gotten into the spirit of it and came up with a few ideas of his own. Now, the dressed-up menu was listed on the small, printed presentation card as:

Wine Country Lettuce Wedge
Breast of Chicken with a Cherry-Pinot Glaze
Duchess Potatoes
Medley of Valley Vegetables

Samantha had chosen chocolate cake for dessert, but Darren had creatively added the option of a blood orange sauce to go with it.

"How're things going?" Cami now asked Darren.

"Fine. Everything's set for tomorrow's wedding, along with regular dining for our guests. Laurel's going to decorate the private dining room after we close down dinner tonight."

"Sounds like things are in control. How's that puppy of yours?"

Darren grinned and held up his hand. Several little red spots covered it. "Oscar? He's really something. It's like having a real baby. He's up at night, runs around like crazy, and is trying to bite my hand off with his sharp little teeth."

Cami chuckled. "He'll get over that as long as he has plenty of chew toys."

"Thanks for the box of toys you sent him. We've already sent for more."

"Another spoiled puppy? I love it! Sophie has more toys than I have shoes, and that's saying a lot!"

They laughed together.

Just before the guests' cocktail hour, Curt's parents arrived. Anxious to meet them, Cami went to greet them.

"Welcome to the Chandler Hill Inn," she said with practiced ease.

Curt's mother smiled. "Thank you. I'm Robin. This is my husband, Tommy, and our boys, Casey and Christopher."

At a pointed look from their mother both teen-aged boys bobbed their heads at her and said, "Hello."

Tommy held out a hand. "Howdy."

Cami shook it, liking his friendly smile and the way his brown eyes warmed. She knew from Curt that they owned a farm. Tommy looked the part with his strong body and weathered, tan face. Robin was a tall woman who stood straight and gazed at the lobby with quiet interest.

"You're in time for our happy hour. I believe Curt and Samantha are already there. Please come in and help yourself to some snacks. We have wine, beer, sodas, and flavored waters to drink."

"That sounds lovely," said Robin. "It's been a long day to get here."

When other guests arrived, Cami said goodbye to Curt's family and went to greet them.

The next morning, Cami stood with Laurel in the small dining room, inspecting the decorating Laurel and two of the crew from The Barn had done in the room.

"It's gorgeous!" Cami exclaimed, staring at the ceiling that had been covered with tiny lights and white silk flowers in a pattern that was both magical and subtle. At the far end of the room, in a little alcove, a small table had been set up with a crisp white linen cloth. Two tall, thick candles were placed on top of it, leaving room in the center for the bouquet of flowers that had been ordered. Rev. James Bliss would perform the ceremony.

"I love having this room separated into two sections the way you've done it, one for the wedding itself and the other for the dinner," said Cami. Three white trellises were set in a line midway in the room, leaving plenty of space for chairs at the one end where the ceremony would take place and two rounds of six in the dining area.

"Good thing this wedding is indoors," said Laurel, looking out the windows that overlooked a small garden. "I don't think this rain is going to let up anytime soon."

"The weather forecaster said very little chance of it doing so," Cami said. "But I don't think Samantha and Curt are going to mind a bit. They're very much in love, and a little rain isn't going to stop them from having a special day."

Laurel smiled. "They're the cutest couple ever. When we heard they couldn't afford to have a photographer, a few of my friends and I decided to surprise them. We've hired Hank Coleman to take photos for them."

"Oh, how sweet!" cried Cami. "They'll love it."

The day evolved like a story in a fairy tale, with one tender moment following another. While the men worked out in the gym, the women sat in a group in the living room. Cami accepted their invitation to join them.

Smiling shyly, Curt's mother, Robin, announced she had a special gift for Samantha. She pulled out a small box from her purse and handed it to Samantha. "I hope you like it."

The usual smile on Samantha's face widened. "I'm sure I'll love it. Should I open it now?"

"Sure. I wanted you to have it for your wedding. It's not every day a woman gets a daughter."

Samantha's smile evaporated as her eyes filled. With shaking hands, she unwrapped the box, opened it, and lifted out a gold locket.

"It was my grandmother's, and now it's yours. It's both something old and something new for your ceremony."

The tears that she'd held back slipped down Samantha's cheeks as she went to Robin and hugged her.

"Do you know how long I've waited for a girl? I knew if I kept having babies they'd turn out to be boys. Besides, raising three active boys is enough for anyone."

"Three great boys," Samantha said. "Especially Curt."

As Samantha took her seat, Justine spoke up. "I've got something borrowed and something blue covered." She held up the lacy blue satin garter she'd worn at her wedding.

"It's yours—for both the wedding and afterwards," Justine said. A blush brightened her cheeks.

"And I have something new too," said Kerry. She handed Samantha a small package. "I saw these here in The Barn yesterday and thought they'd look perfect on you."

Samantha opened the package and held up a pair of dangling pearl earrings. "Oh, I love them! Thank you so much for making this day so special."

Cami sat among them well aware they'd hosted much fancier, more expensive weddings. But this one, with all the care and love that had gone into it, was her new favorite.

CHAPTER TWENTY-THREE

Cami checked the last-minute details with Laurel, talked to Darren, and then made sure James Bliss was set to perform the ceremony. She was paying especially close attention to having a wedding in the private dining room because she'd come up with a new marketing idea. This intimate space was perfect for second marriages for couples who wanted a tasteful, small wedding in a luxurious setting. Laurel had even suggested to Samantha that she let the inn use photographs of their wedding for promotional materials, and she'd readily agreed.

As Cami stood on the sidelines in the background, listening to the harpist they'd brought in for the wedding, she waited like the others for Samantha to appear.

Curt stood with his father by the makeshift altar, next to Rev. Bliss.

The music suddenly changed to "Here Comes the Sun." Everyone stood and turned. A soft gasp of delight filled the air as Samantha and her Uncle Patrick walked toward them. Samantha wore a crown of white daisies in her auburn hair and carried a bouquet of colorful gerbera daisies. Against her sleeveless, white, ankle-length silk dress, the flowers gave the effect of looking as if they were freshly picked from the garden. Tears sprung to Cami's eyes as Samantha and Curt exchanged looks of such love, her breath caught. She immediately thought of Drew. He made her feel the way Samantha was looking now.

Like the whole affair, the ceremony was short and sweet,

complete with declarations of love and promises to keep.

After the ceremony, a place was hastily made at a table for Rev. Bliss, who'd decided at the last minute that he could stay for the celebration.

As the salad course and then the main course were served, Cami's heart swelled with gratitude for Darren's sensitivity. He had garnished each guest's plates in a way to make a beautiful presentation.

Cami left the guests to their meal and went into the office to check on things. She was going through a stack of notes when the telephone rang. Seeing the California number, Cami's pulse quickened. She picked up the phone.

"This is Camilla Chandler. May I help you?"

"Hi, Camilla? This is Paul Gardener, Congressman Kingsley's assistant. He's planning a visit to Portland and would like to drive down to Chandler Hill to meet with you. Will that be possible?"

"Of course. I'd love to meet him. He's welcome to stay here. I'll make arrangements anytime they're needed."

"We're hoping the trip will take place two weeks from today, but some things still need to be worked out with the committee in Portland. Go ahead and book him a room, but please understand we may have to cancel at the last moment."

"Thank you so much! I'll hold a room for him. And, please, thank him too. I appreciate this opportunity to talk to him."

Cami hung up the phone and got to her feet. She kicked off her shoes and did a little dance across the carpet. The opportunity of being able to talk to the man who might be her father was a dream come true!

"What's going on?" said Becca stepping into the room.

Cami jerked to a stop. "Just some good news, I hope. What about you?"

"I'm ready to leave. Do you need me for anything?"

"No, go ahead. I'm about ready to head home myself. Laurel has things under control, and I'm beat."

"It was the best wedding," said Becca. "Simple, but beautiful. I change my mind about what I want every time we hold another wedding here."

Cami smiled. "I'm sure when it's time to get down to final plans for you, you'll have it figured out. It'll probably be a piece of each wedding."

"That's it. I'll have to decide how to put it all together. How are things going with you and Drew? Dan says Drew seems really happy."

"He's the best guy ever," Cami said, aware her voice had become breathy with emotion.

Becca grinned. "It sure sounds like it. See you later."

As Becca left, Cami picked up the phone to tell Drew the good news and then set it down again. As before, she'd keep her news from both Drew and Rafe. It was best that way. She'd be heartbroken if things fell through, and both men would be angry at the congressman for disappointing her. And even though they'd be upset with her for not telling them ahead of time, they each had a lot on their minds with the opening of new acreage at Taunton Estates Winery for their special Lettie's Creek Wine.

At home, Cami still bubbled with excitement. She picked up Sophie and squeezed her. "Guess what, Soph? I may meet my father. I know you don't get to spend time with your father, but at least you know who he is."

Sophie licked her cheek and then, at the sound of a truck pulling into the driveway, she wiggled to get down.

Cami smiled as Drew got out of his truck and headed inside. The day was getting even better.

###

One morning in early July, Cami walked the land outside her home observing the growth of the grapes with satisfaction. As had been forecast, this looked as if it was going to be an excellent year. An early harvest might even take place if the sugar content of the grapes indicated they were ripe for picking. Rafe stepped out of his cabin and looked around.

Sophie saw him, barked, and ran over to him.

He greeted her by rubbing her ears, waved to Cami, and approached her. "Think it's gonna be a good year. Both Chandler Hill and Taunton Estates grapes are flourishing."

She smiled and gave him a quick kiss. "We just have to keep things going well for a couple more months."

"Yeah. Let's hope the weather holds. California has had some pretty bad storms."

"It's always a worry if the weather begins to act up. Have time for a cup of coffee?"

He smiled. "I always have time for you, sweetheart."

They walked to Cami's house in easy silence. Rafe enjoyed gazing at the land as much as she. No doubt, his thoughts dwelled in the past, while she couldn't stop thinking of what the future held.

Cami made fresh coffee for them and placed a small bowl of fresh-picked raspberries on the table for them to share.

"Are you getting more excited about your river cruise?" Cami asked.

"Actually, I am. They keep sending me information offering side trips, and it should be a nice little vacation. I'm thinking of taking them up on some earlier excursions and will leave earlier in August than I'd thought. Drew can handle things on his own. If that goes well, I'm going to hand over more of the operation to him."

"I think Nonnee would be very pleased to know you're looking forward to the trip. It's what she hoped for."

Rafe shook his head. "I can't believe she was working with a professional to overcome her fear of flying so we could take this trip together. She'd tried before, you know. She said that watching me take off to pick you up in Africa was one of the hardest things she'd ever done."

"You've always been there for me, Rafe. I remember how scared, how confused I was after my mother's death. And when I saw you, I knew I'd be safe."

"Yes, we've had a special connection from the time you were just a toddler," said Rafe, blinking rapidly.

Cami's phone rang. She picked it up and checked Caller ID. A California number she didn't know. Thinking it might have something to do with Congressman Kingsley, she clicked on the call. "Hello?"

"Hello, Ms. Chandler? This is Howard Dickinson. We met at my son's wedding."

"Yes. You're George's father. I remember you well. How can I help?"

"As you may recall, I'm advising Rod Mitchell on the sale of his winery. I received a call today from a Mr. Jonathan Knight. He says he worked for Chandler Hill for several months. Is that correct?"

"Yes-s-s," Cami answered cautiously. A sinking feeling had already affected her stomach.

"He has put together a group of people who might be interested in buying Lone Creek Winery. I thought I'd better get some references."

"I see." Cami wasn't about to offer any information freely without knowing more about the deal. "Are his partners winemakers?"

"Mr. Knight claims several of them are interested in

learning the business."

"What about Jonathan?"

"He has an idea about building an inn on the property. He managed Chandler Hill Inn and would like the opportunity to do his own thing after resigning from your operation."

Cami couldn't hold back. "He didn't resign from Chandler Hill. I fired him. Jamison Winkler was my lawyer handling this. I suggest you call her. I'd prefer not to be involved in this any further."

"I appreciate your candor, Ms. Chandler. It seems the requirements we set up for prospective buyers are making it hard to find a reliable one. I do note, however, that Bernard Arnaud is on the team and is reputed to be a knowledgeable vintner."

"I wish I could help you, but I can't. As I suggested earlier, I'd give Jamison Winkler, my lawyer in L.A., a call. She can provide you with more information than I'm willing to give. Good luck. By the way, Justine and George were here for a friend's wedding recently. They looked terrific and are very happy together."

"Yes," said Howard. "It's been a nice match. Thank you for taking my call. Goodbye."

"What's going on?" Rafe said, giving her a worried look.

"You'll never guess who's trying to buy Rod Mitchell's place. Jonathan Knight and Bernard Arnaud and other buddies of Jonathan's."

His eyes rounded. "*¡Ay Dio mio!* What a disaster!"

"Yes, I know. It's bad enough having Rod run the place. The two of them are ten times worse." A heavy feeling tightened Cami's stomach. "I suggested to Howard Dickinson he call Jamison Winkler. I want to keep a distance from any further conversation with him. He's counseling Rod on the sale of Lone Creek Winery."

" A wise idea to keep out of it," Rafe commented. "Rod can be a very nasty person. And Jonathan and Bernard have already shown themselves to be that way. I worry about you."

"No need," said Cami with a new resolve to stay away from dealing with anyone at Lone Creek Winery. It was almost laughable to think that's why Bernard and Vanessa had wanted joint advertising. He'd want people to think Chandler Hill and Taunton Estates would welcome them into the business.

Rafe called Drew and asked him to come to Cami's house to discuss the situation.

Later, Cami called Adam Kurey. As her winemaker, he was a valued member of her team. His grandfather, Ben, had worked for Chandler Hill in the early years of Nonnee's ownership and had stayed with her until her death. It was he and his son, Scott, who'd trained Adam.

When he heard the news about Jonathan and Bernard teaming up to run a winery, Adam laughed. "Jonathan thinks he knows about making wine, but he doesn't. And Bernard might have been involved in making wine in France, but the grapes here are different and require a lot of care, as you well know."

Cami paused before speaking. "Have they approached you to work for them?"

"As a matter of fact, they have. I couldn't believe it and laughed in their faces. My family has been allied with yours for almost fifty years. And, as far as I'm concerned, that isn't going to change."

Cami let out the breath she'd been holding. "Thank you. I appreciate that very much. I consider you family."

"The wife, the kids, and I appreciate all Lettie and you have done for us—stepping in to pay hospital bills when we couldn't. I'm not going anywhere. Besides, you and I have some fun in store, coming up with a few new wines."

Cami felt a smile spread across her face. "Yes, we do. We can't let Taunton Estates wines get ahead of us."

"Damn right," said Adam, chuckling. "I'll let you know if I hear anything more about either one of those guys."

"Thanks," Cami replied, so relieved she wanted to cry. Competition in the valley was usual, but the cutthroat antics of Rod, Bernard, Jonathan, and Vanessa were out of line.

Two days later, Jamison Winkler called Cami. After they exchanged pleasant greetings , Jamison said, "I just got off the phone with Howard Dickinson. I'm glad you gave me the heads-up on him and the deal he's thinking about because he peppered me with questions."

Cami tensed. "And?"

"And I think I pretty much convinced him that these are not reputable people. I told him I wouldn't want to deal with them on a professional level. He sounded grateful to get the straightforward information I gave him."

"Thanks for doing that. I appreciate it," Cami said. "When are you and Wynton coming for a visit?"

"Not for a while," Jamison said. "The girls are looking at different colleges, and we're taking a lot of trips with them. But as soon as we can, we'll return to Chandler Hill. Uh-oh. I'd better go. I have a call on the other line. Thanks again for including Wynton in your art show. Next year, he'll plan to be there again."

"Fabulous," Cami said, hoping Bernard wouldn't continue to try to undercut her efforts to make the show bigger and better next summer.

CHAPTER TWENTY-FOUR

August entered the summer season in a storm cloud. Outside, rain and wind swept the area. Inside her office, Cami was nervously awaiting her visit with Edward Kingsley, who was arriving incognito under the name of Ned King. They'd agreed to meet at the inn that evening, and though the meeting was over eight hours away, Cami couldn't stop her nerves from twanging like the strings on an old banjo. Realizing that actually seeing him would probably keep her tongue-tied, she'd prepared a list of questions to ask him.

Restless, she got up from behind her desk and headed to the kitchen for another cup of tea to settle herself. The lobby was full of guests waiting for limousines or vans to pick them up for trips to the different wineries. Inclement weather didn't prevent a visitor from imbibing a sip or two of wine. On days like this, with nothing better to do, more than one guest had stumbled into the hotel at the end of the day and gone directly to bed, their heads spinning.

Cami swung into the kitchen. Liz, was overseeing cooking staff.

"How's the new mother?" Cami asked her, giving Liz a teasing smile.

"Oscar and I are doing fine." Liz beamed at her. "But dachshunds sure are stubborn, aren't they?"

"Oh, yes," Cami replied, remembering all the tussles of will with Sophie. "Okay, if I grab a cup of tea?"

"Sure thing," Liz said and turned back to rolling out pie dough.

Cami carried her cup of tea into her office and turned on the TV for the morning weather, hoping last night's storminess had cleared the way for some beautiful days ahead.

Sighing at the paperwork that lay on her desk, Cami sat and took a sip of the hot tea.

"More on Congressman Edward Kingsley after the break," came the announcer's voice.

Cami groaned, "Not again." She wondered what it must be like for Lulu to hear stories about her father's infidelities. Lulu had defended him so fiercely.

Seconds later, the television flashed a picture of Edward Kingsley on the screen. "Fifty-four-year-old Edward Kingsley is dead of a heart attack he suffered early this morning in Portland, Oregon. Doctors at the Provident St. Vincent's Medical Center assured us they did everything they could to revive the congressman, but it was of no use. An autopsy is planned. Right now, all we know is that he came to Portland to attend a meeting of strategic advisors to deal with the charges he faced. As some of you may know, Congressman Kingsley had hopes of campaigning for president, but in light of the recent allegations, he was struggling to hold onto his office."

Cami's teeth began to chatter as chills ran through her body, numbing all thoughts but one. *Now, I'll never know the truth.*

The screen pulled up a picture of a stately home and showed pictures of Lulu and a pretty blond woman, who was Edward's wife. "We haven't been able to talk to any of Congressman Kingsley's family. His assistant, Paul Gardener, will issue a statement later this morning."

Another series of ads came on the television.

Someone knocked on her door, and Cami turned from the television.

The door opened, and Becca stuck her head inside. "Did you hear the news? Lulu's father is dead! A heart attack." She glanced at the television and then turned to Cami.

"I'm so sorry. I know you wanted to meet him someday."

Cami burst into tears. Her hopes of talking to him were gone. She'd never know if he was her father or why he'd agreed to talk to her. At the deep sense of loss that swept through her body, she felt as if someone had cut her open.

Like a mosquito bite that someone couldn't leave alone, Cami sat in her office watching the bad news on television over and over again, unable to stop the disappointment that kept surging through her. When Paul Gardener came on, he spoke with genuine sorrow.

"Congressman Kingsley's wife, Rosalie Stockton Kingsley, expresses her appreciation for the support that is already coming in for her and her daughter, Louise. She requests that in lieu of flowers, all donations be given to the American Red Cross. Some of you may remember that Edward and Rosalie's only son drowned at the age of ten. Some say it was this sudden loss of her son that has kept Rosalie withdrawn from society."

The television screen showed a picture of Rosalie and Edward together and then a clip of Lulu with her father. Tears came to Cami's eyes when she realized how devastated Lulu must be with all the rumors about her father and then his sudden death.

She picked up a pen and wrote a note to Lulu, not stopping to edit, but simply to tell her how sorry she was and that if she needed a break, she was welcome to use the facilities at Chandler Hill.

Before she could change her mind, she addressed the

envelope, sealed it, and put a stamp on it. Dabbing at her eyes, feeling as if every bone in her body had turned to rubber with grief, she told Sophie it was time to go home.

The little dog, who accompanied her to her office most days, marched to the door and waited for her to catch up.

Glumly, Cami picked up her purse and headed out. The day that had promised so much had turned into a disaster.

When she pulled into the driveway, Drew's silver truck was already there. She felt her throat thicken with emotion. She needed him—his strength, his love.

Sophie barked and wiggled to get out of the SUV. Cami opened her car door and Sophie rushed into her lap to be lifted down onto the ground. As soon as her paws touched the driveway, Sophie was off and running.

Drew caught the dog and lifted her up into his arms. Tail wagging furiously, Sophie licked his cheeks and then wiggled to get down.

Laughing, Drew grinned at her and said, "Next?"

"You haven't heard the news?"

Drew's expression grew serious. "What are you talking about?"

She started to fill him in on Edward Kingsley's death and paused, unable to speak for a moment. Her vision clouded with tears.

"Go on," he urged her. "He was in Portland with supporters and what happened?"

"He's dead! He died of a heart attack! They tried to revive him and couldn't!" Tears slid down her cheeks in woeful, silvery trails.

Drew wrapped his arms around her and rubbed her back. "I'm sorry, hon. I'm really sorry. I know you hoped to talk to him one day."

She pulled away from him. "You don't know the worst part. He was going to meet me here at the inn tonight. He made a reservation under a pseudonym. I was finally going to find out if he was my father."

"What? Coming here? When did you set that up?"

Heat colored her cheeks. "I know I should have told you, but I thought you and Rafe might object."

Drew studied her, his expression thoughtful. Then he slowly nodded. "You're right. I would've discouraged you. Rafe too. And now you have to go through this. I'm sorry, honey."

Cami nestled against his solid chest, wishing there was a better way to get an answer. If Edward hadn't been forthcoming, she'd planned to take a glass or a coffee cup that he'd used and try to get his DNA from that. She already knew Lulu wouldn't cooperate. Especially now.

"Let's go inside," said Drew. "It's hot out here. I've been working in the fields all day, which is why I haven't been near a television. When I got home, I took a shower and came right over here."

She looked up at him. "I've watched hours and hours of the news, stuck to the television like a magnetic screen saver, too interested to walk away. Too disheartened to try."

Drew gave her a squeeze of encouragement. "Aw, Cami, life is full of unanswered questions—'what if' and 'what now' things. It takes a certain amount of faith just to get through a day. Sometimes, it's best to forge ahead and let things play out on their own. You know?"

Cami nodded, but didn't mention that one of the reasons she wanted to know about her father was to have the medical history knowledge he could give her, because she was beginning to think of having children someday. With Drew.

CHAPTER TWENTY-FIVE

O ver the next few days, Cami continued to watch the news for any updates on Edward Kingsley. Lulu had talked about her father's plans to run for president, but Cami had no idea how much of that had already been put into motion. And she wondered how the changes in plans affected Lulu. It was one thing to be a president's daughter, living in the White House, and quite another to be the daughter of a man defamed by his actions. She thought back to Justine's wedding. Lulu had been so self-assured, so in control until Cami had questioned her. Had she known or suspected that something was off with her father? Was that why she'd lashed out at Cami? To protect him?

The press camped outside the Kingsley home hoping for any tidbit they could grab. And when Lulu and her mother refused to meet with them, the rumors started and were perpetuated by speculation and hearsay. Even in these days of irresponsible press reporting, this seemed beyond cruel. Lulu's mother was described as an alcoholic, her daughter as a spoiled brat. Cami fumed at the portrayals. Lulu had graduated from college, and, as Cami had overheard at the wedding, was planning on taking a break as a substitute teacher to work on her father's campaign. And even if Lulu's mother had a drinking problem, it wasn't right to make it public.

While the inn was running smoothly and the grapes were

ripening, Cami worked with Adam in the winery, cleaning out barrels, and making arrangements for the harvest and crush. As predicted, it looked like a very bountiful year.

Rafe met with Cami and Drew to work out a distribution of duties while he was away on his river-cruise vacation. He was sticking to his decision to go to Europe ahead of the scheduled cruise to take part in some of the pre-cruise travel specials.

"I just need to be sure everything will be taken care of while I'm gone," said Rafe. He turned to Cami. "You'll handle my personal finances, and Drew will take care of the books for the winery."

"Right," said Drew. "Just like we've talked about."

Cami and Drew exchanged looks. As the time of departure for him grew near, Rafe was both excited and worried about being away.

"I think it's great that you're doing this, Rafe," said Cami.

A smile spread across Rafe's face. "I think so too. I dreamed about Lettie the other night. She and I were sipping wine in a Paris café. Strange, huh?"

"No. Sweet," said, Cami, returning his smile.

Feeling as excited as he, Cami helped load Rafe's luggage into her car. His morning flight from Portland would take him to Seattle and then a non-stop directly to Paris.

Of all the trips Cami had taken to and from the airport, this was one of the most exciting. She felt Nonnee's presence as she slid behind the wheel. The trip she and Nonnee had planned was finally taking place. More than that, she and Drew were being trusted to take over for Taunton Estates Winery. For Cami, it was more than a challenge for doing that; it was an excellent indicator of how the two of them could work together in business. Though neither had brought up the subject of marriage, Cami knew that marriage to Drew would mean working together to maintain both Chandler Hill and Taunton Estates. If they couldn't do it well, the relationship would never last.

Uncharacteristically chatty, Rafe carried on a conversation about the list of things he intended to see in Paris. The Louvre and the Eiffel Tower were right at the top of it. Cami added a few things to his list, remembering how romantic, how wonderful Paris had been when she'd spent time there with Bernard. Despite the disappointment with that relationship, Paris remained one of her favorite places.

Cami pulled up to the curb and waited while Rafe removed his luggage from the car. Turning to her, he waved, his smile wide.

Cami fought the unexpected sting of tears as he entered the terminal. He'd always been a person she could turn to when she needed someone to talk to without judgment. Even more since Nonnee's death. Now, with this gift, he was free to have fun away from the pressures and worries of his business.

Back home, Cami checked in with the inn and then went about preparing dinner. Drew was not only coming for a meal, he was bringing a few of his things to her house so they could try living together for a while.

A bark of excitement from Sophie announced Drew's arrival. Smiling, Cami went to meet him.

Drew set Sophie down beside his suitcase and swept Cami into his arms. "This is how I want to end all my days." His lips met hers, soft and demanding, sending excitement racing through her. His kisses never failed to arouse her. And now, he was hers to enjoy with a new freedom.

When they pulled apart, they simply stared at one another. Then, without a word, they headed for her bedroom. Sophie followed, her feet tapping the wooden floor behind them.

When they reached the room, Cami stared down at the dog.

"No, Sophie. You stay here."

The dog looked from her to Drew and back to her again, then lay down with a soft groan.

Cami and Drew smiled at each other. In the several weeks they'd been together, Sophie had learned they meant what they said.

Inside her bedroom, Cami turned to Drew. "Welcome home, dear."

He chuckled at her humor. "Music to my ears." He lifted her into his arms and carried her over to the bed. "Now let me show you a proper welcome."

Cami's body grew hot with anticipation. Drew was such an exciting, generous lover.

Later, lying naked beside him, Cami traced the planes of his muscled chest with her fingertips. Brown hair was lightly scattered across his skin. Placing her hand over his heart, Cami could feel the wild thumping of his heartbeat begin to slow. Their lovemaking was free. And afterwards, Cami liked cuddling with him while they talked softly to one another.

Drew looked at her and grinned. "So far, day number one of living together has been great."

"So far?"

"We still have a few more hours to go." He wiggled his eyebrows playfully.

Cami laughed and welcomed him into her arms.

Later, after a hastily put together dinner, they worked to settle Drew's things in the closet, a couple of designated drawers in her bureau, and in the bathroom.

"Looks like everything fits," said Drew. He placed his sneakers on the floor of the closet and gazed at the shelves filled with her shoes. "You think you have enough shoes?"

She bit her cheek. She studied the footwear, lined up in varying colors and shapes. "I need them all. Each pair is meant to go with a specific outfit either for work or for casual times."

He shook his head. "Women and shoes. I don't get it."

Cami lifted her hand. "Hold on. You brought a tool box here, along with your tool belt?"

"Yeah, well you never know when I might need them," Drew protested.

She arched her eyebrow at him. "Case closed."

They looked at each other and laughed.

Living together was a great idea, Cami thought, watching Drew and Sophie play fetch on the front lawn. It had taken her a few days to get used to the way the bathroom looked after Drew took a shower, or how his clothes never quite made it to the hamper. In return, though, Drew helped her with the cleanup after dinner and was becoming very proud of his grilling capabilities. And, of course, Sophie loved him and the extra attention he gave her.

Things at the inn were good too. Laurel was handling weddings nicely, Imani had become an indispensable part of the team, and Becca was her right-hand person whom she could trust with almost anything. For the first time in months, Cami felt herself relax in her role. And when a postcard arrived from Rafe telling them he was having a wonderful time, Cami decided it was time for a little vacation herself.

Sitting on the deck with Drew one night watching the sun set, Cami turned to him.

"Let's go to the coast for a couple of days. The wedding party at the hotel will be gone by noon on Monday. We could leave that afternoon and come back Wednesday morning. What do you say?"

"I like the idea, but only if I can get Rafe's nephew to be on site."

"He lives right there," Cami said, confused.

"I mean handling the tasting room as well as overseeing the office." Drew gave her a thoughtful look. "I'm wondering if Taunton Estates Winery shouldn't expand the tasting room by offering more than snacks. Maybe a regular lunch, someday."

"It's something to think about. But can it wait until Wednesday afternoon?"

He chuckled. "I'll let you know. In the meantime, we can have our own stay-cation here. Come here, Cami." He set down his glass of wine and patted his legs.

Smiling, she hurried over to him and settled in his lap. She loved the way he held her, giving her a sense of protection at the same time his kisses made it clear how much he'd like to see her undressed.

Cami sighed and got to her feet. "If you want dinner, I'd better get to work. You're grilling salmon tonight, OK?"

"That'll be fine. I'll use a little flavored olive oil and seasoning rub and then I'll serve it with a lemon wedge."

"Sounds delicious. I'll take care of the salad and garlic bread." As Cami walked away, Sophie made a dash for Drew. Cami knew without turning around that he'd picked her up. They were so adorable together.

The anticipation of a mini vacation with Drew kept Cami busy as she went through the weekly financials. Though she checked numbers daily, she liked to track weekly figures for future planning. August was a busy month, but the best wedding months were February, June, and September.

When the intercom buzzed, she paused. "Yes? What is it?"

"Are you free? I need to show you something," said Becca.

Cami knew from the sound of Becca's voice that the news wasn't good. "Okay. I'm here."

A few moments later, Becca marched into Cami's office and slapped down a magazine on top of Cami's desk. "Better read this."

Cami opened the local travel magazine to a page marked A Dream Wedding and stared at a picture of Bernard, Vanessa, and a young woman Cami recognized as one of Justine's bridesmaids. Her stomach tightened.

Nan Richards was a pretty girl whom Cami remembered as being competitive with the others in Justine's wedding party. She'd overheard Nan make a few statements about who had the best tan, the nicest dress for the wedding, and other petty details Cami had thought silly at the time.

She read the article with growing dismay. Nan was quoted as saying the wedding planning at the Lone Creek Winery was the easiest and classiest in the valley. She went on to say she'd been in a wedding party at another known wedding venue in the area and compared to it, Lone Creek Winery offered the best advice and the most for the money. She explained both Vanessa and Bernard had helped her plan and execute a wedding with an elegant European flair. Descriptions of wedding details were offered, and then the article ended with this quote from Vanessa: "A dream wedding is what every woman wants. Here at Lone Creek Winery we strive more than others to give our bride and groom everything they need to make their day special." Nan was then quoted as saying: "Older properties tend to do the same thing over and over. Try something new, something better, and make your wedding dreams come true." It showed Nan in a beautiful, white dress with a lace veil and kissing a nice-looking man.

Studying the photograph, Cami shuddered. It was a picture of a perfect bride and groom set against a background of flowers on an oversized trellis that looked exactly like the one Cami had had constructed at Chandler Hill.

"Well, what do you think?" said Becca, pacing the room. "What an ungrateful, backstabbing bitch! I got Vanessa the job, and she's turned on us."

"I think we need to call the editor of the magazine and arrange for her to come see us. It's time we got a little more publicity anyway. And with the governor's daughter booked for a late September wedding, we have plenty of ammunition with which to fire back. After you make that call, why don't you phone Justine? I'd like to hear what she knows about the wedding that took place at the same time as Samantha's wedding here. I bet there's a lot more to the story than this."

A slow grin spread across Becca's face. "Sounds like a plan. I like it."

After Becca left, Cami leaned back against her chair and let out a long sigh. All the training and insight Vanessa had been given at Chandler Hill was now being used against them. And Bernard? He'd do anything to get back at her for refusing to become involved with him. He was that kind of guy. She wondered how she could have been so stupid not to have seen that earlier.

Fighting frustration, Cami turned back to her computer. Imitation might be a form of flattery, but she hated it had come to this.

Monday morning was bright and clear with a promise of more days like it to come. As Cami bid goodbye to the parents of the bride, she held back the urge to do a little dance. As soon as she could get packed, she and Drew would leave for the coast. Becca and Dan had agreed to stay at the house to take care of Sophie.

The rugged Oregon coast along the western edge of the state had three regions: north; central; and south. Cami had opted for the city of Cannon Beach in the north with its long, sandy beach, shops, and restaurants. But, really, she didn't care where they stayed. Any place with Drew would be special. Away from the pressures of their work, they'd have a better opportunity to get to know each other in a different setting.

They left McMinnville and headed for the coast. Taking the coastal route would be a little slower, but it would give them the chance to see the Central Coast too. Maybe they'd even buy some Tillamook cheese to take with them. In the Cannon Beach hotel she'd booked, they'd be able to gaze at Haystack Rock. If they were lucky, they'd see the tufted puffins nested on the rock. Spring was the best time to see them because, during mating, their gray bodies brightened with color. But now, in late August, the puffin chicks would be ready to fly to open sea with their parents. She'd brought along her binoculars hoping to see them.

Cami smiled at the memory of Nonnee's delight at the birds on a trip they'd once taken to the coast. Never one to miss teaching Cami a life lesson, she'd pointed out how fast and furiously the stocky birds had flapped their wings to keep themselves aloft. "Just when life seems to be dragging you down, darling girl, you need to flap your wings as hard as they're doing. Don't ever give up. Hear?"

Recalling that moment, Cami filled with determination. No matter how much competition the inn faced, she'd work to succeed. And it if meant flapping her "wings" like a puffin, by damn she'd do it.

"A penny for your thoughts," said Drew turning to her for a moment.

Cami smiled at him. "If I said I was thinking about puffins, what would you say?"

He laughed and reached over and squeezed her hand. "By the look on your face, I'd say you're thinking about a whole lot more than birds. Want to talk about it?"

Cami shook her head. "It can wait." She had no intention of ruining this special break with Drew with talk of troubles.

They stopped at a little seafood restaurant and brewhouse north of Tillamook. The red-painted door on the rustic building sided with weathered, gray clapboards beckoned them inside.

"Is the bar okay? The tables look pretty full," said Drew, standing inside the doorway.

At her nod, he led them to the bar.

The bartender greeted them and handed them menus. "Hi, folks. What can I get you?"

"I'll have the local pale ale," said Drew. "How about you, Cami?"

"The same." She studied the menu. "Mmmm ... I'm going to have a bowl of clam chowder. I'm saving crab for tonight."

"Guess I'll have a cup of that and a fish sandwich," said Drew. "Love all this seafood right off the boats."

Sitting at the bar with him, Cami saw Drew as a stranger might. With caramel-colored hair and light-brown, alert eyes, he reminded her of a lion. She smiled at the thought. In many ways, he was her protective lion. Strong and kind, he boosted her self-confidence when she sometimes felt overwhelmed.

Their food came quickly and efficiently. As Cami savored the creamy chowder, she drifted into and out of the conversations going on around them. It felt marvelous to just float along in a state of contentment, knowing these people were not about to make demands on her. They were not her guests, and she was not responsible for their happiness.

CHAPTER TWENTY-SIX

The hotel wasn't fancy, but that suited Cami just fine. She wanted simple. After they unpacked and settled in, Drew said, "C'mon! Let's take a walk on the beach."

Cami grabbed a light sweater and headed outside with Drew. Puffy clouds, like dollops of whipped cream on a sea of blue-gray, drifted across the sky, playing a game of hide and seek with the sun. Though the weather was pleasant along the shore, the temperatures were moderate—in the low seventies—and an onshore breeze made it seem cooler when the sun was hidden by the clouds.

Cami breathed in the salty air and let out a happy sigh. The smooth sand beneath her bare feet was warm from the sun. Seagulls swirled in the air, their gray and white bodies circling above them as they called to one another with raucous cries. Cami recognized a couple of black oystercatchers walking along the shore in search of unsuspecting candidates for their meals. She'd always admired their solid black bodies, bright red beaks, and pink legs. Most of all, she was fascinated by their eyes, which had a bright yellow iris and red eye-ring.

They were only one of a number of shore bird species in the area searching tidal pools and the edges of the water for mollusks and other tidbits.

Drew took her hand.

She smiled at him, and they headed south to get a closer look at Haystack Rock. Its craggy surface rose from the water, a huge reminder of the volcanic lava that had formed it and the more than two thousand other stacks along the coast. She knew that because it had been a science quiz question in the fourth grade.

Because of the low tide, Cami and Drew were able to walk to the base of Haystack Rock. Above them seagulls squawked, and puffins flew in and out of the grassy coverings hiding their chicks. Suddenly a large number of seabirds took flight from the rock, circling nervously as a bald eagle glided above the surface of it, looking for an easy meal.

"Wow," Drew murmured softly. "Nature is putting on a show for us."

They stood silently, watching the eagle until it flew away in search of another meal. With its departure, birds flew onto the rock once more and resumed their noise as if this threat had never occurred.

Cami followed Drew back to the sand, and they headed in the opposite direction toward a bar Drew had read about. The sun was lowering in the sky, and though it wouldn't set for another two hours, the clouds at the horizon had captured some early pink coloring.

At the Whale's Tale bar, they found seats on the outside deck and sat among the group of tourists exclaiming over the nice weather and the beauty around them. Cami liked being reminded of such things. Living at Chandler Hill where every scene seemed worthy of a postcard picture, she realized she'd forgotten how to relax enough to simply enjoy her surroundings.

"Nice spot," said Drew.

"It's gorgeous," agreed Cami. She lifted her glass of pinot noir in a salute to him. "Hopefully, the weather will hold."

His brow furrowed. "We've had so little rain, I'm beginning to worry about the grapes."

"I think we're going to have an early harvest."

"Looks that way. I didn't say much to Rafe about it because

I didn't want him to have an excuse to cancel his trip."

Cami lifted her glass. "Here's to him and a fantastic harvest!"

Grinning, Drew clinked his wine glass to hers. "Yes!"

Sitting comfortably, finishing the last of their selection of appetizers, Drew said, "I'm ready to go back to our room. Are you?"

"Yes. I'm beginning to be so relaxed I don't want to do anything else."

"Anything?" Drew teased.

She laughed. "We'll see."

Later, in their hotel room, Cami stretched like a well-fed feline. She'd found she had a lot more energy than she'd thought. She turned to Drew lying beside her. "I love you, Drew."

He brought her closer to him. "Love you, too."

Cami knew from his experience with Vanessa, he wouldn't say anything about marriage, but still she wanted to know where she stood with him. "Do you think ... Where are we going with this?"

He rolled over on his side and cupped her face in his hands. "I love you, Camilla Chandler. I really do. But I'm in no position to ask you to marry me. Not yet. I'm working on a couple of plans, and then I'll be ready, if you are."

"What plans? You'll still work for Rafe, won't you? He needs you. I need you."

"I'd like property of my own," Drew said. "Rafe and I have talked about my buying a section of land but I want more than that. I intend to talk to him about it after he returns from vacation."

Cami desperately wanted to be able to tell him about Rafe's

plans, but she couldn't. She'd promised to keep it a secret.

Drew broke into her silence. "Hey, sweetheart, trust me. I'm not about to break your heart. You're too precious to me."

"I know," Cami said, wishing she felt more secure about their relationship. Bernard had dumped her in a hurry, and though Drew was a much different man, he could change his mind about her too.

The next morning Cami was deep asleep when she was aroused by something tickling her cheek. She brushed it away. "No, Sophie. Not now."

She felt a tug on her earlobe. "Better wake up, Sleepyhead. It's another beautiful day."

Cami groaned, rolled over and faced Drew. He grinned at her. Wearing a white tee-shirt and cut-off jeans, and with his hair still wet from a shower, he looked ... well ... delicious.

Her smile grew wider when she realized he was holding a cup of coffee out to her. She sat up. "You sure know how to wake someone up."

He laughed. "You were sleeping so soundly, I didn't want to disturb you. But it's nice outside and this is our only full day here at the beach."

She took a sip of the steaming hot liquid he'd offered her and let out a sigh of satisfaction. Sunlight streamed through the blinds on the sliding-glass door in tempting, lemony stripes that promised more of the same. Her thoughts turned to the inn. Normally, the first thing she'd do after getting up was to check for messages and take a quick look at the numbers. She pushed those thoughts aside and patted the bed beside her. The first thing she was going to do today was give Drew a morning kiss he'd remember. She set down her coffee cup and nestled in the arms he held out to her. At home, they'd each be doing a different task, but this was vacation, and she wanted to enjoy it.

After a lazy breakfast, Cami and Drew took a long walk on the beach. Sun glistened off the waves rolling into shore, shore birds scurried along the hard-packed sand at the water's edge, and in the distance Haystack Rock was a majestic presence.

Cami had been to the beach plenty of times, but it had never seemed as magical as it did right then. They ambled across the sand. She knew from her old science class that the tidal pools here were special because of the gifts from the sea they held. In addition to the red, green, and brown algae, the pools were home to limpets, sea urchins, and other species.

Standing beside Drew, Cami studied one of the tiny pools. "Look! A sea star! My favorite! And it's a sign of good luck!"

"Cool," said Drew, squatting for a better view.

"Because Coos Bay and Sunset State Park are among the best places to find things like this, it's special to find such a treasure here."

Drew stood and tugged her to him. "Look what a treasure I've found."

Cami laughed and gave him a quick hug. "Corny, but cute."

They continued on their way, and then Drew broke into a jog. Holding her arms out to the sky, feeling as free as the birds whirling above her, Cami took off running behind him.

Later, sitting on the outside deck of one of the restaurants in town, Cami felt more relaxed than she had in years.

"Having a good time?" she asked Drew.

He grinned. "Yes. It's a beautiful area."

"Wish we could get to Tillamook Rock Lighthouse. I bet the views from there are spectacular."

"At one mile offshore, not much to see except the

coastline," Drew commented. "Still it would be fun to see."

"How about meandering around town this afternoon? I'd like to pick up a book at the book store and check out some of the art galleries. Does that sound okay?"

Drew shrugged. "Sure. we have some time to kill. Dinner reservations aren't until seven."

After finishing their meal and paying the bill, Cami and Drew headed out. At each art gallery, she attempted to speak to the owner. If they weren't available, she left her business card and an old flyer of the art show at Chandler Hill.

"The more people we can get interested in it, the better it will be," Cami explained to Drew who'd chosen to sit outside one of the stores on a bench.

"Take your time. I'm not going anywhere except maybe to the pub for a cold beer."

She laughed. "Okay, I'll meet you there. I have one more person to see." The owner of the Pink Puffin Gallery, Iris Cowell, was someone she knew from her previous visits to Chandler Hill. It was especially important to Cami to invite her to participate in next year's show.

Cami entered the gallery and stopped to gaze at her surroundings. Colorful artwork and handcrafted items met her eyes from every space inside—on the walls, in cabinets, and on shelves. It was, she decided, like stepping into a rainbow.

Iris saw her and waved. Leaving customers to browse under the watchful eyes of an assistant, Iris came over to her. "Cami! I haven't seen you in ages? How are you?"

Cami gave her a quick hug. Not much taller than her grandmother, Iris was a warm and shining presence with her alert green eyes and ready smile. "I'm fine. How are you? We've got to get you back to the Chandler Hill Inn. In fact, that's why I'm here."

As Cami explained about the art show she was arranging for next summer, Iris' smile disappeared and a frown creased her forehead. "Oh, my dear! I just made arrangements with the Lone Creek Winery for an art show to be held that very same weekend."

Cami felt the blood leave her face and then rush back in a hot flood of color. "The Lone Creek Winery? The very same date?"

"I'm afraid so. Vanessa Duncan sent out an invitation last week and when she phoned me today, I agreed to do it."

"But I'd already planned the show at Chandler Hill. She's stolen another one of my ideas." Cami felt like throwing up.

"I'm sorry. Why don't you plan to have your show before hers?" Iris said, looking contrite.

"It's too late. I've already signed up some of the artists who showed this year. I can't change the date now. It's the only weekend a lot of them have free."

"Why don't I call Vanessa back and explain to her that I'm going to appear in your show and suggest she change her date to sometime in the late fall?"

Cami felt the sting of tears. "You'd do that for me?"

"Yes, for you and for Chandler Hill. Your grandmother did a lot to promote my work when I was struggling to set up a business. Now it's my turn to repay that debt."

Cami hugged Iris. "Thank you! I've been fighting a battle with the people at Lone Creek. They're out to make my life difficult. Competition is one thing; this is very different."

"Hmmm. I saw the article about weddings at Lone Creek. It sounds like they're doing a great job. Vanessa mentioned to me they're trying a new concept for the outdoors people who want a different kind of wedding. They're building a luxury campout for the bride and groom to be used after the celebrations at the winery. A clever idea."

Cami reluctantly nodded. "She's good at her job, but she shouldn't try to get ahead by hurting us."

"She confided that her fiancé is about to become the owner of the property. Maybe that's why her actions are as aggressive as they are."

Cami's mind spun. *Bernard had proposed to Vanessa? The deal with Bernard's group to purchase the Lone Creek Winery was going through? What next?*

Iris placed a hand on Cami's arm. "Don't worry. Chandler Hill has been in business for a long time."

"But they're making it sound as if we're old-fashioned and boring," Cami blurted.

"The only way Chandler Hill could be called old-fashioned is the way you bring class to what you do, my dear. The people who come to you for rest, relaxation and, yes, weddings, know what excellent service you provide. No one can copy that."

Cami didn't think it was that simple. Rod Mitchell had clashed with Nonnee, and now Bernard and Vanessa were doing everything they could to undermine her. In her mind, she could see Nonnee's face and hear her voice. "Remember, you are a Chandler and a Lopez." She straightened. "Let's talk about my art show and then you can make your call to Vanessa."

CHAPTER TWENTY-SEVEN

As she and Drew drove back to Chandler Hill the following day, Cami wasn't surprised to receive a phone call from the Lone Creek Winery. However, she'd thought it would be from Vanessa, not Bernard.

"Cami, you're asking for trouble," he said, his French accent pronounced by anger. "Vanessa has told me what you have done about her art show. Be careful. We don't want anyone to disrupt our plans for the future."

"You mean your attempt to buy the Lone Creek Winery?"

"Who told you that?" Bernard asked, caught off guard by her remark.

"I'm not at liberty to say," said Cami. "And by the way, congratulations on your engagement to Vanessa. I'm sure the two of you will be happy together." She forced herself to keep from sounding snide.

"Is that another of your rumors?"

"She's calling you her fiancé," said Cami, wondering if Vanessa was pushing this relationship too far, too fast, as she'd done with Drew.

"We've talked about it in passing, but nothing is official. That's beside the point of this call. I'm warning you that if you try to pull another stunt like the one you did for the art show, I'll make sure you never get a starred review for the inn again," Bernard said with enough growl to make her believe him.

She clicked off the call and glanced over at Drew driving the car. "Bernard is upset about the art show, and he says he's not officially engaged to Vanessa. I'd hate to see her get hurt by that cad." She and Bernard had once talked about marriage too.

"After all Vanessa has done to ruin your business, I'm surprised you even care," said Drew.

Cami remained quiet. She'd been deeply wounded by the insensitive way Bernard had dumped her. And even if Vanessa was someone she didn't like, she wouldn't want any other woman to be treated like that.

Once back at the hotel, Cami hurried into her office to see what she'd missed. A stack of messages and colorful notes awaited her on top of her desk. She quickly leafed through them then called Becca, Gwen, and Laurel to arrange a meeting for the next morning. She'd been gone only two days but a lot had happened. A child running in the swimming pool area had slipped and fallen on the pool deck, requiring a couple of stitches in his chin. Even though the child was technically at fault for running, the inn would take care of any expenses not covered by insurance. One of their restaurant hostesses had been placed on bedrest for the remainder of her pregnancy, leaving an important post vacant. Another employee working in The Barn had quit to go to work for Vanessa.

On the plus side, a last-minute fall wedding had been booked by the great-granddaughter of a well-known movie actress. Though it would involve extra work to make the occasion perfect, it was an important contact.

The next morning, Cami sat in her office with Becca, Gwen, and Laurel. "There's a lot we need to catch up on," said Cami. "Thanks for handling things while I was gone."

"I found out something interesting," said Becca. "I've followed up with your request to keep an eye on the property next door. One of my spies at Lone Creek Winery told me that they're planning a special venue for outdoorsy couples who want an entirely different kind of wedding. They're erecting a fancy, upscale tent for the wedding couple. Gourmet food, excellent wine, and candlelight will be part of the luxurious setting and service."

"Yes," said Cami, irritated all over again. "Iris Cowell at the Pink Puffin Gallery in Cannon Beach told me that when I went to sign her up for the art show. That's how I discovered Vanessa was planning an art show for the same date next summer as ours. It's another of her attempts to make things difficult for us."

"Whaaat?" Laurel shook her head. "When is this nonsense with the competition going to stop. Doesn't she realize we'd all do better to cooperate?" As head of the wedding department Laurel Newson wasn't about to be on the losing end of any contest. Smoothly competent, she privately fussed and fumed each time she lost a bid for a wedding.

"I'm afraid she doesn't get it," said Cami. "What's more, she's under the impression that she and Bernard are engaged. She's calling him her fiancé, but when I talked to Bernard, he said they'd merely talked about it. I'm afraid she's in for a big disappointment."

"The two of them alone are bad, together they're impossible," grumbled Gwen. "I shudder each time one of them comes into The Barn. I know they're looking for ideas to make their own, but I can't ask them to leave."

"No," agreed Cami. "You're doing such a great job of managing The Barn you tempt them."

Gwen shook her head. "Bad news, those two."

"Vanessa may be trying to hurt our wedding business, but

it's not working. We're holding steady," said Laurel. "Sometime this fall, we're getting an article in the magazine that featured Lone Creek Winery. And I left you a message regarding the Silverstone wedding."

Cami held up the note. "Thanks. Fill me in on the details."

"Allison Silverstone, whose father is a big producer in Hollywood, is flying in from L.A. this afternoon. She wants to meet you and go over the plans. The wedding is to be a small, private one without any paparazzi around."

"Why here?" Cami asked. "We have lovely weddings, but she could go to Paris or Italy or any other place in the world."

Laurel's blue eyes sparkled. "She said there's a special story behind her decision to use Chandler Hill for her wedding. That's why she's flying up here today, your first day back on the job."

"Excellent!" said Cami. "Can't wait to meet her." She turned to Becca. "The report concerning the poolside accident has been completed for our lawyer and insurance company?"

Becca bobbed her head. "The accident should never have happened. The little boy was out of control, splashing people in the pool, running on the pool deck, and being obnoxious. His mother did nothing to stop him, simply kept on reading her book. You know, one of *those* guests."

Cami groaned softly. Not all guests were pleasant to be around. "And what about the replacement in the dining room? Any luck on finding a new hostess?"

"We can use Bess temporarily, but she can only work two of the four nights we need her. I've called Rose at Nick's to see if she's available." Becca shook her head. "This is such a bad time of year to be trying to find new help."

"Tell me about it," said Gwen. "Thankfully, my staff will cover for the salesperson Vanessa stole from us. But if she takes any more of my people, it would hurt us."

"Have any of you heard rumblings from the staff regarding any possible problems?" Cami studied the faces of the three smart, loyal women she not only respected but had grown to love.

"The temporary staff I use for weddings can be a little iffy about their time commitments, but the core of them are reliable," said Laurel.

"Let's hire extra help for the upcoming wedding," said Cami. "This could be an important one with a lot of good experience for us."

After receiving a call from the front desk, Cami headed into the lobby area to welcome Allison Silverstone. From a distance she admired a tall, thin woman with blond, almost white hair dressed in skinny white jeans and a billowy turquoise top talking to the desk clerk. The rolling piece of Louis Vuitton luggage at her feet was slightly battered, indicating travel.

"Welcome to Chandler Hill Inn," Cami called, stopping in surprise when Allison turned to her and smiled. Allison's eyes were a startling, stunning green.

Hand held out, Cami moved forward mesmerized by the color of those eyes.

"You're Camilla Chandler," Allison said, studying her. "We might have more in common than you think."

"What do you mean?" Cami's gaze settled on the wide smile spread across Allison's face.

"Is there someplace we can talk in private?" Allison said, glancing around the busy lobby.

"Sure. But wouldn't you like to get settled in your room first?"

Allison shook her head. "I'd rather sit and talk."

Putting on her professional smile, Cami said, "Okay. We can leave the luggage here behind the desk. Won't you come with me to my office?"

As Cami walked beside Allison down the hallway, she quietly studied her. Glamorous but not overdone, Allison presented the picture of a sophisticated woman. Cami guessed from the confident, business-like manner in which she handled herself that Allison was in her thirties.

Cami opened the door to her office, indicated for Allison to go inside, and followed her. Allison stood in the middle of the room turning slowly in a circle, taking everything in. Then she walked over to Cami's favorite photograph of Rex and Kenton Chandler. The two of them smiling into the camera were striking in appearance. There was a light in Rex's eyes and an impishness to Kenton that she'd always found endearing. Nonnee had this color photograph enlarged and framed to look very much like a portrait.

Allison reached out and touched the glass that covered the photograph gingerly. She turned to Cami. "This is your family?"

"Yes. Rex was the original owner of the inn and the vineyards. His son Kenton was killed during the Vietnam war era and didn't spend much time here. It was my grandmother, Violet Chandler, who got the inn up and running, along with the winery."

"Ah, here she is," said Allison, studying the photograph of Nonnee. "A striking woman. I can see such strength in her face. Yet, there's a sweetness about her that one couldn't miss."

"Yes, she was both tough and gentle. I loved her dearly."

Cami walked to her desk and waited for Allison to take a seat in one of the chairs in front of her.

After settling in her chair, Allison said, "I've got a story to tell you. It's why I've chosen Chandler Hill Inn for my private, quick wedding away from the shine of Los Angeles. Do you have time to listen?"

Certainly," Cami said. At this point, she wouldn't let Allison leave without telling her.

After Allison had accepted the glass of water Cami offered her, she cleared her throat. "My family has lived and worked in Los Angeles and Hollywood forever. My father, Arthur Silverstone, is a well-known producer. My grandmother, his mother, was married to a film editor respected for his Academy Award winning work. It is my grandmother, Anne Gable, who is responsible for bringing me here. She died recently, and I was given her house and everything in it. In going through her belongings, I came upon some information about my great-grandmother, Darla Rose, an actress in the forties." Allison paused, then studied Cami. "Do any of these names mean anything to you?"

"No, I'm afraid not. I really don't follow all the Hollywood news," said Cami.

"Well, I didn't know that much about my family until I did the work for my grandmother. Maybe it's my upcoming wedding and the baby I'm carrying, but I've taken a sudden interest in my family's history. Much to my parents' distress, I've waited for the right man to come along before marrying anyone." Her smile was charming. "Better to wait than to make a mistake."

"I can see how important this might be to you, but why are you telling me?"

Allison continued. "In my grandmother's old papers, I found a bundle of letters between Rex Chandler and Darla Rose. Apparently, they loved each other, but the studio wouldn't let them marry. Can you imagine? There's no mention of any children, but I thought I'd check with you. I mean, maybe you and I are related!"

Cami shook her head. "I'm sorry, but I don't think that's possible in any case. You see, I carry the Chandler name, but my grandfather was not a Chandler, he's a man by the name of Rafe Lopez, a close friend of Kenton Chandler's. It's something that's almost never mentioned because my mother had a difficult time with it."

"I know Violet, your grandmother, has passed. How about your mother?" Allison asked eagerly.

Cami drew in a long, painful breath. "My mother is gone too. She died in an accident in Africa when I was just six. My grandparents raised me."

"Oh, dear! How awful!" Allison reached across the desk and squeezed Cami's hand. "Thank you for listening to my story. I was hoping to tie up a loose end of history."

"I understand completely. It's something I've been trying to do myself recently."

"Guess we all like to know who we are and where we came from," said Allison giving her a sympathetic look.

"You have no idea how important it is to me. You see, Nonnee, my grandmother, grew up in foster homes and had absolutely no information about her parents. It's different today, but back then it was sometimes impossible to know anything about them."

Allison's gaze settled on her. "I wish there had been some unknown connection between us. I like you already."

Cami grinned. "Me too. Now, we'd better talk about that wedding of yours."

"Yes, even though it isn't real family, I have a connection to the Chandler Hill Inn that feels very nice, as if I belong here and my great-grandmother somehow knows it."

As it turned out, planning the wedding Allison wanted was easy. She was a woman of definite tastes.

"A midweek wedding will suit your needs much better than planning for a weekend," Cami said, grateful once more for the improvements they'd made to the garden, the area around it, and the lawn space outside Chandler Hall. "We can block off the area around the garden, which will give you all the privacy you want for the ceremony itself. The small dining room is available for your dinner, and Chandler Hall is entirely yours, if you so choose."

An hour after filling out the sheet of information for all departments, Cami said, "I think we're all set. Two weeks from today, we'll be ready for you."

"Thanks." Allison beamed at her. "It's going to be perfect. My parents, Graham's parents, my best friend and her husband, and Graham's three siblings and spouses will make up the wedding group. I want the smallest, most non-Hollywood wedding as possible. Luckily Graham has agreed."

"What is Graham like?" Aside from the fact that he was an accountant to the stars, Cami knew nothing about Graham Watson.

The pink flush that washed over Allison's cheeks was telling. "He's a doll! One of my friends told me I was wrong to marry a boring old accountant, but she's been married three times."

Cami easily joined in the laughter and then waited for Allison to continue.

"Graham is forty-five, divorced for many years, and is anything but boring. Besides, I like a down-to-earth guy who's not enthralled with all the fake Hollywood stuff. It's all make-believe, you know."

"I can imagine," said Cami. "I've never been attracted to the rich and famous in that group."

Allison stood and gave Cami a big hug. "We should have been related. It would be such fun to discover a new member of the family."

Cami stood back and smiled at her, hiding her disappointment. She'd hoped for that very thing with Edward Kingsley, and that was never going to happen.

CHAPTER TWENTY-EIGHT

That night sitting on the deck after dinner, Cami held Sophie in her lap. The dog hadn't left her side since she'd come home from the short vacation with Drew. Stroking Sophie's smooth fur, Cami's thoughts turned to the events of the day. She gazed out at the landscape wondering if she'd ever know who her father was.

"You're awfully quiet, sweetheart," Drew murmured, giving her a worried look. "Everything all right?"

She shrugged. "I didn't get the chance to tell you about my visit with Allison Silverstone." She gave him the details. "I guess everyone needs to know who they are and where they come from. The awful part of not knowing is being worried about the worst, or manufacturing something so far from reasonable it becomes a mental game. A destructive one. I can't imagine how my grandmother dealt with not knowing anything about her heritage."

"At least you know who your grandparents and mother are. Then there's someone like me who had a mother who left. As the saying goes, 'You can choose your friends, but you can't choose your family.'"

Cami gave him a worried look. "Do you think I should ask Lulu for a DNA test?"

Drew shook his head. "No. That poor woman has gone through enough. I know you're anxious to learn if there's any connection there for you, but you're going to have to drop it for now and maybe forever."

Cami sighed. "You're right."

As if fate was confirming Drew's viewpoint, a few nights later, as they turned on the nightly news, Cami heard an announcement that sent chills through her. "Rosalie Kingsley, the widow of Edward Kingsley, has been hospitalized after being found unconscious in her home by her daughter. Mrs. Kingsley was treated in the past for a problem with opioids. That is suspected now. The family is asking for privacy at this difficult time."

Cami placed a hand over her heart. "Oh, my God! How awful for Lulu. I'm so relieved I never called her."

"And you hoped you might be part of this family? You're lucky not to be. Poor Lulu," said Drew with a note of sympathy she appreciated.

In the days that followed, Cami's thoughts stayed on Lulu. She took out a piece of notepaper and wrote a brief, but tender message of encouragement to her and again offered her a place to stay should she need to get away.

As before, she slipped it into the mail before she could change her mind.

The days fled. As busy as she was with the inn and the upcoming wedding for Allison, Cami's thoughts turned to the upcoming harvest of grapes. She could hardly wait for the picking and crushing of them. Everyone in the valley was optimistic about its being a superb year.

The day before her wedding, Allison arrived with her fiancé. Graham Watson was anything but boring in appearance. Tall, with short black hair, classic features and a smile that brightened his hazel eyes behind the horned-rimmed glasses he wore, Graham, with his easy smile, won

Cami over right away.

"After you're checked in and settled in your room, give me a call. My extension is 100. We'll meet in my office and go over the notes for the wedding with Laurel. She's been working on the details you've requested."

"Okay," said Graham. "I've got my own notebook with notes."

Cami and Allison exchanged glances filled with humor.

Allison gave Graham a loving squeeze. "I can't do anything without him."

He grinned. "So, I'm a notetaker. That shouldn't be a problem. Right?"

"Don't change one bit," Allison said, giving him a sizzling look that brought a flush of color to his cheeks.

They were, Cami thought, adorable together.

Later, sitting with them in her office with Laurel, Cami realized how proficient Graham was with the details. Allison had very specific ideas about how she wanted things done, and Graham had written every one down.

After the plans had been made, Cami said, "The cocktail party is about to start. Why don't you go have a drink, and you and your guests can relax before your big day tomorrow."

Allison checked her watch. "Mother and Daddy should be here by now. I want them to meet you, and Laurel too. They'll be so happy to be here. It's not every day they finally get their daughter married."

"They almost paid me to do it," teased Graham.

Cami chuckled, but saw the look of love Graham gave Allison.

Cami was struck by how un-Hollywood Arthur Silverstone appeared. Of average height and a bit on the dumpy side, the sharp intelligence in his sparkling blue eyes enhanced his looks. She was pretty sure he wouldn't miss a detail of the setting. His wife, Evelyn, was a willowy blonde who was charming. In preparation for the wedding, Cami had read about them and learned that though Evelyn had the beauty for film, she was too tall to work comfortably with many of the actors. Arthur had been enamored of her from the moment he'd met her. Instead of becoming a star, she married him, became a mother to Allison, and served as a leader in doing charity work for older, retired actors who needed financial assistance. They were a well-respected couple in Hollywood.

It was interesting to see how much they adored their daughter. At thirty-eight, Allison had given them despair over her ever being married and producing a much-awaited grandchild. Now, she was doing both.

The rest of the wedding party was as down-to-earth and humble as Allison and her parents. And when Graham's family arrived, she was amused to see the teasing he got from his three brothers, who ribbed him about being the last to marry. Cami could see how Graham, serious and a bit on the shy side, might have been overwhelmed by his brawny, loud siblings, ten, eight, and six years younger than he. They, their spouses, and Graham's parents joined Arthur and Evelyn for dinner. Allison's friend Sybil and her husband had been caught at LAX with a delayed flight.

Once Cami was assured the wedding party was content with their private party in the small dining room, she slipped away from the inn. Laurel was in charge and doing a great job.

In the hotel business, even the best-laid plans go awry, Cami thought, staring glumly at the still dark sky and hearing the tapping sound of rain on the windows. She wondered how

Allison and Graham would like an indoor garden wedding.

She climbed out of bed and picked up Sophie, being careful not to wake Drew. Though the dog would hate it, she had to go outside. Then, Cami would allow her to sneak back into bed with Drew while she herself took a shower to get ready for work. *Oh, to be the dog!*

Smiling at the thought, Cami stood aside while Sophie did her duty and came trotting back toward her, giving Cami a look that made it very clear she was not amused by being forced out of a warm, comfy bed on such a rainy morning.

As she placed Sophie back in bed, a hand reached out and grabbed her arm. "Where do you think you're going?" said Drew playfully.

She laughed. "I have to get to work."

"Your guests are not going to be up demanding your presence at this time of morning. Come back to bed."

She almost succumbed to the suggestion, then reminded herself that she needed to make sure Allison's wedding party was taken care of. Laurel wouldn't be in until later.

When Cami walked into the inn and saw Arthur sitting in the living room sipping a cup of coffee, she was glad she hadn't stayed with Drew any longer than she had. This was a chance for her to find out more about Rex Chandler, a man her grandmother adored.

"Good morning, Arthur. Did you sleep well?"

He smiled. "Very well. But I'm an early riser. It looks like the weather isn't going to cooperate with us. The weatherman on television said the rain will stop this afternoon, but it's going to remain unusually cool and damp."

"Yes, I heard that too. In the past, with situations like this, we've held indoor weddings in Chandler Hall and they turned out to be beautiful. I'm going to suggest to Allison to do that."

"Guess you need the rain," said Arthur.

"Yes, it's been a mixed summer weather-wise for our guests, though we are expecting an excellent crop of grapes." Cami hesitated then said, "May I ask you a few questions about your family. I understand your grandmother, Darla Rose, and Rex Chandler wrote love letters to one another."

He patted the seat on the couch next to him. "Sit down. I've been wanting to talk to you about it."

Curious, Cami lowered herself onto the couch and faced him.

"After Allison showed me the love letters between Darla and Rex, I did a little investigation of my own. Their relationship remained a well-kept secret through the years, with each marrying someone else." He shook his head. "It's pretty amazing to think of the power of some of the Hollywood studios back in the day. But it's a beautiful love story. I'm thinking of suggesting it as a script for a movie. I gather you're the last remaining member of Rex's family. Would you be agreeable to something like that?"

"But I'm not a real member of the family. Not by blood anyway," said Cami, aware how her mother must have felt when she'd first been told that Rafe, not Kenton Chandler, was her father.

"Still, through your grandmother, you've inherited all that was his, including his name," persisted Arthur. "I'll have my lawyers look into it, but I need to know how you would feel about doing a project like that."

"I'm inclined to say yes, but I need to talk to my grandfather. Then I'll get back to you. What about Rex's ex-wife?"

"She's not alive, and with Kenton being their only child together, the issue becomes moot."

"I'd love to see the letters someday."

He smiled. "I can arrange that. They're really quite lovely."

"Thanks. Done tastefully, it could be a very special story. Nonnee often talked of Rex and how special a person he was." Cami rose and shook hands with him. "I'll get back to you on that. Now, I'd better see to your daughter's wedding."

He chuckled. "Anything she wants is fine with me. Evelyn and I have waited a long time for this."

As Cami headed to the kitchen she thought of families, how different some of them were. She wished she'd gotten more information from Nonnee, but each time questions had arisen they'd remained swamped by a sea of unknown facts.

CHAPTER TWENTY-NINE

Having the wedding indoors proved to be an inspired solution to the unpredictable weather outside. Cami stood in the shadows off to the side observing the small group as they settled in a semi-circle around Allison and Graham. The flower-bedecked altar, the soft music, and the muted lighting in the small section of Chandler Hall that had been blocked off made the perfect background for the live trees and pots of flowers that had been brought in for the occasion. In the rafters above, twinkling lights added a nice touch to the space. When not in use for weddings, the potted trees and flowers were spread around the property.

Cami listened as the minister began the service. As she did each time, her eyes welled. She thought of Drew and wondered when she might hear those words for her. She knew he loved her, but she wished he didn't have so much pride. Yes, she had inherited land, the winery, the inn. But she knew very well he wasn't after her money. Not like Bernard. Besides, he was going to have land of his own someday through Rafe. In the meantime, she needed him to help with hers.

The ceremony was as lovely as Allison herself. Her voice trembled as she recited her vows, and when Allison listened to his vows, her eyes glistened with tears that matched Graham's. Their love was so obvious.

Laurel handed Cami a tissue. "Have one of mine. I've learned to have them ready. Weddings like this always make me cry."

Cami smiled. "Me too. I'm going back to the inn to see to

our other guests. Are you ready there?"

Laurel nodded. "Everything's all set. We'll move them into the small dining room for the dinner. Thank heavens, it's finally stopped raining."

The main dining room was packed. Rainy weather either drove guests away or brought them here in groups looking to add a little brightness to their days. Tonight was one of those nights.

Becca was standing by, overseeing the new hostess they'd brought in. When she saw Cami, she smiled. "Dori's doing a great job. And I've checked the small dining room. Liz is overseeing the service there."

"Very good," said Cami. Liz Bullard liked to handle the service for private dinner parties.

As she was leaving the small dining room, the wedding party headed in her direction.

Allison, wearing an A-line, jewel neck, tea-length dress of white chiffon hurried over to her. The simplicity of the dress gave a stunning effect as Allison seemed to float toward her. "Thank you! Thank you! Everything looked beautiful for the wedding."

Cami returned her hug. "I loved it too. And you look gorgeous!"

"The dress is perfect," Allison said. "My mother and I picked it out."

Cami smiled but a painful pang stung her. She'd been thinking of weddings, but who would help her pick out a dress when the time came?

The days that followed the rain were hot and dry. Some thought too dry. The heat held its breath over the valley adding to the worry about the upcoming grape harvest not being as spectacular as originally thought.

Cami kept busy at the inn. Early fall was an especially busy time for the hotel, and this year, like others, rooms were being filled.

Becca came into her office and plopped down in a chair in front of Cami's desk. Giving her a worried look, she said, "Guess the latest? The luxury tent at Lone Creek Winery is completed and looks great. According to the waitress who went to work there and who is a friend of Dori's, it's the sexiest thing ever. The first wedding of its kind will be held there in two weeks. It's a super deal with one of the travel magazines scheduled to cover the event, which they're calling 'love under the stars.'"

Cami held up a hand to stop her. "Don't worry. There's a time and place for everything. Let's just sit back and see how it goes. I'm not going to try to copy every little thing they do. We're known for classy, upscale weddings, and that's what we do best."

Becca let out a long sigh. "You're right. Every time I see Vanessa, I get upset with her all over again. You think you know someone, and they prove you wrong."

"I know," said Cami with genuine sympathy. "The whole situation drives me crazy, too."

That night, Cami and Drew sat on the deck and discussed the new luxury tent and the wedding program around it.

"You're right," said Drew. "You stick to what you do best. You've always had competition, though it's never been as blatant."

"Do you know how much I love you?" Cami said, rising to her feet and going to him. Clasping his face in her hands, she lowered her lips to his.

With a quick, smooth movement, he pulled her into his lap. "There! Now I have a better hold of you."

Purring softly inside, she nestled up against his chest and inhaled the spicy, sexy smell of him. His heartbeat matched hers. She hugged him tightly, wishing they'd always feel this way about one another.

When his lips met hers and then his tongue did a dance with hers, she told herself not to worry. Each time they were together, it was like this.

Later, after making love, Cami stretched out beside him and fit her body to his. Loving him was such a soul-satisfying thing. He nourished her in a way nothing else could. She thought of Rex and Darla, Nonnee and Kenton, and Nonnee and Rafe. They'd all been great loves, too.

Cami stirred in her sleep, uneasy. Something was not right. She rolled over to her other side and curled up again. She needed her sleep. Tomorrow was another busy day.

Sophie circled and settled down once more next to her.

Drew, as usual, slept soundly.

Cami was drifting at the edge of a dream when that nagging feeling of something wrong came back to her. She looked around sleepily. The house was quiet.

Her eyelids closed again.

She felt a nudge behind her. Sophie whined.

Cami sat up. Smoke!

Heart thumping in her chest, Cami jumped out of bed and raced to the sliding-glass door that led to the outside deck. The sky held an orange glow.

"Drew! Wake up! Fire!"

She grabbed Sophie, raced down the hallway, and stepped outside. The orange-yellow glow was coming from the property to the north of her.

Barefoot, in only an oversized T-shirt, she ran out onto the front lawn. Here the smell of smoke was overwhelming. Flames were visible in the sky and a roar filled the air.

"Oh, my God!" she screamed. "It's Rod Mitchell's place, and it looks like it's heading this way. We have to get out! I have to go to the inn!"

"Hold on! I'll get dressed and drive over there to find out what's happening," said Drew in a smooth, firm voice that quieted Cami. "You call the inn and warn them that there's a fire in the area."

"Oh, my God! What if the fire comes here?"

"Remember, I insisted on making fire breaks around your property and Rafe's. Even so, sparks could cause damage here or at the inn. In case we have to evacuate, pack up your computer and important papers while I go see how bad it is. I'll be right back."

The sound of sirens split the night air, sending a frisson of fear through Cami as she raced to the house. Barking, Sophie stayed right at her heels.

As Cami searched for everything she wanted, she wondered what had caused the fire. They'd had rain a few days back, but the summer had been a dry one. She thought of the rows of grapevines and wondered how they could ever survive. The 2017 wildfires in California wine country had ruined many crops and vineyards.

Trying to hold herself together, she worked quickly to fill a couple of suitcases with papers, photos and items she considered irreplaceable. Funny, she thought, with the many material things she had or had been given, it came down to so few items of true importance. She leaned over, picked up Sophie, and hugged her to her chest.

When Drew pulled his truck into the driveway, she ran

outside to greet him. "What is it? How did the fire start? How bad is it?"

He held up a hand to stop her. "Whoa! One thing at a time. It looks like the fire started in the grove of trees where the luxury tent and facilities were set up. Rumor is that Vanessa and Bernard were spending the night there, fell asleep, and let the campfire keep burning. The wind kicked up a spark and with the dry weather we've been having, sent everything up in flames."

"Oh, my word! Are they okay? Is the house okay? Anybody on the property hurt?" Cami's stomach churned with acid at the thought of someone getting badly burned.

"Everyone is fine. The fire department is getting a handle on the fire. Looks like they won't be able to save most of the vines, but the house is intact and being protected." Drew shook his head. "It's bad, but it could be a lot worse."

"I'm calling Becca and the inn and then heading there," Cami said. "Guests will be upset and I want to keep them calm." She studied Drew. "You don't think I have to worry about things here?"

"I honestly don't think so. Our fire department is joined by two others in the valley. At this point, the fire is contained but will continue burning. I'll stay here. With Rafe's property on the far side of you, I'm not worried about the fire reaching it. But I'll call there to make sure his nephew is aware of everything and will keep an eye on things."

Cami embraced him. "I'll get my things and then leave."

Drew helped her load the suitcases and other items into her car. He leaned in and kissed her. "Be careful. I love you."

"Love you too," she replied. Then she and Sophie took off for the inn.

Even though quick action had tamed the fire, the glowing sky behind her resembled a fiery monster attacking the land.

At 4:00 A.M. inside the inn, guests were sitting in the lobby area, conversing with one another, their faces creased with worry. The night clerk, a young man Gwen had suggested for the job, was in their midst.

Cami walked into the group. "Hello! For those who haven't met me, I'm Camilla Chandler, owner of the inn. I'm sure you're wondering what is going on. First of all, I want you to know you're safe here. The fire is at the Lone Creek Winery, and I'm told it's being brought under control by the capable fire fighters of our local fire department. A few other departments have shown up, as well. Secondly, if any of you have breathing problems, I suggest you stay inside. Our air conditioning system should help keep the indoor air relatively clear, but the air quality outside isn't healthy right now. Last, but not least, we'll be refreshing the coffee service area momentarily for those of you who might not choose to go back to bed."

Cami studied her guests. Many were wearing the white terry bathrobes that were placed in each guest room. Others had obviously hastily dressed with odd combinations of clothes and were looking harried.

Cami turned as Becca rushed up to her. "What can I do for you?" she asked Cami.

"You can help me in the kitchen. We need to set out some snacks and refresh the coffee service area with fresh coffee, bottles of water, and a selection of juices."

In the kitchen, Becca gave Cami a worried look. "Did you hear? Vanessa and Bernard could have been killed. They were asleep inside the tent when everything caught fire. They barely made it out alive. All their personal belongings were left behind in the tent, which is why they couldn't call for help right away. Rod Mitchell made the call to the fire department from his house."

"Were they drinking? Is that why they didn't notice something was wrong?"

Becca shook her head. "I don't know for sure, but I would guess so, which complicates the matter."

"I bet Rod is furious about it," Cami said. Rod Mitchell was nice to his neighbors only when he wanted something. He and Nonnee had fought for years.

"This is going to devastate Lone Creek Winery, not only the vineyards but the wedding business too. And goodbye to the luxury tent idea."

"What a mess. I wonder what will happen to his plans to sell the property?"

"Who'd buy it now?" Becca said. "It's such a shame."

CHAPTER THIRTY

By the time Cami left the inn, breakfast was underway for the guests. Instead of driving home, she went to Lone Creek Winery. A number of cars were parked by the entrance, no doubt belonging to the volunteer fire fighters in the area who must have responded to help the Fire Department. Cami drove up to Rod's house, parked the car, and got out.

Standing on the driveway, she surveyed the land beyond it. Burned and charred vines clung to trellises in straight lines across much of the landscape, marring its beauty. The sight of that hard work gone to ruin made her queasy.

She turned and headed to the front door. Neighbors took care of neighbors in situations like this, even if one of them was as difficult a person as Rod Mitchell.

Rosita Fernandez came to the door. She'd been Rod's housekeeper for years. "Hello, Cami. How are you?"

"I'm fine, but you must be overwhelmed by all that's happened. I'm here to see if there's anything I can do to help. I can have food delivered or, if necessary, offer Rod a place to stay."

"Who's there?" came a deep voice from behind Rosita.

Rod's face was covered with black soot, his hands too. "Rod, I'm so sorry for all that's happened. I'm here to see if there any way I can be of help. Do you need food? A place to stay? Anything?"

He nodded grimly. "I need to borrow some of your people. It's going to take some time to check all the vines for viability. We'll need to assess the pH levels of the soil, remove any burnt patches, check the strength of the trellis support systems, and trim away scorched vines, leaves and branches. It's a hell of a mess out there."

"I'll talk to Adam Kurey about sending a couple of men on his crew to help you. I'm sure others will do the same. Good luck to you, Rod."

"Thanks, Cami." He paused. "For a minute, you reminded me of your grandmother. You look a lot like her, you know, and she would've done what you're doing for me now."

Cami lowered her head, touched by his words. She waved goodbye and walked away, her mind spinning with ideas.

When she got home, Drew was just stepping out of the shower. He wrapped a towel around his waist and gave her a kiss. "Hi, how are things at the inn?"

"Okay. I'm glad I went. Fire and smoke make people nervous, and I was glad I could reassure my guests that they'd be fine. Becca arrived soon after I did and helped me prepare refreshments for everyone. I waited until things were settled into a more normal routine before leaving, and then I stopped at Rod's on the way home."

"How is he?" Drew asked. "I've already committed one of Rafe's staff to help with the cleanup."

"He seemed shaken by all that's happened. I forget how much older he is than Rafe, but he was showing his age. Any news beyond rumors about Bernard and Vanessa?"

"Neither one was around. I understand they each got superficial burns on their hands and arms trying to put out the fire and get their things from the tent. They were sent to the hospital for burns and smoke inhalation."

"What is going to happen to Lone Creek Winery?" Cami asked. "Rod's house escaped flames, but so many of the vines looked terrible."

"One whole section might be ruined, but I think the rest

will be recoverable. And along the south end, there wasn't any damage at all. Still, I can't imagine Rod will get the big buyer he was after."

"I hope whoever buys it will be someone willing to work hard to restore the land," said Cami. "It's a shame. I didn't like the way Bernard and Vanessa were acting toward me, but I certainly didn't wish for anything like this to happen."

Drew shook his head. "Neither did I. It's hard to imagine anyone here in the valley would want to hire either one of them. You know how close knit we all are."

"I think you're right." Even knowing Bernard might be out of her life gave Cami no satisfaction.

She took off her shirt and set it aside.

"Hey! What are you doing?" Drew asked, giving her a sexy grin.

"I have to get cleaned up so I can get back to work."

Drew took off his towel and dropped it to the floor. "Great. I'll help."

Later that week, Cami was putting together Drew's favorite chicken casserole for dinner when he called.

"Hi, I just wanted you to know that I won't make it to dinner. And don't wait up for me. I'll be late getting home."

"Oh? Anything I should know about?"

"Just a lot of details I need to take care of. See you later."

Cami hung up the phone wondering what was going on. She'd started in on the casserole again when Becca called. "What's up? Want to meet for dinner? Dan is working on some special project, and I want some company."

"Come on over. I'm just putting together a casserole, Drew's favorite, and I could use some company myself."

"I'm on my way. Thanks, Cami."

When Becca arrived, she handed Cami a bouquet of yellow sweetheart roses. "Thought I'd share these. They're from Dan for the seven-month anniversary of our engagement. They're too beautiful to leave at home."

"How nice! I'll put them on the table so we can look at them while we eat. How about a glass of wine?"

"As long as it isn't from Lone Creek Winery. Some people are hoarding bottles of it, thinking those wines will never be the same. Silly, huh?"

"Yes, because they weren't that great to begin with. Rod isn't a vintner, and Bernard, for all his big talk, isn't either."

"I heard Vanessa is going back to New York and taking Bernard with her. They're trying to get jobs at some of the upstate wineries in the Finger Lakes region."

Cami shook her head. "Another disaster, no doubt."

"At least having them gone will be better for Chandler Hill."

Cami smiled. "Laurel has received several requests from brides who'd booked with Lone Creek Winery. Though I wish it were under different circumstances, she's excited about it and so am I."

"I can't wait for my wedding. I've brought a couple of pictures of wedding gowns I want to show you."

"How nice!" Cami said, wondering when Drew would think the time was right for him to propose.

Later, after choosing a wedding dress for Becca and enjoying a meal together, Cami realized how important it was for her to have a girlfriend like Becca. Working as hard as she did, it was difficult for Cami to set aside time for evenings like this. She understood as much as she loved Drew, she needed girlfriends too.

After Drew had missed three dinners and had taken a

private trip into Portland, Cami finally confronted him one morning. "What is going on? You keep saying you're taking care of details, but I need to know if it has to do with Rafe's winery."

"Yes and no," he said mysteriously. "I promise I'll be home for dinner tonight. Will you do me a favor and order some Beef Wellington from the inn and one of their special lemon tarts for dessert?"

"What's the occasion?" she asked, studying the smile on his face.

"The details I've been working on. You'll see." He kissed her goodbye and headed out to his truck, whistling.

Cami frowned. It wasn't like him to keep secrets. *Details? What did that mean? They'd talked about expanding the tasting room at Rafe's. Was that what this was all about? Some sort of surprise for him?*

In her office, Cami was still mulling over Drew's activities. After work she'd drive over to Rafe's and see for herself what he might be up to.

Becca entered her office, stopped, and frowned. "What's the matter?"

Cami shook her head. "Oh, it's this suspicious activity of Drew's. He keeps telling me he's working on details. I think I know what it might be. We'd talked about expanding the tasting area at Rafe's."

Becca clicked her fingers. "That's it. Dan has been working on a special project. He won't tell me what it is, but now it makes sense if he's working for Drew."

Cami felt a smile spread across her face. Of course. That's what it was about. The dear man was surprising both her and Rafe.

For the rest of the day, Cami was filled with satisfaction. Drew's project would be a heartfelt gift for Rafe. She did as he'd asked and ordered Drew's favorite dish from the inn. She'd have it delivered around eight o'clock and make sure everything was nice for his big surprise reveal.

CHAPTER THIRTY-ONE

Cami left the inn early. Drew wanted this evening to be special, and she was going to play along. At home, she changed out of business clothes and put on a filmy skirt he'd admired and pulled a cotton sweater over her head. In a shade of seafoam green, the sweater offset the red in her hair and brought out the sparkle in her brown eyes. She decided to wear Nonnee's grape necklace and slid it around her neck, clasping it with satisfaction. Nonnee would love Drew's kindness and the loyalty he showed Rafe.

Standing back, she gazed at herself in the mirror, then went to the kitchen to feed Sophie, who trotted at her heels, barking with expectation.

With Sophie fed, the table set, wine uncorked, and the menu ordered, Cami went out onto the deck to await Drew's arrival. Next week, the harvest of the grapes would begin, and Rafe would be home from his trip to Europe. It had been over a year since Nonnee had died—a year full of angst and self-doubt, of triumph, of finding a true love.

Lost in thought, she was startled by Rafe's voice calling, "Hello."

She whirled around. "What are you doing here?" She ran to him and wrapped her arms around him. "Welcome home! I'm so glad you're back. So much has happened."

"Yes," Rafe said. "I know all about it. Drew has informed me." He patted her back and hugged her close. "I couldn't stay on the trip another day. I missed you."

She looked up at him and smiled. "I missed you too. But I

thought you were enjoying the trip. Didn't you have a nice time?"

"The river cruise was fabulous. But staying an extra ten days was too much. I wanted to be here with you and Drew for the harvest. It should be an excellent year."

Drew approached them. "A good year for many reasons. Let's sit and have a glass of wine, and I'll give you all the details."

At last, Cami thought. She couldn't wait to hear what Rafe thought of his surprise.

While Drew poured the wine, Cami put together a tray of camembert cheese, garlic stuffed olives, and crisp wheat crackers.

After they were all seated on the porch, Drew lifted his glass. "Here's to the future!"

Rafe and Cami responded, "To the future!" in a chorus of excitement.

They'd taken a sip of the wine when Drew set his glass down. "As you know, Cami, and you now know, Rafe, I've been working hard to make something happen. I can now tell you exactly what it is." A broad smile crossed his face and lit his eyes. "Dan Thurston, Rafe's nephew, José, Adam Kurey, and I are now the proud owners of the Lone Creek Winery."

Cami's jaw dropped. "You mean you haven't been expanding the tasting room at Taunton?"

Drew's surprise was equally telling. "What? No. I wouldn't do that without Rafe's permission."

"You want to expand the tasting room?" Rafe asked.

"It's something we talked about," said Cami. She turned to Drew. "It's wonderful news, but what about your work at Taunton Estates?"

"That's why I'm here," said Rafe. "Drew called me, and I told him what I had in mind for him with the Taunton Estates vineyards and winery. It's one reason the bank approved the loan for Lone Creek. Drew will be the major holder of the property. And by combining a lot of the work, both properties can be handled well."

"What about Chandler Hill? Adam is my winemaker." Cami couldn't hide her dismay.

"He's still going to be loyal to you, but he will help me and José with the winery at Lone Creek. With your permission, we'll all be working together."

Cami hesitated only a moment. The three wineries lined up together could do things more efficiently. As long as the quality of her wine wasn't affected, it would be fine.

"Deal," she said, rising to give Drew a hug. "Wow! You've got as much land as you can handle now."

"It's all in the details," he said, laughing at the way she arched her brow at him.

Rafe stood. "Now, if you two don't mind, I'm heading home to sleep in my own bed. Remember, on European time, it's still my bedtime."

Cami walked him to the front door and hugged him tight. "I'm glad you're home. I love you so much."

"Love you too, *cariño*."

"Want me to drive you home?" Cami asked.

Rafe shook his head. "I want to walk the land and make a stop along the way."

Cami knew he was talking about sitting in the special grove of trees with his memories of Nonnee and their time together. "I understand. See you tomorrow."

When Cami returned to the deck, Drew was standing at the railing looking out at the rolling hills. Color from the leaves of the hardwood trees among the pines dotted the hill.

"Beautiful, isn't it?" Cami said, coming up beside him.

He turned to her and smiled. "You're beautiful." He

lowered himself to one knee.

"What are you doing?" Cami asked softly.

"I'm asking you to marry me. Will you, Cami? I want to spend the rest of my life with you, living and loving, growing grapes, and making wine and babies." He opened a small, black velvet box. Inside lay a gold ring with a large, round diamond flanked by two emerald-cut diamonds.

Sophie bounded over to Drew, jumped up on his leg and turned to Cami with questioning eyes.

"Are you two ganging up on me?" With her heart pounding with joy, she was finding it hard to breathe.

"Will you marry me, Cami?" Drew asked, his eyes full of love for her.

"Yes! Yes! I will marry you, Drew Farley, and love and live with you forever and ever."

He rose and pulled her into his embrace. "I love you more than you know, Cami. I promise to make you happy."

"You already have," Cami murmured, lifting her lips to his.

When they finally pulled apart, Drew said, "Let's put off dinner for a while."

She was about to agree when the doorbell rang. Laughing at the timing of the delivery of their dinner, she went to answer it. She'd make sure Drew was satisfied with both dinner and her.

Later, after making love with him, Cami glanced at the ring on her finger. It was gorgeous. But it was only a symbol of the love they shared. She thought ahead to her wedding and wondered as she often had how everything would work out. Surely Rafe would agree to walk her down the aisle. There was so much to be thankful for.

Becca was waiting for her in her office when Cami arrived.

"So, we know now what the project is. Dan is very excited about being a part-owner of a winery. He's already coming up with plans to improve it."

Cami held her hands behind her back and beamed at her. "Drew is excited about it too. In fact, he's asked me to marry him." Cami thrust her left hand out in front of Becca.

"Oh, my God! It's beautiful!" Becca hugged her. "But you can't get married before me!"

Cami laughed. "I won't. I promise. I've waited a long time to find the right man. I want to enjoy being engaged to him. Besides, we're all going to be busy. It's looking like a very good year."

CHAPTER THIRTY-TWO

As Cami had predicted, things became hectic with the harvesting and crushing of grapes. Though the inn was busy, she spent as much time as she could with Adam, testing the grapes, making sure they were being handled properly. And when it came time for tasting, she found she'd inherited her grandmother's palate. Maybe, she thought, in time I can act as the winemaker for Chandler Hill. The future loomed delicious and worthy of tasting.

As Cami was reviewing the weights of the grapes and looking at other data regarding the harvest, Becca burst into the office. "There's someone here you need to speak to. She's checking in right now."

Cami frowned at her. "Who are you talking about?"

"It's someone important to you," Becca said, giving her an impish grin. "Someone named Louise Kingsley."

Cami felt her eyes widen. She dropped the pen she was using and looked up at Becca. "Lulu?"

"Yep. She's checking in for two nights. And, for once, no weddings are scheduled. You should be able to have plenty of time with her."

Cami was unable to stop the flutter of nerves in her stomach. "Maybe she's coming here to warn me again to stay out of her business. Her life is so mixed up right now."

"Maybe she wants simply to take you up on your offer to relax here for a while, like you told me. Whatever the reason, Cami, you need to try to resolve things between you."

Cami nodded and stared out the window, so lost in thought

she failed to see the squirrel busily moving about. *After all Lulu had been through recently, was Becca right about Lulu coming to Chandler Hill to simply relax? Or was Lulu up to more trouble?*

As Cami placed a call to the front desk, her emotions swung from high to low, each positive thought countered by a negative one. *Had Lulu received her notes of condolence? If so, did she consider it a threat of some kind? But then, why hadn't she called?*

"Chandler Hill Inn and Winery. It's my pleasure to serve you," came the voice on the line.

"Please ask Ms. Kingsley to come to my office." Cami wanted to greet Lulu in her own territory.

A knock at the door brought Cami to her feet. Taking a deep breath, she walked over, opened the door, and stared at Lulu standing in the hallway.

"You asked to see me?" Lulu looked young and uncertain, not at all like the confident, outgoing young woman she'd been at Justine's wedding.

"I thought we should talk. Please, won't you come in and have a seat?"

"I received your two notes. That's why I'm here." Lulu's eyes filled. She gazed at Cami with such a forlorn expression that Cami's heart twisted with sympathy.

"Please. Let's sit down." Cami indicated one of the two leather chairs in front of her desk.

As Lulu lowered herself into a chair, Cami took the one facing her and began speaking. "I never wanted to hurt you, Lulu. You or your family. I just wanted the truth. Only that."

Lulu clasped her hands, drew a deep breath, and slowly let it out. "I hope you'll forgive me. I've been awful to you. And now that I'm more or less alone with no one to protect, I need to make that up to you."

"I'm sure you were doing what you thought you should," said Cami softly. "After everything that's happened, I understand."

Lulu shook her head. "You don't know what my father was like. He was a light in a dark room, attracting all sorts of people to him, like moths to a flame. Though he was charming and pleasant, he was driven to succeed at anything he did. He dreamed of doing so much for this country as president. Of course, the way things turned out, that was never going to happen. Not after those women came forward with claims of sexual assault. God! What a nightmare!"

Cami reached over and took hold of Lulu's hand. "I can't imagine what you've been through. First that, then the heart attack, and then your mother. I hope you have a lot of friends around to help you."

Fresh tears filled Lulu's eyes. "A few, not many. It's amazing how something like being publicly shamed exposes other people for who they really are—fair-weather friends. That's another reason I'm here. Even after the way I treated you, you took the time to write to me. Not once. But twice. You deserve more than my thanks for that." She sighed sadly.

Cami waited for her to speak again.

"When I was going through some of my father's papers, I found a letter from Autumn Chandler. I think you should have it." Lulu pulled out a worn envelope from her purse and handed it to Cami.

With trembling fingers, Cami took it.

"You'd better read it," prompted Lulu. "It's important."

Scarcely breathing, Cami opened the envelope and pulled out the plain sheet of white paper addressed to Edward Kingsley. Her eyes caressed every letter as Cami read:

Dear Ed, I hope you are fine and moving ahead

with your plans to do government work. With your blazing smile and determination to carry on good projects, you seem so suited to it. In reading about you lately, I was surprised to learn that you are now committed to marry another woman, someone chosen for you by your ambitious father. We share a daughter from our brief affair, but I won't stand in your way. In order to avoid hurting you or your family, I have decided to end what was, for me, an extraordinary relationship. Please don't contact me again. It's best that way. With love, Autumn Chandler.

Cami looked up from the letter in her cold fingers and through a mist of tears stared at the woman she now knew was her half-sister.

Lulu's tears matched her own. "I swear I didn't know anything about them being together or about him with any of the others. The family lawyer says there are no other children of his. Just us." She lowered her head in her hands and sobbed. "I'm sorry. I'm sorry."

"Hey, it's not your fault," Cami crooned, attempting to calm her. "Both of our parents made those decisions on their own. My mother was very adamant about not telling me or any of the family who my father was. I realize now how much she must have loved him."

"Look at the envelope and the page inside, Cami. They're worn on the edges as if someone had read the note over and over again," said Lulu softly.

They stood and stared at one another, aware of what that meant.

"We're family now. Sort of. Right?" said Lulu hesitantly. "I mean, I have nobody else, not really." A tremor went through her.

Cami wrapped her arms around Lulu. "Shhh. You won't have to be alone. I promise. Come with me. I want to show you something."

They left the inn and walked toward the grove of trees that meant so much to Cami. "I didn't want your father's name, or his money, or anything else," Cami said, looking over the land. "I'm a Chandler and a Lopez, and that's more than good enough for me."

"He wasn't the man I thought he was," said Lulu sadly. "But my father did a lot of amazing things for others. That's what I have to hold onto."

As they walked, Cami thought of families. They weren't necessarily made up of the people who were born into it. Some people left holes behind. Others filled them with new beginnings. She glanced at the younger woman beside her. Maybe Lulu would find happiness here. And peace.

A hawk circled in the sky above them, a brown swirl in a palate of blue. Cami barely remembered her mother, but she felt her presence in that moment. Her mother had been a brave, independent woman—Nonnee's daughter in so many ways.

Cami gazed at the hills around her. She, like Nonnee, had always loved the land. They were alive with the grapevines that lined them, promising rich harvests in more years to come.

She'd come home to keep a promise to her grandmother, and what a gift it had turned out to be. Coming home had provided her with family, the one she had, the one she hoped to have with Drew someday, and the one she'd willingly share with Lulu and others who needed her.

She lifted her face to the warmth of the sun, certain this

was where she should be. Here at Chandler Hill, she and others would thrive because love was such a big part of it.

A soft breeze caressed her cheek. In the whisper of air around her, she heard Nonnee's voice. "Welcome home, darling."

Thank you for reading *Coming Home*. If you enjoyed this book, please help other readers discover it by leaving a review on Amazon, Goodreads, or your favorite site. It's such a nice thing to do.

Enjoy an excerpt from my book, *Home at Last* – A Chandler Hill Inn Book (Book 3 in the Chandler Hill Inn Series.)

CHAPTER ONE

Louise "Lulu" Kingsley sat on the deck of Camilla Chandler's house and wondered how she could be so lucky as to live in a place like Willamette Valley, Oregon. The journey to reach this point was more than painful—it had almost destroyed her. But here, at Chandler Hill, she felt she'd found her true home at last.

Staring out at the rolling hills and the rows of grapevines devoid of their fruit after harvesting, she saw the goodness of the land, its beauty and, most of all, the comforting assurance of more harvests to come. She thought of this continuity of life as a renewal of her own.

If Cami hadn't offered her a place to stay and a job in an entirely new location, Lulu wasn't sure she could have survived the last year of family misfortune and scandal. For anyone who didn't know much about her, they'd think her life as the daughter of a rich, powerful man who'd one day wanted to run for president of the United States was a privileged, easy one. But the man who tied her to her newly discovered half-sister was a man of too many appetites, and it had hurt others, including her ailing mother and her.

The understanding shown by the half-sister she'd never

known growing up meant the world to her. Cami came from a long line of kind, generous Chandler and Lopez families. Living and working at The Chandler Hill Inn and Winery was more than an ordinary situation. For Lulu, it meant finding a loving place in the world, one she'd desperately needed.

"I thought I'd find you here," said Cami, stepping onto the deck and standing behind her. "I love to sit here and gaze out at the land too. It's very peaceful toward the end of the day and, as always, I think of Nonnee. My grandmother's love of the land was the foundation for everything that's been done here with both the inn and the winery."

Lulu turned around in her rocking chair and smiled up at Cami. Not much older than she, Cami's big heart matched her usual smile. Though Cami wasn't as tall as she and had totally opposite coloring, their facial features were astonishingly alike. Among other things, they shared a tiny quirk— misshapen ear lobes, a genetic inheritance from her father. Lulu wished she had Cami's strawberry-blond curls like Cami's grandmother, but her hair was straight and dark like her father's.

"How'd your day at school go?" Cami asked, sitting in a chair next to her.

"Pretty well," Lulu said. "Every kid in the fourth grade tries to act up with a substitute teacher, but I really got their attention when they realized I speak Spanish. My father insisted on that, and I'm glad he did. I'm hoping to be able to volunteer to teach a special tutorial class for second-language students after the winter break."

"Sounds good. Until then, Gwen is very pleased to have you help out at The Barn from time to time. I explained it was temporary only. It won't be long before the holiday season and we'll be crazy busy. Even busier than now. Then we'll all have to concentrate on the upcoming year."

"I love being part of the staff," said Lulu, meaning it.

Cami gave her a sweet smile. "Sweetie, you're much more than one of the staff; you're family now, and we intend to use your marketing and sales skills here at the inn and the other two properties."

A warmth filled Lulu. Being part of a real, healthy family was such a gift. An only child after the death of her younger, ten-year-old brother, she'd always longed for siblings. And though Cami's so-called family consisted of a whole group of people who weren't necessarily related by blood, it was a close-knit group. Cami's grandfather, Rafe, was a wonderful man who'd been very kind to her. They'd formed a bond over the fact that her father and Rafe's daughter, Autumn, had met and fallen in love, producing Cami.

Cami nudged Lulu's arm playfully. "By the way, I think Miguel was disappointed you weren't at the strategy meeting today."

Heat flooded Lulu's cheeks. Miguel Lopez was one of the most handsome men she'd ever seen. Like his great-uncle, Rafe, he had hair so dark and shiny it resembled the wings of a blackbird or the smooth coat of a panther, she couldn't decide which. His straight nose, dark, intelligent eyes, and full, kissable lips had every young girl in the valley swooning in the wake of his sexy butt. The very reasons Lulu had no intention of ever getting involved with him.

"How did the meeting go?" Lulu asked. "Are the three vineyards able to set up a joint purchasing program for supplies, advertising, and other services?"

"We're ironing out details, but yes, it's moving forward. With you about to begin handling the marketing for all three, it simplifies those matters." Cami grinned at her. "So glad you're here."

"Thanks for letting me take the substitute teaching day. I

know how difficult it is to find teachers at the last minute, especially those who speak Spanish. But I know things have been difficult for you lately with the marketing and how much you now need someone to step in and take over a large portion of it for you." She'd been intrigued by the story of how Cami's fiancé, Drew Farley, along with Dan Thurston, Adam Kurey, and José Lopez had ended up co-owners of the Lone Creek Winery after a fire had destroyed part of its acreage. She'd been even more fascinated to learn that Cami's ex-boyfriend, Bernard Arnaud, had taken off with Vanessa Duncan, who used to work on marketing at Chandler Hill.

Sophie, Cami's black-and-tan miniature dachshund, barked and ran to greet Rafe, who stepped onto the deck.

"Hi, come join us," said Cami, rising and pulling a chair over to their group. "The sun will be setting soon, but it's still pleasant outside for this time of year. In fact, I was thinking of trying a new pinot noir release from Taunton Estates." Her eyes sparkled as she teased, "You, as owner, might want to judge it for yourself."

Rafe laughed. "I think I should, especially if it means I get to spend time with my two favorite women." His gaze swept over them, bringing a smile to all three.

It was this kind of banter that Lulu loved most. Rafe was such an honorable guy. In his seventies, he was a quiet man who lived and loved and worked hard. He still mourned Lettie Chandler, Cami's grandmother, who'd passed away over a year and a half ago. She was the love of Rafe's life and always would be.

Cami went to get the wine and glasses, leaving Lulu and Rafe alone. In Spanish, Rafe asked, "How did the teaching go?"

She replied in the same language, "Pretty well. I'm glad I could help, but I don't know how much of that I can do. I'm going to be needed more and more at the inn."

Rafe nodded and switched to English as Cami joined them. "It used to be that things got quiet after the harvesting of the grapes and all the hoopla that went with it. But the Chandler Hill Inn with its spa and special vacation and bridal packages has kept business going throughout these months. Christmas, the New Year, and Valentine's Day are big deals here now."

"I can't wait for the Christmas celebration. I'm hoping to convince my mother to make the trip here. I think it would do her good."

Cami continued pouring the wine into the three glasses. "How is she doing?"

Lulu couldn't hide the sadness in her voice. "With her, I never know. There is no cheerfulness, no excitement about anything. Her depression never ceases, even with the drugs and alcohol I know she's sneaking. I've talked to the doctors about it. They try to discuss other options with her, new medicines and therapies. Heaven knows, she's tried a lot of programs, but nothing seems to work. My counselor has advised me that aside from encouragement there's not much I can do."

"It's so sad," said Cami, setting down the wine bottle on the table and distributing the glasses of wine.

"I'm learning that it's not my job to keep her spirits up and help her stay sober," Lulu continued. "I was made to feel responsible for her after the death of my brother."

"He drowned when he was ten. Right?" Cami said.

"Yes, it changed our lives dramatically," said Lulu. "Nothing's ever been the same since."

Cami rose from her chair and wrapped her arms around Lulu. "I'm so sorry."

Lulu allowed herself a moment to relax and let go. She'd lived with disappointment and pain for so long, it felt unfamiliar to accept this sign of acknowledgement. *If only I'd been there when Eddie decided to go swimming alone at the beach.*

Rafe broke into her musing about the guilt she carried and always would. "Okay, ladies! Let's taste this wine. I'm hoping it's as good as my new marketing director says." His words brought a smile to Lulu.

They'd just proclaimed the wine excellent when Drew arrived. He kissed Cami hello and sank into one of the chairs on the deck with a soft groan. "Ah, it's good to be home. I've been working with Dan on the last bit of cleanup and updating of the house at Lone Creek. He and Becca are hoping to move in next week."

"I'm so happy for them," said Lulu. "I know how excited Becca is to have a house of her own."

"Yes, it's a fair deal all around," Drew said. "They got the house for a good price, and we owners are assured of cooperative people living there after the fire in the vineyards a couple of months ago." He glanced at the glass of wine Cami handed him. "What do you think? Is it as good as I thought it'd be?"

"It's lovely." Cami grinned at him. "I can't wait to get more involved in Chandler Hill wines. Then I'll really test your work."

Rafe laughed. "I knew it was a good idea to put these two up against each other. Both Taunton Estates and Chandler Hill wines are already great, but I suspect they'll be even better with Cami and Drew competing against one another."

Lulu laughed with the others.

Drew turned to her. "We're going to have a big party to celebrate Becca and Dan's moving into Rod Mitchell's old house. Miguel told me to tell you to be sure to come."

Lulu rolled her eyes. It sounded just like him. "I'm

planning on coming to it because Becca has already invited me. She has a teacher friend she wants me to meet."

"I've met Ross Coughlin," said Cami. "He seems very nice, and he's easy on the eyes too." She laughed when Drew arched his eyebrows at her. "Don't worry. You are too."

"Is this Ross Coughlin the young man who started the after-school program at the middle school?" asked Rafe.

"Yes, that's what I've been told," said Cami.

"Good, because in the spring, I'd like to be able to volunteer on my time off," said Lulu. "I enjoy being with the kids."

"You're so good with the kids who come to the inn," said Cami. "I really admire that."

"Thanks." Lulu hadn't told anyone this but working with the kids at school made her feel as if she was making amends for the time she'd let her younger brother down. She'd talked to a psychologist about it and knew it wasn't her fault that he'd drowned, but she always felt better after being with other kids who needed her attention.

As for herself, she wasn't sure she wanted children of her own, not when it required making sure they were safe from all the dangers of the world.

About the Author

Judith Keim enjoyed her childhood and young-adult years in Elmira, New York, and now makes her home in Boise, Idaho, with her husband and their two dachshunds, Winston and Wally, and other members of her family.

While growing up, she was drawn to the idea of writing stories from a young age. Books were always present, being read, ready to go back to the library, or about to be discovered. All in her family shared information from the books in general conversation, giving them a wealth of knowledge and vivid imaginations.

A hybrid author who both has a publisher and self-publishes, Ms. Keim writes heart-warming novels about women who face unexpected challenges, meet them with strength, and find love and happiness along the way. Her best-selling books are based, in part, on many of the places she's lived or visited and on the interesting people she's met, creating believable characters and realistic settings her many loyal readers love. Ms. Keim loves to hear from her readers and appreciates their enthusiasm for her stories.

"I hope you've enjoyed this book. If you have, please help other readers discover it by leaving a review on Amazon, Goodreads, or the site of your choice. And please check out my other books:

The Hartwell Women Series
The Beach House Hotel Series
The Fat Fridays Group
The Salty Key Inn Series
Seashell Cottage Books
Chandler Hill Inn Series
Desert Sage Inn Series

ALL THE BOOKS ARE NOW AVAILABLE IN AUDIO on Audible and iTunes! So fun to have these characters come alive!"

Ms. Keim can be reached at **www.judithkeim.com**

And to like her author page on Facebook and keep up with the news, go to: **https://bit.ly/3acs5Qc**

To receive notices about new books, follow her on Book Bub - **http://bit.ly/2pZBDXq**

And here's a link to where you can sign up for her periodic newsletter! **http://bit.ly/2OQsb7s**

She is also on Twitter @judithkeim, LinkedIn, and Goodreads. Come say hello!

Acknowledgements

As mentioned in Book 1, I gratefully acknowledge Wayne Bailey's help in answering questions about grape growing and making wine. Our stay at Youngberg Hill and meeting him and his family was exactly what I needed to transform my ideas for this series into written word.

As always, I thank Peter and Lynn Mapp for editing, and Lou Harper for the book covers.

Made in the USA
Middletown, DE
28 April 2024

53606161R00189